The
Golden Hand
of Duntisbourne Hall

FastPrint
Publishing
www.fast-print.net/store.php

The Golden Hand

Copyright 2013 © L.P. Fergusson

ISBN: 978 178035 581 8

A catalogue record for this book is available from the British Library.

First published 2013 by
Fast-Print Publishing
Peterborough
England

An environmentally friendly book printed and bound in England by
www.printondemand-worldwide.com

Mixed Sources
Product group from well-managed
forests, and other controlled sources
www.fsc.org Cert no. TT-COC-002641
© 1996 Forest Stewardship Council

PEFC Certified

This product is
from sustainably
managed forests
and controlled
sources

www.pefc.org

This book is made entirely of chain-of-custom materials

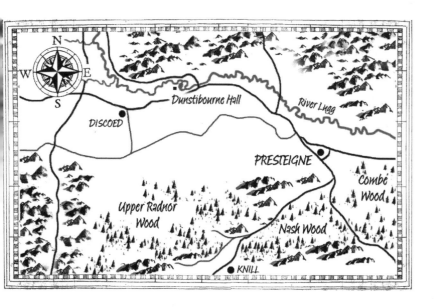

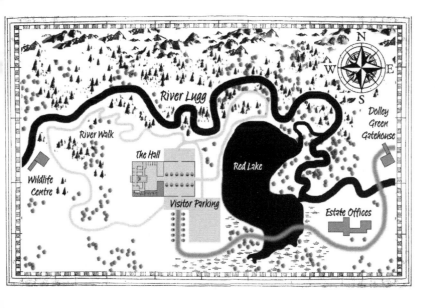

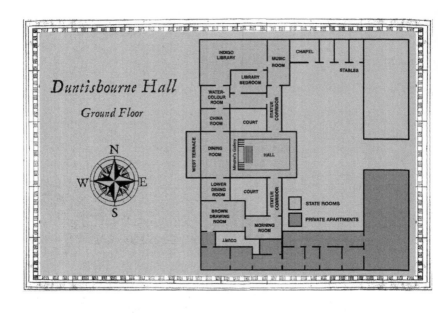

Duntisbourne Hall

Ground Floor

INDIGO LIBRARY

MUSIC ROOM

CHAPEL

LIBRARY BEDROOM

STABLES

WATER-COLOUR ROOM

CHINA ROOM

COURT

STATUE CORRIDOR

WEST TERRACE

DINING ROOM

Minstrel's Gallery

HALL

LOWER DINING ROOM

COURT

STATUE CORRIDOR

BROWN DRAWING ROOM

MORNING ROOM

STATE ROOMS

PRIVATE APARTMENTS

COURT

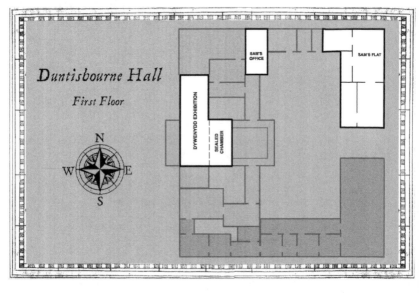

Duntisbourne Hall

First Floor

SAM'S OFFICE

SAM'S FLAT

DYWENYDD EXHIBITION

SEALED CHAMBER

To Chris, as ever

– 1 –

By the time the wedding guests were making their way towards the great hall for dinner, the evening sun was slipping low over the Black Mountains and casting a final glitter of light across the waters of the Red Lake. The north side of Duntisbourne Hall was already deep in shadow, the only illumination coming from three windows in the undercroft behind which a makeshift cloakroom had been created for the evening, and it was these pools of light that exposed the figure of a man approaching the Hall with some stealth. On reaching the building he slowed his pace further and moved into a position between two of the windows where he pressed himself flat against the stone and surveyed the darkness around him. Satisfied that he was the only person out on the north side of the Hall that evening, he rolled himself cautiously along the wall towards the edge of the low window and, being careful not to make himself visible to anyone inside, peered into the room.

A girl in her twenties with the wide candid features of the Welsh was tidying the coats. Occasionally she paused to caress a fabric with her fingers or to brush her lips across the fur trim of a cuff. She was wearing a long white apron like a waitress and when she turned away it seemed to frame and accentuate the tightness of her jeans. A sturdy overnight bag in the style of a leather Gladstone had been left on the floor a short distance from the coat rack and as the girl bent forward to grab the handle on the top and lift it, the watcher inhaled sharply. She checked the label and stood to locate the coat that belonged to the same owner, then bent once more to stow the bag in its correct position. Satisfied with her work she ran her hands down her apron and into the pocket at the front, drawing out a packet of cigarettes. Hearing her footsteps approach the window, the watcher pushed himself back against the wall. He heard her struggle with the latch and then the window opened out above him and he saw the silhouette of her head on the ground in front. There was the click of a lighter – he saw a plume of smoke rise above the pane of glass and lightly disperse in the evening air as she exhaled.

All of a sudden the girl blew out a lungful of smoke, flicked the lighted cigarette down onto the grass and banged the window shut, forgetting to latch it so that it swung open a fraction as her shadow moved away from the pool of light.

'There you are, Jess,' a woman's voice said. 'Staff supper's about to start. You'll have to hurry up or you won't be through before the guests finish dinner.'

'Coming,' she replied.

The watcher waited for a few more minutes before approaching the window once more. Swinging it open, he held onto the sill and placed the toe of his shoe against a stone which stood proud of the wall. With some effort and a great deal of grunting, he managed to haul himself up onto the window ledge and, taking a few moments to check that the room was indeed empty, pitched himself in and stood for a moment blinking in the light. Darting over to the coat rack, he began to pull the bags out from underneath the coats. He immediately discarded carrier bags, kicking them to one side. Eventually he located the Gladstone bag he had seen Jess stow and, still panting, although his task had not been physically challenging, lifted it gently and carried it over to the far corner of the room which was in shadow. Crouching down he pressed his fingers on the catch and caught his breath as the latch clicked up. Easing the top open with gentle precision he peered down into the bag then began to take out the contents one item at a time – a folded skirt, a shirt, a soap bag, a cream-coloured cardigan with mother-of-pearl buttons and finally a pair of tights, worn and mis-shapen like the discarded skin of a snake. Confident that the case was now empty he stood and seemed to be about to unbuckle the belt of his trousers when a gale of laughter from the corridor stopped him dead in his tracks. Flustered he stared down at the clothes strewn on the floor but when he heard the door of the room open and the laughter increase in volume on the other side of the clothes rack, he turned and stumbled back towards the open window.

'Hey!' a woman's voice shouted. 'What on earth . . . ?'

He hurled himself onto the sill, swinging his legs round and over before launching himself out into the darkness. Unfortunately the prong of the casement stay snagged on the inner seam of his trousers, pivoting him round as he leapt, and with a yelp of pain and fright he landed heavily on the grass below. Looking back towards the window he saw that the two women had reached it and were glaring down at him.

'Come back here!' the older woman shouted.

He scrabbled to his feet and began to stumble away through the darkness clutching his inner thigh, and as he pressed on further towards the Red Lake the shouts of the two women at the window died away.

– 2 –

At the southern end of that great Jacobean pile on the borders of Wales, Max Black was standing on his own in the brown drawing room. He was feeling uncomfortable in his dinner jacket – the dress shirt was tight around the collar and the evening was hot. He had been staring at the eighteenth-century chandelier in the centre of the room for some minutes puzzled as to why it occasionally trembled and hoping that this interminably dull evening might be enlivened by its sudden descent earthwards. The din of the wedding party reached him in waves and he glanced down the state rooms and wondered if anyone was actually going to wander along and look at the rooms. He doubted it. Noel Canterbury was stationed in the lower dining room to remind guests that they had to leave their drinks on the table before entering the state rooms, and Max thought this was enough of a disincentive to ensure no one would come. Still, he was earning half a day's wages for standing here for a few hours and when the guests went through to eat, he and his colleagues would dine in the buttery on the same food as the guests were being served in the great hall.

He usually enjoyed being at Duntisbourne Hall in the evening when it was dressed up for a function. The atmosphere was different when the shutters were closed along the west front and the lighting was low and intimate, oil paintings barely visible during daylight hours glowing under the picture lights, but the Hall hadn't been the same since Sam Westbrook left. The erotic exhibition was complete and had been hailed a success, and her work as curator here was done. Despite a few abortive attempts to keep the spark of a relationship going he was coming to the conclusion that it was spluttering out, smothered by the geographical distance between them. It was beginning to look as if they probably would end up as jolly good chums, just as Sam had once predicted.

Max sighed and stared around the room. The furniture behind the ropes was looking faded and worn: he could see slivers of brass standing proud of the Boulle-work cabinets, horsehair sprouting from the armrests of the sofas, foxing speckling the mirrors on the pier glasses. Everything in the room looked tired and shabby.

He felt a vibration against his chest and pulled his mobile phone out of his jacket pocket. The caller was his daughter.

'Daddy! My Daddy!' Charlotte said, the salutation she had used ever since she spotted her father dabbing a tear from his eye one Christmas when they were watching *The Railway Children* together.

'Hi, sweetie,' Max said, glancing down the state rooms to make sure the head guide wasn't in view before moving deeper into the brown drawing room where he wouldn't be so visible. 'What's up?'

'Just ringing to see how you are.'

'OK. Well, I'm at work.'

'Still?'

'Doing an evening function – and I can't really chat.' Max gazed up at a painting of the first Earl of Duntisbourne and waited. Charlotte didn't usually ring to see how he was.

'The thing is, Dad, I've run up a bit of an overdraft this year and I was thinking about working during the summer to pay it off instead of travelling.'

Or asking me to pay, Max thought. 'That seems a sensible idea,' he said.

'Problem is, the sort of job I can get down here only just covers my rent and food and everything so I was wondering – if it wouldn't be too much trouble – if you'd ask at the Hall and see if there are any jobs going over the summer. Then I'd see lots of you and it'd be really good fun.'

'Sweetie, we're on minimum wage here.'

'It's the same as working in a bar or a shop but without any expenses. '

'Define "without any expenses".' There was an ominous silence on the other end of the phone. 'Charlotte?'

'I thought it would be fun, that's all. Never mind.'

'No, Charlotte – wait. Do you mean move back home again?'

'Only for the summer – but it doesn't matter. Forget it.'

'Max! What on earth are you doing?' Bunty Buchanan was standing beside him in the double teapot position. She was wearing a full-length plaid skirt and a velvet waistcoat but this stab at evening wear made her no less intimidating. 'Put that mobile away at once. What are you thinking? You're meant to be on security. How on earth can you see what's going on if you're nattering on the phone? Put it away this instant.'

'It's my daughter.'

'I don't care if it's the Queen of Sheba. Put it away.'

'Sorry, Charlotte,' Max said, 'I've got to go. I'll ring later.'

'Now turn it off,' Bunty said. Max had learned not to argue with the head guide and did as he was told. 'I came down here to tell you that the guests are going in to dinner in the next few minutes.'

'Right.'

'You can start making your way down for supper.' Turning, she headed back along the state rooms. Max reflected that she really did treat her team as if they were polo ponies – then he reviewed that thought. Bunty had far more respect for her animals than she did for the guides working for her. Max had built a successful career in the real world for nearly twenty years before taking early retirement to bring up his daughter alone, and he always found it difficult to choke back a rejoinder when Bunty spoke to him as if he was a schoolboy. He watched her bustle down the state rooms, grey hair bouncing on the pie-crust collar, flat country shoes accentuating the thick ankle of the well-bred matriarch. Once she had passed the lower dining room the slim figure of his colleague Noel Canterbury slipped into view. He too was in evening dress but having spent so many years in the Far East, his knack of mismatching waistcoat, dicky bow and pocket handkerchief, gave him, despite his age, the colourful air of a showman. Noel was looking amused.

'You could have told me,' Max said.

'Honest to God old chap, I didn't see our ever-vigilant head guide until she swept past me and fell on you like an ocean – or I would have warned you.'

'Would you?'

'Course I would.' Noel peered beadily at him for a moment but then his smile faded and he said with genuine concern, 'You OK, Max? You've seemed a bit down in the dumps lately. Still pining after the lovely Mrs Westbrook?'

'Of course not,' Max lied.

'Come on then, let's go and have supper. That's the last of the stragglers on their way through.' Max looked down the state rooms and saw a sweaty blonde in a huge evening dress downing a glass of champagne as if it was the last drink she'd ever have. She put the empty glass back on the improvised bar and left the room, clattering unsteadily on her heels. 'They'll probably let us have a glass or two of wine – if there's any left,' Noel added.

The wedding guests had decided to use the great hall as the

dining room and the official dining room as the bar, and it was through this room that Max and Noel sauntered as they made their way along the west wing of the Hall towards the indigo library and down into the buttery. On the way Max was aware of his friend's scrutiny and eventually Noel said, 'The phone call. Not bad news, I hope?'

'No, no. Not at all. It was my daughter, Charlotte.'

'Who's reading English at Bristol?'

'Yes. She seems to think it would be a good idea to get a job here over the summer.'

'Really?'

'And move back in.'

Noel stopped dead in his tracks and laid a consoling hand on Max's shoulder. 'Good God, man! No wonder you're looking so chapfallen. That's the most ghastly news.'

They fell into step beside one another once more. 'I love her to bits–' Max said.

'Goes without saying.'

'We get on incredibly well–'

'Of course.'

'I would cut off my right arm for that girl–'

'– and you'd rather do that than live with her again.'

Max smiled. 'I don't want to live with anyone again.'

'Oh really?' Noel said. 'I'll not take issue with that rather sweeping statement but I would advise you in the strongest possible terms to do everything in your power to foist her off somewhere else. Janet and I have hordes of children and stepchildren between us and the only way we survive them is with a strict three-night rule – no one stays longer. Nor, I might add, do we when we visit them.'

'Easy to say – but there's no point worrying about it at the moment. My darling daughter hasn't got what you'd call stickability. She could well change her mind before the start of the summer break.'

By the time they reached the buttery Laurence Cooke and Edwina Lemon, the other two guides on duty for the evening, were seated at a table near the window. As the two men approached the counter where the food was laid out Noel glanced across the room and muttered, 'We'll have to join them. I can't leave poor Laurence in the lurch. Good grief! What is that woman wearing tonight?'

'Mutton dressed as lamb?'

'Mutton dressed as mutton.'

Edwina, or Weenie as she preferred to be called, had stripped her jacket off and was leaning forward nattering at Laurence. The strappy top was made of a slimy fabric which had flopped forward and was bowing at the front, showing more chest than was palatable. Max thought it was a mistake for a woman to reveal a cleavage once it was made up of a cluster of creases instead of just one. The liver spots across her chest from years of sunbathing were poorly concealed by several strings of costume jewellery which matched the chain of the mock-Chanel handbag she had cast onto the table. Her make-up was thicker than usual and the lipstick had bled into the corners of her mouth making it look like a ragged gash. She had back-combed her hair – brittle from years of bleaching – into a helmet of peroxide curls so thick with lacquer that any potential lover would need the protection of gardening gloves to run his fingers through them.

'Yoohoo!' she shouted, waving a skinny arm in their direction. The bangles at her wrist clattered up her arm like quoits on a stick and Laurence flinched away from the wrinkled armpit inches from his face. 'Come and join us. We're over here.'

'She's like a boxer dog's arsehole, that woman,' Noel said piling his plate up with an assortment of crudités.

'What on earth are you talking about?' Max said.

'Her sexuality, of course. You don't want to look at it but your eyes keep being drawn towards it because it's so obviously on display, and then you wish you hadn't caught an eyeful.'

'You really can talk a phenomenal amount of nonsense.'

'Right. What do you fancy drinking?' Noel had picked up a bottle of Duntisbourne Hall Merlot, one of retail's less successful ventures into the world of fine wines. 'It's this or the Chardonnay. They're both a little astringent, as I recall. The Merlot has an unattractive nose of burnt match and wet dog with just a hint of skunk, qualities you may feel are thankfully lost the moment the thin wine reaches the palate but alas all too swiftly replaced by a taste that skilfully combines a pungent papery quality with a slap of ethyl acetate. You may prefer the white, but I should warn you that this particular variety embodies everything one has learnt to dread from the word Chardonnay – wet straw, a hint of caramel verging on burnt sugar with the long finish of artificial sweetener. I think the Merlot is probably the lesser of the two evils.' Max nodded mutely and accepted the proffered glass.

'No Roger tonight?' Weenie said as they sat down. 'I was sure I saw his name down on the list.'

'They called me at home last night,' Noel said, 'and asked if I minded covering for him.'

'Did they? You didn't say.'

'Why would I?'

'I just thought you might have mentioned it. It's nice to know who the team are before you pitch up, that's all,' Weenie said. 'I wonder why Roger couldn't make it.'

'I believe the Hogg-Smythes had tickets for *Scalding Toad* in York,' Laurence said. He appeared to be younger than the majority of the guides but he had been an actor during the sixties, habitually cast as the clean-cut, impeccably dressed Englishman, and this was a look he maintained, despite the fact that he had been 'resting' for many more years than he had trodden the boards.

'*Scalding Toad*?'

'It's a new opera by a local composer, I think.'

'Good grief!' said Noel. 'If there's one thing worse than opera, it's modern opera. And York. Why trek all the way over to York when you can see a perfectly good production in Birmingham? If you like that sort of thing.'

'I think his wife is very into opera,' Laurence said.

'Poor man.'

'Yes, poor Roger,' Weenie said. 'I would say he's rather uxorious.'

'What?'

'Roger said the other day that we should all try to learn a new word each week, Noel and then use it as often as possible. Uxorious means overly submissive to a wife and I think that describes poor Roger to a T.'

'Oh – pussy-whipped.'

'Noel!'

'Anyway, how do we all think the evening's going?' Noel said, spreading a roll with a pauce square of butter. 'Seems the trustees are happy to lend the old Hall out to every Tom, Dick and Harry provided they come up with the cash but why they insist on providing room wardens for the evening is beyond me. In all my years doing functions here the only question I've ever been asked is "Where are the loos?"'

'I've had those young men simply fluttering around me all evening – much to the consternation of their girlfriends, I might add.'

'Drunk to a man, every one of them.'

'Not at all. They were asking me some very penetrating questions.'

Max's attention was beginning to waver. He didn't want to drink very much and Noel had been right, the Merlot was fairly unpleasant. He gazed out into the gardens beyond the window where white flower heads in the borders along the north walk glowed more brightly as dusk descended, and as he looked he was sure he saw a movement.

'I think somebody's out there,' he said.

'Probably one of the guests popped out for a smoke.'

'No. Someone's running,' and he stood up and walked over to the window. The others didn't take much notice – Weenie was holding court about the sin of bossy women – and as his eyes became accustomed to the darkness he could just make out the squat figure of a man limping into the night, one hand clasping his inner thigh.

'There is someone out there,' he said. 'It's not a party guest, I'm sure of it,' but the man had disappeared into the shrubbery at the end of the walk.

'Come and sit down, Max. What's the matter? Wish you were out there having a cigarette too, I suppose.'

'Not really,' he said returning to his seat.

'How long since you gave up?' Weenie asked.

'Must be nearly two months now.'

'And all for nought, Max, eh?'

'Stop it, Noel.'

'He gave it up for the love of a good woman and she instantly fled back to London.'

'Who do you mean?'

'Weenie, are you the only person here at the Hall who doesn't know that the beautiful Mrs Westbrook stole the heart of my good friend here?'

'Oh,' she said, 'and I always thought you fancied me,' and she reached out across to give Max a playful bash on the shoulder but instead sent Laurence's glass of wine spinning across the table. He pushed his seat hastily backwards but the rivulet of wine had already reached the end and splashed onto his trousers.

'For goodness' sake, Weenie!' Laurence said as Max and Noel grabbed handfuls of paper napkins and swabbed the growing pool on the table.

'Sorry, Laurence. Here. Let me dab it off your trousers for you. I'll be very gentle.'

'Get off. I'll do it myself.' Laurence stuffed a wad of paper napkins into his crotch and began to mop away. 'Honestly, Weenie. Control yourself.'

'Just can't. You know me – I like my gin cold and my piano hot. I tell you, I'll still be dancing on tables when I'm eighty.'

'Next year then.'

Alone in the ladies' cloakroom Weenie pulled her lipstick across her mouth and pouted at her image in the mirror, then placed her fingers along her jawline and moved her skin up and backwards towards her ears, smoothing her neck and returning her chin to the contours of youth. Turning her head from left to right she wondered whether she should seriously consider more plastic surgery. She had had a little work done around her eyes back in the eighties and hadn't enjoyed the experience. The surgeon was cheap but had rooms just off Harley Street which gave her confidence. He had worked on her lids under local anaesthetic and sent her home in a taxi with no instructions other than to wear dark glasses for the next few days. When she woke in the night to find she had bled copiously into her pillow she had been unable to reach him by telephone and although within a few months the bruising had subsided and she was reasonably pleased with the results, she vowed never again to have work done on the cheap. However, two decades had passed since then and the light in the ladies' cloakroom was unforgiving – if she had the money she would definitely book herself in. After all, she had the body to carry off a younger face – not an ounce of spare fat on her.

She wondered if a time would come when refusing to consider cosmetic surgery would be considered bad manners. Visitors with terrible teeth outraged her as much as the hugely overweight. It smacked of slovenliness, a lack of courtesy to those to whom you spoke because you couldn't be bothered to spend a bit of money and endure a little discomfort to get them fixed. Was cosmetic surgery so very different? Would people be offended if her turkey neck became more wobbly or the skin beneath her eyes began to bag once more?

For as long as she could remember Weenie knew that the gaze of the world was upon her and as a result she played out her life as if she was under a spotlight, an audience of people watching her every move, analysing her every nuance, admiring her poise and éclat even when she was alone. As a young woman she had been extremely attractive and arriving in London during the sixties she used her natural attributes to their full advantage. She had been educated at a second-rate girls' boarding school but when her beauty was at its zenith, her lack of knowledge and wit was of little concern. If you are so beautiful that merely removing your clothes is enough to enslave any man, there really is little point in learning other skills. She had cultivated a few – for example, she could monitor everyone in the periphery of her field of vision to make sure their eyes were turned towards her and when she set her cap at a man she could check out if he was susceptible to her snare by holding his gaze for just a few seconds longer than expected. If he responded with a wary glance away then back again, she would move in for the kill before the night was out. Back in those days in London she knew when she walked into a room that she was the honey-pot around which the drones swarmed.

She sighed. Noel, Max and Laurence had bidden her goodnight and left – that never used to happen. In the old days, one or even two of them would have offered to see her to her car or better still, asked her back for a nightcap. Not that she was particularly interested in any of them – Laurence was a hopeless case, a waste to womankind, and Noel made her uncomfortable because she suspected he was laughing at her and she never understood why. As for Max – well, she had to admit she thought he was rather scrumptious but she had tried her smouldering gaze on him several times and he had responded by staring back and frowning as if he thought she had spotted something stuck between his teeth.

No, her disappointment tonight was that Roger Hogg-Smythe had put his name down to be a room warden for the evening but had cried off at the last minute and now she knew why. He had gone out for the evening with his wife. With another sigh – this one more of resignation than irritation – she popped her lipstick into her bag, clicked it shut with a snap, put on her raincoat and stepped out into the summer night.

It was exceptionally dark in the courtyard and to her surprise Weenie felt a little jumpy. She remembered that she had had the sense to put a torch into the pocket of her raincoat before she came out that evening and although the small beam of light made her progress quicker, it did little to soothe her anxiety and she was annoyed with herself for feeling the need to check deep and darkened doorways along the route. Once away from the building and heading towards the southern exit of the courtyard which led out to the public car park which the guides had to use, she paused momentarily to admire the bleak magnificence of the Park as a sliver of moon, thin enough to cut, began its slow ascent from the horizon up into the deepening indigo sky.

She hurried across the gravel towards her car, the only vehicle marooned at the edge of the car park and pressed the key fob so that she could hop in and lock the doors quickly. However, as she pulled away from the Hall she felt the haunting beauty of the countryside tugging at her heart, little tendrils of memory of a time when a night like this would have been an opportunity to lie down on the grass and make love. She slowed the car halfway up the long drive and pressed the window button. It glided down and a sharp cold air began to fill the car. She breathed deeply, inhaling the scent of mist and earth.

Suddenly she was alert. Out of the corner of her eye she had sensed a movement in the rear view mirror. She swung herself round in the seat, pushing up a little to peer backwards over the headrest. She could see a few feet of road behind, illuminated faintly by her brake lights, the cloud of exhaust tinted pink and swirling as if someone had passed through it, and at the very edge of the pool of light she saw it again – a movement, this time accompanied by the faint sound of gravel underfoot – and then it was gone.

Under normal circumstances her heightened sense of potential romantic drama would have fed off the incident but for some reason she felt an eerie certainty that this was not someone like Roger waiting in the shadows for a lovers' tryst. She looked around the wall of darkness hemming in the car and slowly moved her hand to the window button. The pane of glass whispered back into position and taking her foot off the brake, she let the automatic engine pick up speed. It was only when her headlights swept an arc onto the open road that she became of aware of the thumping of her heart.

– 3 –

BS Moreton sat at his kitchen table staring out at the garden. Patricia had closed the curtains along the front of the house to stop the sun from damaging the soft furnishings but the windows in the kitchen and conservatory were open and the smell of the wallflowers in the beds around the terrace came to him on the breeze that fluttered through the house. It was going to be a beautiful summer's day but BS had no intention of putting his nose outside the door – nothing could lift him from his world of deep despair. He reached down and scratched around his ankle, the skin underneath the monitor sticky and irritated in this hot weather. They said it would be like wearing a heavy wristwatch, people forget they've got it on in next to no time, but he never forgot that it tethered him like a hobbled horse.

'If you want something to do,' Patricia said as she came past with a basket of wet clothing, 'you could get out there and mow the lawn while I hang this lot up.'

In response, BS lifted his foot and pulled up the leg of his trousers, exposing his pale ankle and tether.

'For pity's sake BS, stop being so histrionic. You know perfectly well you can go as far as the perimeter of the garden without any problem. You're being ridiculous.'

'And you know perfectly well that if this thing goes off I'm back inside that terrible place.'

'It wasn't a terrible place.'

'How would you know?'

Patricia put the basket of washing onto the table and leant against the edge of it, her mouth tight with impatience. 'If you don't pull yourself together, the rest of this year is going to be intolerable.'

'It's intolerable already.'

'Why? You're home now.'

BS pressed down on the table and pushed himself up onto his feet. 'Where's my stick?' he said. 'I'm going to the study.' Patricia bent down to retrieve it from the floor before disappearing into the garden without another word. Once she had gone BS sat down again, hooked the stick into the crook of his arm and dropped his head into both hands. The weight that dragged him down was hopelessness and, in the words of John Donne, the place it dragged him was the damp of hell.

His maudlin introspection was interrupted by the tinny jingle of the telephone in the hall. BS lifted his head, leaning slightly to peer out through the windows of the conservatory to see if Patricia had heard it and was running in to answer the call. It went on and on ringing – the answerphone didn't cut in, she must have turned it off again – and with a groan of irritation he hauled himself up onto his feet again and, leaning on the stick to relieve the weight on his knee, rocked his way down the corridor and picked up the receiver.

'May I speak to Mr Moreton, please?'

'Who is this?'

'Is that you, BS? I thought I recognised your voice. It's Arthur Matthews.'

The name was familiar – it conjured up a man in his late thirties, shy and self-deprecating but with an open, pleasant face.

'Arthur! How are you?' BS said, still wracking his brains to place the fellow. He had a feeling there was a connection with Duntisbourne Hall but he couldn't for the life of him think what it was.

'Did they ever get that disabled lift installed?'

Of course – he was a young architect who had come to the Hall to design a lift that would be passed by English Heritage. The project had eventually been approved but never got any further as the Earl baulked at the expense and thought the ramps were adequate for the purpose. BS agreed with the Earl. When Duntisbourne was built no one worried about wheelchair access.

'Not the last time I was there,' BS said.

'The reason I've got in touch is that I've been asked to design a secondary exit from the new exhibition and I don't seem to be getting anywhere with the CEO or the Earl.' BS was silent, his mind racing. 'I remember you had an encyclopaedic knowledge of the building and wondered if I could come round and pick your brains.'

'I don't work there any more.'

'I know.' There was an awkward pause. 'Sorry to hear about that.' BS wondered how much Matthews had heard – not a great deal, he imagined, or he wouldn't be phoning him for advice.

However, he remembered that he had liked the young architect and it would be good to spend some time discussing interesting issues with someone intelligent for a change, but not if it meant helping the Earl or any of the trustees at Duntisbourne Hall. They had sold him down the river, betrayed him and slung him out. They had subjected him to the humiliation of the police, the courtrooms, prison. He had appeared on the front cover of the local newspaper, a humiliating photograph of him looking shifty and feckless, thousands of issues on the breakfast tables of a community who had until then admired him for his position, his knowledge, his moral standing. They had made an example of him for all the world to see and utterly destroyed his reputation and his life.

Arthur Matthews filled the silence by saying, 'I know I probably shouldn't have rung but you always had such knowledge at your fingertips, you were so insightful, your analysis of the evidence that wonderful Jacobean building offered up was so intelligent.'

'Why – thank you,' BS said. At least someone appreciated him – these were accolades that had been absent from his life for a very long time.

'So do you think you could spare a few minutes of your day to have a chat about it? I'm sure you're a very busy man but is it possible you could find the time to fit me in?'

'Time?' BS coughed out a derisive laugh. 'That's one thing I seem to have plenty of these days.'

'I managed to get hold of a copy of the plans from 1805,' Matthews said laying the sheets of paper across the top of BS's desk while BS snatched pots of pens and piles of papers out of the way to make room. Matthews smoothed the folds down with the palm of his hand and BS felt around in his shirt pocket for his reading glasses.

'The exhibition is on the first floor above here,' Matthews said, drawing a finger in a square over the dining room, 'and if you look at its dimensions on the plan of the upper floor you can see it doesn't quite fit. I've been up and measured the exhibition and there's a partition wall here – it sounds hollow when you tap it – but I can't work out what's on the other side. It seems there's a space next door.'

BS leant forward, pushing his glasses up the bridge of his nose, and peered down at the plan. 'Hmm, I see what you mean.'

'I thought at first it was an old box room because it's certainly room-sized and externally you can see window spaces which must have been bricked up at the beginning of the seventeen hundreds, but it doesn't appear to have an entrance. Did you ever hear stories of a priest's hole in the building? Something of that nature?'

'It looks too large a space for that, surely.'

'OK. The other thing I wondered was if it could be interstitial space created as a result of the complexity of the western front of the building.'

'Rather like the relieving chambers in the pyramids.'

'Interesting idea.' BS glanced up. He could see Matthews didn't agree but he felt the respect the young architect had for his knowledge.

'Why is anyone interested anyway?' BS said.

'I have to find some way of creating a fire exit from the exhibition because without one, the Hall is in breach of building regulations.'

'Oh – they're back on that hobby horse again, are they?' Back in the spring BS had been determined to prevent the erotic artefacts in the Dywenydd Collection from going on public display and had hoped the impossibility of creating a fire exit within a Grade 1 listed building would prevent its further development. He had been wrong. They had been so determined to create their new money-making concern, the powers that be simply ignored the problem and went ahead with the exhibition anyway. He chuckled to himself that now they were probably going to have spend a great deal more money sorting it out.

'It's a shame the trustees didn't think of this when the exhibition was being planned,' Matthews said. BS smiled benignly. 'Anyway, I think we could bring people out of the exhibition through that space above the dining room and then construct a circular fire escape externally which would be obscured by the Doric column to the left of the west terrace.

'Interesting.'

'I can only estimate the size from the outside at the moment but thought you may know if it was a proper room or not.'

BS turned away from the plans and, leaning against the desk, removed his glasses once more and held the temple to his lips, nonchalantly nibbling at the tip. 'I wonder,' he said.

'What?'

'Well, there was a story going back over three hundred years.'

'Yes?' The architect left the table and sat down on one of the office chairs with great care as if fearing a swift change of position would disrupt BS's train of thought.

'I wonder . . .'

'Tell me – please.'

BS drew up the other chair and sat down. 'Yes – it's coming back to me now. How much do you know about the history of the Hall?'

'Not a great deal, I have to admit.'

'Well, the first Earl of Duntisbourne bought his title back in 1571 – I'm afraid to say he made his fortune in the slave trade but the less said about that, the better. The second earl, Lord Siegfried, was said to be the lover of Queen Elizabeth I and it was he who built Duntisbourne Hall down here in Shropshire. There was a legend about his son, Lord Edward, which lost popularity but which I always thought was one of the most dramatic and heartbreaking of them all.' He could see the young man's eyes glitter with intrigue and he settled down to his saga.

'Edward Falkenstein –'

'Oh, I thought the family name was Faulk.'

'It is now. They dropped their Germanic-sounding name at about the same time as our royal family stopped calling themselves Saxe-Coburg-Gotha and became the House of Windsor.'

'Right. World War I.'

'Precisely.' BS felt a deep connection to this intelligent young man. 'It was back at the turn of the sixteenth century when Edward Falkenstein became the third Earl of Duntisbourne. He was strongly anti-catholic and refused to spend time at court during the reign of James I, preferring to occupy himself with farming his estates around Duntisbourne Hall. In spite of the attentions of several wealthy landowners with daughters of marriageable age, he married his childhood sweetheart, Maria, in 1619 and within a year she was pregnant. In February 1620 she suffered a long difficult labour and within hours of the birth of an heir, William Siegfried, she died.'

'Oh dear.'

'Indeed. Now, the earl was beside himself with grief, utterly inconsolable. He even refused to hold the infant Viscount William, his heir, insisting that this son had been responsible for the death of his beloved Maria. So intense was his grief that his family feared for his sanity and to their horror and distress, in September of the same year he slipped away to Plymouth to join a group of anti-Catholic Puritans.'

'Surely not the Pilgrim Fathers?'

BS stabbed an approving finger at Matthews. 'Spot on,' he said. 'He set sail for the New World aboard the *Mayflower*.'

'Good heavens! He left the luxury and wealth of his estates for the life of a settler.'

'Indeed he did. Perhaps the hardships he suffered soothed his grief because he eventually remarried. She was a homely woman called Henrietta and they had two children, first a little boy who was named Edward after his father – they called him

Teddy apparently to avoid confusion but I always thought The Honourable Teddy sounded like a children's book from the 1950s.' BS chuckled to himself at his analogy. 'The following year a daughter was born – now, what was her name?'

'Does it matter?'

'It'll come to me in a minute, I'm sure.' BS raised his hand to indicate that he needed complete silence to drag this insignificant progeny's name from the recesses of his brain but after a few moments he said, 'No, no – it's quite gone.'

'So Lord Edward found happiness in the end,' Matthews said as if he wasn't remotely interested in the little girl's name.

'Unfortunately not.' BS shifted his weight in his chair to relieve the pressure on his back and said, 'Wait a minute. Let's have some refreshment before I continue.' He heaved himself up onto his feet and limped over towards the door, leaning out into the corridor and calling, 'Patricia. Are you in the kitchen, pet? Could we have a couple of coffees in here, do you think?'

There was a pause and then BS heard her say, 'I'm busy. Make it yourself.' He pursed his lips, worried the architect had caught the tone of her voice, but returned to the room wearing an indulgent smile and said, 'She's rather busy at the moment.'

'No problem,' Matthews said. 'I didn't want one anyway. Please go on.'

'Well, he returned to England with his new family in 1643 but all of them had great difficulties integrating. Lord William had run the Duntisbourne estates very well in his father's absence and resented the return of his father. He couldn't establish a pleasant relationship with his half-brother, Teddy, and the resentment between these two half-brothers was mutual. The Honourable Teddy,' again BS paused for an amused snort, 'remained much closer to the earl but of course, he could never inherit the estate. Anyway – perhaps to get away from his warring sons – the earl joined the Royalists and made his way up to Lancashire.'

'Oh no! The ill-fated Battle of Preston.'

'I'm afraid so. The earl was killed on 19 August 1648, a day of fierce fighting in driving rain.'

'All hopes of a Royalist comeback dashed.'

'A terrible defeat for the Royalists but a magnificent victory for Cromwell's New Model Army.'

'And a tragedy for the family.'

'That's not the end of it. When news of the earl's death reached Duntisbourne, something strange happened. In a gesture of reconciliation those two half-brothers, Lord William and Teddy, made the long and dangerous journey together to collect their father's body which they bore, still caked with mud from the battle, back to Duntisbourne Hall.'

'Extraordinary.' Matthews breathed in and leant back in his seat once more, then glanced over at the plans laid out on the desk and frowned. 'But what has that got to do with the space above the dining room?'

'Ah – well, I'm coming to that. Although the body of the earl is buried in the crypt underneath the chapel, it was said that his wife and daughter – oh, what was that wretched girl's name?' BS sighed heavily.

'It really doesn't matter.'

'Not to you maybe.' BS shook his head, irritated with himself. 'Be that as it may, the two women had prepared a room for the arrival of the body, a place where the earl could lie in state, his brave wounds exposed for all to see that despite his anti-Catholic sympathies, he was a Royalist through and through. When a respectable amount of time had passed, his wife finally gave permission for him to be cleaned and dressed for burial and she instructed her builders to seal the room off as a permanent shrine to her beloved Edward.'

'And you think that space could be the room where he lay in state.'

'It's right next to the master bedroom in the private apartments. The dowager countess would have wanted to have him near her.'

Matthews chuckled to himself and stood again to lean over the plan. 'It's a nice idea and if it's true, it would certainly be large enough for my plan. Why hasn't anyone ever investigated it?'

'No point. It was never rumoured there was anything valuable in there and no one's going to start pulling walls down to check an empty space.'

'Looks like that's what I'm going to have to do.' The architect turned and smiled at BS. 'I knew you'd have the answer.'

'That's very flattering of you.'

'How do they manage without you?'

BS shrugged. 'They've got no choice.'

Embarrassed, Matthews looked at his watch and said, 'I really shouldn't take up any more of your time, you know. You've been most helpful.' He started to roll up the plans and BS watched him with a sinking heart. He was going to have to see him to the door, stand on his threshold and wave him goodbye, then return to the tedium of his life, a prison more irksome than the one he had left, a gaoler more spiteful than any he met after his trial. Feeling deeply despondent, he led the way down the corridor, the young architect walking behind.

They shook hands at the front door and BS said, 'I have enjoyed our little chat this afternoon.'

'As have I. It was good to see you again.'

Instead of releasing the young man's hand immediately BS paused for a moment and looked out towards the drive, thinking. 'Oh, I've remembered something else,' he said.

'Really?' Matthews had turned imperceptibly towards his car but BS was determined to keep him talking for a bit longer.

'Yes. Another interesting snippet about the third earl. When he returned from the New World he brought back with him two pairs of the new breed of bird – the turkey – and it is from these two pairs that all of today's turkeys have descended.'

'That's really fascinating,' he said but BS sensed a trace of indulgent pity in the architect's smile.

Matthews made his way to his car but as he opened the driver's door BS called out, 'If there's any other information you need, please give me a call.'

'I shouldn't need to pester you any more, I'm happy to say,' he said, one foot already planted in the footwell, his hand holding the open door to stabilise himself. 'I could have waited until the new person arrived but I wasn't confident they'd be able to help.'

'New person?'

'Yes, apparently someone's arriving in a few day's time – your replacement.' He shut his door and started the engine but then rolled down the window and called out, 'They won't be a patch on you.'

After the architect had driven away BS stood for a few moments at the open door. He could hear a collared dove cooing its monotonous call from the branches of the lime tree and a blackbird chip-chipping in the hedge to the left of the drive. He gazed around until he spotted the neighbour's cat sitting further down the hedge, the tip of its tail twitching back and forth in the dirt. It was baiting that poor blackbird. 'Chip, chip, chip,' it went, on and on, trapped in a pointless stream of irritating noise which was having no effect whatsoever on the cat.

BS set out across the gravel, swaying onto his stick with each step. As he neared, the cat turned its head and watched him over its shoulder with a supercilious expression. He raised his stick above his head and shook it saying, 'Shoo!' – not loudly, his neighbour might be out in the garden. The cat didn't move, so with difficulty BS bent down and gathered up a handful of gravel which he threw towards it. It landed short but a couple of pieces bounced up and tapped the cat lightly on its back. It was enough – it turned and stalked off towards the gate, in no particular hurry, slithering between the bars and around the corner.

The blackbird chipped two more times, the intervals longer, but then peace flowed back into the garden and BS limped towards the house. By the time he had shut the door and made it to his office, the bird had started chipping again.

– 4 –

Duntisbourne Hall had opened its doors in the 1950s as had so many stately homes in Britain after the war. When the Labour government swept into power in 1945, death duties were raised to an all-time high and this, coupled with a dramatic decrease in the number of people willing to go back to working as domestic servants, left many peers with few choices – they could resign their great mansions to dereliction and ruin or follow the example set by the Marquess of Bath at Longleat and turn to trade. When the Earl of Duntisbourne embraced the idea, the house was open for a limited number of days, but now it was open seven days a week and Sunday was the most unpopular with the staff.

Weenie didn't mind working on a Sunday but then she was not in a position to turn down work of any kind. This morning she was manning the door with Nerys Tingley. She liked Nerys; they made a good team because despite her seniority in years of service (Nerys was governess to the Earl's children when the Hall opened in the 1950s and one of the first guides) the old lady did as she was told and as a result they got on very well indeed. Weenie felt she had a duty of care to her companion because a number of years ago Nerys had had some sort of breakdown and had been forced to take several seasons off on medical grounds. She had returned to lighter duties looking older and more fragile, and although in the course of a day their conversation was far-reaching and varied – the plot of the current soap opera, the increase of obesity among the visitors, the latest news from the private side – Weenie felt she would be breaking a code of friendship if she pumped Nerys for details about her time away from the Hall. She was, however, happy to hear stories about life at the Hall in the old days.

'The Countess was such a beautiful woman when she was young.'

'I know,' Weenie said, 'I'm often mistaken for her.'

'She's the most normal of them all because she came from rather ordinary stock, which is probably why she was able to relate better to the children. Mind you, when they were young she was hardly ever around and as for the Earl – he was as bad-tempered then as he is now and the children used to try his patience. Life was much happier when he was away.'

'Just as it is now,' Weenie said.

'I used to love the summers in Monte Carlo.'

'Ah yes – lovely summers in Monte Carlo,' Weenie said, 'rubbing shoulders with people like Anita Ekberg and Jean-Paul Belmondo.'

'The family had a house out there – it was like something out of a Scott Fitzgerald story, built on a cliff with terraces running down to the sea and palm trees. I was very sad when they decided to sell it – and there were the estates in Ireland, near Bantry Bay, but I never got to go there. The Earl usually visited by himself, probably to shoot with the local landowners, I imagine. It must have been quite a large estate because the wages were very high.'

'Now come on, Nerys – you couldn't possibly have known about the wages.'

'But I did. I did. I used to help with the bookkeeping when the children were away at school. I tell you, something odd was going on over there. I often wondered if the Earl was siphoning funds off from the Hall and over to Ireland to avoid death duties.'

'What nonsense,' Weenie said. She walked out onto the steps

and turned her face towards the sun, imagining she really had been in Monte Carlo in the sixties, sprawled on the mahogany of some glorious boat in her bikini. She had once spread herself out on the deck of friend's sailing boat on the Norfolk Broads and had never been asked again. Her boyfriend at the time told her the owners had been unable to remove the sun oil from the wood and the thought amused her – the idea that her form was imprinted on the planking for eternity like the ethereal figure on the Turin shroud.

'Good morning Roger,' she said as he came up the steps towards her. 'And how did you enjoy the opera?'

'Dire,' he said.

'What a pity – you should have stuck to your plans and done the evening function with us. The food was lovely.'

'Perhaps I should – but duty called.'

'You are wonderful,' Weenie said. Roger winked at her before sweeping past towards the door up to the guides' room to dump his things. He returned a few minutes later and said, 'Message from Bunty – Nerys is to take the next tour and you, my dear, are to make your way down to the library.'

'Oh, not again. Why can't I stay on the door with you Roger?'

'Boss's orders, I'm afraid. I've got that irritating new boy to break in, the one with all the hair – Rupert is it?'

'Rufus.'

'Bunty does like having men on the door. Besides, you should be bloody grateful – we've got a coach-load of wheelchairs coming in and I'd hate to see you struggling to push them up the ramps – especially in that silly little skirt you're wearing.'

'Really?'

'Not unless I was coming up behind you.'

'Roger. You are awful–'

– 'but you like me.'

This badinage set Weenie off towards the library with a buoyant step and scant concern that yet again Bunty had forgotten she hadn't had a tea break: over the last few months Roger had responded to her questing gaze on several occasions by returning it with a smouldering look from underneath his brows accompanied by a raffish smile.

When he arrived at the Hall a year earlier she had spotted him immediately at the opening pep talk which Simon Keane, the CEO, gave to the staff at the beginning of each season. She was excited that there a was new man at the Hall, someone who seemed dependable and manly. He was tall and well-built, with the upright posture that suggested he might have been in the forces at some stage in his life, and he dressed with flair and style. She struck up a friendly conversation with him as the staff milled around with their coffee cups and discovered he sat on the bench at the Oswestry Magistrates Court. She also guessed he was interested in her. As they chatted she spotted a small crumb of custard-cream filling which had fallen out of the biscuit he was eating and landed on his tie. It was sufficiently distracting that eventually she could stand it no longer and said, 'I'm afraid you've got something on your tie.'

Roger looked down and flicked the tip up towards him between his index and middle fingers. 'Well, so I have,' he said, letting the tie drop once more. He then moved the upper part of his torso towards her and said in a low tone which thrummed with suppressed desire, 'Do you want to take it off for me?'

When the season opened she was greatly disappointed to discover that he didn't work on the same days as her but whenever the staff congregated at a social gathering – which wasn't that frequently – she made a beeline for him and was confident that he very much looked forward to seeing her. Her hard work eventually paid off and he changed his days ostensibly because his working hours had altered but she was certain he had engineered things in order to work the same days as her.

Thrown together at last she realised her deep attraction to him was because he reminded her powerfully of the love of her life, Edgar Lockhart, the man she had adored for most of her twenties and well into her thirties. He was also a married man, which meant that she had spent all of her early adult life waiting. He had provided her with a gorgeous flat off the Fulham Palace Road and it was there that she did most of her waiting, there that she spent her Christmases alone, there that she imagined where his wife was taking him on every one of his birthdays.

Back then she forced herself to dwell instead on the positives. She enjoyed her freedom and appreciated that she was insulated from the drudgery of a married relationship – he only ever saw her at her glossed and buffed best, he never witnessed her shaving her legs or painting her toenails, and she never had to wash his socks, clean up after him or nurse him when another bout of the malaria he had picked up in Kenya laid him flat. When the weekends came and he left town to return to his wife and family she justified taking other men back to the flat for a bit of fun because she knew he was having fun with his wife and besides, she enjoyed living dangerously. She flirted with the frisson of discovery, fantasised about hearing the grumble of a taxi engine early in the morning in the street outside, the thrilling fear that Edgar was about to burst into the flat and find her with a man much younger than himself which would inflame his jealousy and force him to fulfil his promise – renounce his marriage and replace his wife with her.

Weenie was a few months away from her thirty-eighth birthday when she heard the news she had been waiting for for all those years – Edgar's wife had discovered his infidelity and thrown him out of the house. It wasn't Edgar who told her this wonderful news – she found out from a mutual friend who worked with him. When she failed to get hold of him for a number of days she turned up at his office – something she had been too discreet to do before. His secretary said he wasn't in but Weenie heard his voice on the other side of the door and burst through. He was in. He said yes, the story was true but the infidelity hadn't been theirs – he had been involved with someone else for the past two years and it was this third woman he intended marrying when his divorce came through.

Weenie didn't like to brood too much on the following couple of years when she took to her bed for months on end, lost her job and lived on a diet of gin and cigarettes. Besides, Roger reminded her of the good times she had with Edgar – a feeling of excitement that even though he belonged to someone else, he wanted to be with her. It would happen, she was confident of that.

After forty minutes of standing in the library on her own she started to feel rather testy and began craning her neck to see where on earth the next tour had got to. Eventually she spotted the reason for the delay – Nerys had just entered the china room and had four of the wheelchair users in her group.

The door halfway down the library opened and Laurence came wandering in from the statue corridor and up towards her. 'Weenie,' he said as he drew closer, 'Bunty sent me to relieve you. She said go and have your morning break.'

Weenie stretched out her arm and squinted at her wristwatch. 'Morning break? It's nearly one o'clock.'

Instead of commiserating Laurence cocked his head and stepped forward to peer down the state rooms. 'What on earth . . . ? Oh, my lordy lawks.' There was a tremendous commotion going on in the china room and, as the volume increased, Weenie recognised the foul mouth of the Earl.

'Chaos! Chaos everywhere. Can't you do your job properly?' The group was moving fast towards the watercolour room and the Earl towered above them, berating someone who was out of view. 'You've bloody well been here long enough – why can't you get it right? You're just another damned incompetent. I'm surrounded by bloody incompetents.'

Seeing that the Earl had broken away from the group and was surging towards them like a bull loose on the streets of Pamploma, Weenie ducked out of sight behind one of the bookshelves and beckoned frantically at Laurence who had begun to hop ineffectively from foot to foot and was, for some inexplicable reason, covering his genitals with his hands as if he was about to face a free kick.

The Earl burst into the library, spittle flying from his mouth as he bellowed 'Bloody cripples everywhere! Everywhere I look, all I see is bloody cripples. Get them out man – get them out.'

Weenie crept out from behind the bookshelf and hurried into the watercolour room, grabbing a wheelchair from one of the more frail helpers and, swerving to avoid the irate peer, she began to sweep down towards the exit. This finally galvanised Laurence into action and to her surprise he careered past her, making little bleating noises and pushing another wheelchair. She heard him say 'Don't look back, don't look back', and by the time they reached the end of the room, he was well in the lead.

Weenie heard the door to the statue corridor crash shut behind them – the Earl had exited the library – and they stopped to get their breath. She handed the wheelchair back to the helper and began to apologise on behalf of the Earl.

'Don't worry, dear,' said one old lady, 'I'm sure he's under a lot of pressure. It's quite understandable,' and the group continued on their way.

'Honestly Weenie, I do not know how that man gets away with it,' Laurence said. 'However rude he is, the visitors don't seem to mind.'

'He's the Earl. That's enough. It's all to do with breeding.'

'It's nothing to do with breeding any more – it's celebrity and I think it's disgusting. I hope one day something happens to that man to redress the balance. Do you believe in divine justice, Weenie?'

'I will if you will,' Weenie said, then brayed with laughter and stabbed him merrily in the ribs with her elbow.

'Poor old Nerys,' he said, 'she's been in that man's service for years – how could he speak to her like that?'

'Where has the old thing got to, by the way?' Weenie said, turning round to look back up the library. 'I'd better go and see if she's all right.' She retraced her steps and looked back through the rooms to where she had last seen Nerys. She thought for a moment that one of the group must have been feeling faint because she could see people bending and crouching around a figure slumped on one of the chairs. As she walked into the watercolour room she realised the figure was Nerys. Her skin had gone as grey as putty and she was staring down at her hands where her fingers worried a handkerchief in her lap. A visitor must have retrieved the chair from the other side of the ropes and placed it beside the window – it was a Chippendale.

'Come on, Nerys,' Weenie said in an ebullient tone, 'up you get. You can't sit on that. Supposing Bunty catches you. Let's get you back upstairs.'

'That dreadful man,' Nerys said.

'What? I can hardly hear you.'

'That dreadful man. I'm sure I saw that dreadful man.'

'We all saw him but you mustn't let him upset you so much. Come along,' and Weenie helped her to her feet.

They made their way up the winding staircase – too narrow for them to ascend side by side – towards the guides' room. 'Goodness,' Weenie said, flapping a hand in front of her face, 'that soil pipe is humming a bit today.' The pipe beneath the boxing had been fractured for the past eight years and depending on the direction of the wind or perhaps the height of the water table – Weenie wasn't sure which – it intermittently imbued the narrow staircase with the fetor of raw sewage. Weenie escorted Nerys over to the only comfortable chair in the room, then flicked on the kettle and rummaged around in the tin for a tea bag. She spooned several heaps of sugar into the cup and carried it over to her friend.

'All very upsetting,' she said. 'Come on, drink up. The sugar will do you good.'

'It was him,' Nerys said, more to herself than to Weenie. 'I'm sure it was him.'

'The Earl's really upset you this time, hasn't he?' Nerys shook her head slowly but Weenie wasn't sure she was listening. 'Do you want me to get someone to take you home?'

Nerys took a sip of tea and the intense sweetness seemed to shake her back on track. 'No,' she said, 'I'm better off working.'

She gave Weenie a brave smile. 'It's silly – things trigger an awful sense of doom – they warned me it would happen – but I'm better now. I'll go back down. I'm not meant to be on a break. I'll be in dreadful trouble if Bunty finds out.'

Left on her own, Weenie poured herself a cup of hot water, unwrapped the cling film from a slice of lemon she had in her handbag and dropped it into the cup. As she stirred and squashed the lemon slice with the spoon, she wondered if her friend was going a bit loopy.

– 5 –

The following morning Max woke early. He had never been one of the world's best sleepers and recently he had been waking at dawn, so instead of tossing around in bed in the forlorn hope that he might go back to sleep he had got into the habit of pulling on a pair of old jeans and a T-shirt and taking Monty for an early walk.

The countryside around his cottage was seldom busy but as the sun rose and the two of them set off across the deserted fields, the only sounds he could hear were the birds and the panting of his dog as he ran ahead. Max felt for all the world as if they were striding out across the ancient lands of Mercia. The wet and cold spring had held back the plants and now, pumped with moisture, they had exploded into action under the sunshine of early summer. The air was still moist from last night's dew and the fields around him looked like huge puffy eiderdowns as green as emerald, the lines left bare where the tractor wheels had run during sowing, seeming to pin the burgeoning vegetation down like quilting.

He began to climb the shoulder of the hill where the grass was so thick it brushed Monty's stomach as he bounded through it, pressing the blades down against the nap of the sward, leaving a silver trail where the light reflected off the glossy leaves as if the dog was a little dinghy putting out across a green ocean under the moonlight. Each puff of breeze sent silvery swells flowing and rippling across whole fields around the base of the hill and at every footfall lacewings rose up in front of Max before dropping away in waves which glistened in the sun.

When they reached the summit of the hill, Max paused and

gazed around. From this vantage point he could just see the tip of the chimney pot on top of his house poking out above the trees that filled the hamlet and he conjured up an image of Sam Westbrook down there, in his cottage, getting up and making coffee for his return. He sighed. How he wished Sam was here with him on this glorious summer morning.

He let himself back into his cottage with a vague sense of discontent and went upstairs to get ready for work. One of the greatest advantages of working as a guide at Duntisbourne was the hours – the ten o'clock start gave him plenty of time not only to walk the dog but also to have a leisurely breakfast. He took his coffee and toast out into the garden and sat listening to the birds busy around in the hedgerows, nesting and making families.

His pensive mood lingered on his drive to work but Duntisbourne Hall had a wonderful knack of taking his mind off his worries and he trusted today would be no exception. As he approached the entrance, Pugh must have spotted his Land Rover from a distance because the gatekeeper waved enthusiastically at him and was preparing to come out of the box when his phone started to ring. He turned back to answer it but kept on smiling and nodding as Max approached, then beckoned his car through giving him a huge smile and waving a sheet of paper at him as he passed. Pugh was a friendly sort and everyone at the Hall was a bit eccentric but the incident struck him as different in some way.

Max continued down the long drive and spotted fellow guide Claude Hipkiss striding ahead of him. He had learned not to offer the old boy a lift – Claude was the original iron man and liked to keep himself to himself – but this morning it was as if he had been keeping an eye open for Max because as he overtook him, Claude raised an arm and waved at him with enthusiasm, his grin baring uneven teeth like yellow tombstones.

'Most extraordinary,' Max said to himself as he drove on.

He was still puzzling it over as he parked but he was even more baffled when he climbed out of his car and saw Sharon, the Hall's cleaner, stumbling towards him with her arms outstretched.

'Mr Black,' she cried, 'I don't know as I've ever been more pleased with anything in all my born days,' and she clasped him by the shoulders and held him at arm's length. 'Well I must have–' and she planted a smacking kiss on the side of his face – 'and no offence on a day like this. You aren't offended, are you? I haven't taken too great a liberty have I? –But on a day like this . . . '

'A day like what?'

Their exchange was rudely interrupted by a coach driver blasting his horn at them to move out of the way. Sharon shrieked and bounded across the path of the vehicle and Max pressed himself against his car as the coach swept by, throwing up a huge cloud of dust and diesel exhaust.

He brushed at the lapel of his suit and looked around. Everything had gone very still. On the edge of the cloud of dust he could see Sharon backing slowly away, still smiling, and Bunty standing near the gate watching him too. The cloud began to thin and slowly, imperceptibly, the shadow of a figure coming towards him began to form but he couldn't make out who it was. The figure became clearer – he saw a flutter of blonde hair settle back on a slim shoulder and as the dust finally thinned and melted away, Sam Westbrook was standing in front of him.

He stood transfixed. In his head he breathed, Sam, my Sam, but he didn't rush forward and gather her up his arms, instead he gathered himself up inside and came over to greet her.

'Goodness. What a surprise! What are you doing back here again?'

She laughed and shook her head. 'Haven't you heard?'

'Heard what?'

'A memo went out two days ago.'

'What memo?'

'I thought everyone knew by now.'

'Knew what?'

Sam paused then laughed ruefully. 'I'm the archivist of Duntisbourne Hall.'

'You?'

'Well, don't sound so surprised.'

'Sorry. No. I'm not, I'm just – flabbergasted – and delighted. Absolutely delighted.'

They stood facing one another for a few moments until Max said, 'Come on then, we'd better get to work,' and fell into step beside her as they crossed the courtyard together, nodding and smiling at their work colleagues as they went.

'Why didn't you ring and tell me?' he said as they walked.

'I should have, I know, but when they first offered me the post it felt awful – as if I had pushed BS Moreton out of his job so that I could take it myself.'

'Rubbish,' Max said. 'The man was a crook – a charming crook, admittedly, but a crook.'

'And I was the snitch – as I recall.'

'Sam Westbrook. Never in all my dealings with the fair sex have I met a woman who can hold a hurt to herself for as long as you. We went through all that at the time and you did exactly what I asked you to do – you gave BS every opportunity to set the record straight and dig himself out of that enormous pit he had quarried. But he couldn't – he was in too deep.'

'Perhaps – but maybe I was wrong to do what I did.'

'If you hadn't, you could have been cited as an accessory.'

'I'm not sure saving my own skin is a particularly honourable reason for blowing the whistle on someone.'

Max stopped and touched her on the elbow so that she turned to face him. 'Where's all this negativity coming from?'

'I don't know – taking the poor old fellow's job, I suppose. What must the rest of your colleagues think about me now? They were very fond of BS.'

'Of course they were – as was I – and it's possible they might have taken a dim view of your part in the drama if the old boy had just helped himself to one or two choice items over the years, but he was flogging thousands of pounds' worth of treasures.'

'I know, but treasures that were given such scant respect by most of the people here. Now I realise BS had a great admiration for beauty, I can imagine he began by taking custody of a few things that seemed discarded or unloved – he probably felt he was giving them the deference they deserved – and then as time passed and no one noticed they were no longer at the Hall, they must have begun to feel like his and the decision to sell one of them would have seemed very small beer.'

'Of course he had his reasons but that doesn't mean he had an excuse.' Max looked out across the park and sighed. 'You know what, Sam? It wasn't many months ago that I spoke in BS's defence and you were firmly on the side of the prosecution. None of it really matters now – BS is home again sporting a rather fetching house arrest anklet.'

'Is he?'

'Yes, he is – and if you'd kept in touch like you promised, you'd know all that.' Sam had her eyes lowered and Max bent forward to peer at her. She smiled. 'That's better – look, it's a beautiful summer's day and I am delighted to have you back.'

'You're very sweet, Max.'

'Not sure I like sweet.'

Sam laughed. He liked it when Sam laughed.

'Well,' he said, 'I feel the bright and penetrating scrutiny of my colleague Noel watching us from the front door, so I'd better get going. Are you back in the flat then?'

'For the time being, yes. Pop in for a drink after work.'

'I thought you'd never ask.' He bounded away from her, taking the steps two at a time, but before he reached the top she called his name and he turned.

'It's great to see you too, Max,' she said.

'Good start to the day?' Noel said.

'The best.'

'Everyone thought you'd be pleased.'

'Everyone?'

'Yes. The news pretty much dominated yesterday.'

'I see. That explains it.'

'What?'

'The strange feeling I had that I was in a film I watched one Christmas with Charlotte.'

'What did you eventually decide about Charlotte?'

'You don't for a minute believe it's going to be me who makes the decision, do you?'

'No – I suppose not.'

'I rang her last night. She definitely wants to come for the summer so I promised her I'd have a word with Rosemary in the office – with a bit of luck they won't be taking on any more staff this late in the season.'

'I don't know how to break this to you, old chap, but I've a horrible feeling you're going to be out of luck. I walked in with Rosemary this morning and apparently the erotic exhibition is causing a number of tricky problems which the management hadn't thought through properly.'

'Such as?'

'Age restrictions to start with – they don't want to risk breaking any indecency laws and of course it's different country by country. Here it's eighteen, the States twenty-one, and in many countries, it's illegal – full stop.'

'I thought the whole thing about the exhibition was that it wasn't pornographic.'

'Mute point but not one we humble guides need to wrestle with. The only reason I'm telling you is that they have decided to set up a kiosk dedicated to selling tickets for the Dywenydd Collection because proof of age can be checked and there'll be a list of warnings that have to be read before a visitor can buy a ticket. They need some extra bods to man it.'

'OK.'

'You could keep quiet about it – your daughter would never know.'

'I can't do that – the alternative is she sets off travelling again and I don't think my nerves could stand another summer of that. Maybe it's not such a bad thing – she won't be working inside the Hall, which could have been problematic.'

'Why? You worried she might put a spoke in the wheels of your romance?'

'Not at all. I'm far more worried that she's going to embarrass me.'

'Flighty, is she?'

'Just a bit too pretty for her own good.'

When five o'clock finally arrived and the doors were locked behind the last visitors, Max left the shadow of the Hall and walked across the courtyard into the warmth of the evening sun towards the stable block and the flat that Sam had occupied during the spring. Dipping into the shadow once more as he entered the archway, he made his way up the stone steps with a sense of rising excitement and he tapped a jaunty tetrad of knocks on her door.

'Max!' she said. 'Come on in.' As he moved forward, she stepped to one side and he wasn't able to plant the welcoming kiss on her cheek that he had been planning. 'I want you to meet someone.' Behind her he spotted the polished toe of a brogue and as he followed her into the sitting room he saw it was attached to a man who rose to his feet as he entered. 'This is Hector Schofield – he's been down for the day researching a book he's writing on John Wilmot, the second Earl of Rochester.' Max sensed that she was talking with more haste than was necessary. 'His train back to London doesn't leave until eight so I invited him to join us. Hector – this is a colleague of mine, Max Black.'

The visitor placed a warm palm into Max's hand and shook it firmly. 'Very nice to meet you,' he said.

'Right.'

'Do sit down, both of you. What can I get you to drink, Max?' Sam said. 'A beer?'

'Yes. That would be lovely.' He sat down in the chair on the other side of the fireplace and appraised the stranger.

Hector Schofield was probably a few years younger than him. He was dressed as you would expect a man from London to dress for a visit to the country – jumbo cords, a mustard sports jacket with a dark blue shirt and no tie. His hair was brushed straight back from his forehead, accentuating the widow's peak between his receding temples. Max had often noted that men who retained a thick head of hair past their forties frequently wore it too long and Schofield's curled densely onto his collar at the back. Despite the darkness of his hair he had the sandy complexion of a red-head, the skin dull and rough across his cheeks suggesting that as an adolescent he had suffered from acne, but instead of this blight-ing his good looks it seemed to confirm his manliness – a sign that abundant levels of testosterone had been pumping around his body throughout his adult life. Max took an instant dislike to him.

'Lord Rochester, eh?' Max said. 'He was an Oxford man, wasn't he? I can't think of any connection he could have with Duntis-bourne Hall.'

'You wouldn't think so,' Schofield said, leaning forward in his seat towards Max and placing his elbows on his knees in a pose of familiarity as if they were two friends having a chat in their drink-ing club, 'but you'd be wrong.'

'Would I?'

'It was the publicity surrounding the Dywenydd Collection that alerted me to the possibility that an extraordinary item once used by that fascinating and dissolute rake may have fallen into the hands of your very own wicked earl.'

'And did it?'

Sam joined them and handed Max his beer. 'We don't know yet,' she said. 'There's still a great deal that the inventory of the collec-tion has to tell us. The more I study it, the more I realise it's actual-ly a sort of journal – minutes almost – of the raucous meetings that the ninth earl held with his cronies, and there do seem to be hints that a particularly odd artefact was brought to Duntisbourne Hall by an officer in the Royal Navy – William Augustus Montagu.'

Schofield intervened. 'Sorry, Sam – it's a bit complicated. It may be best if I explain,' and he nodded at her and smiled. 'This officer was the illegitimate son of the fifth Earl of Sandwich.'

'The sandwich man.'

'No, no, that was his father. No, the fifth earl – Hinchinbrooke – you know, Eton and the Guards and all that – was the great-grandson of Lord Rochester.'

'I didn't think he left an heir,' Max said.

Schofield paused and the hint of a frown rippled across his brow. 'He did as a matter of fact, but the boy died when he was about eleven and the earldom became extinct. The Rochester estate was divided up between his three surviving daughters and it was one of these – Elizabeth – who married the third Earl of Sandwich. Their son predeceased them so her grandson eventually took the title of the fourth Earl of Sandwich and it was he who was the eponymous inventor of the sandwich.' Max was beginning to feel exceedingly bored. He had enough trouble remembering all the earls of Duntisbourne and at least they were relevant to his job – he had little interest in this interminable family tree. He glanced over towards Sam but she seemed to be listening to Schofield with rapt attention.

'OK, so that's the culinary side wrapped up,' Max said. 'Why don't you cut to the chase and tell us how this involves the Dywenydd Collection?'

'Oh, sorry,' Schofield said, 'I didn't mean to bore you.'

'Not at all.' Max was aware that Sam was looking at him and wished he hadn't sounded testy. 'I'm obviously eager to tie the story down to Duntisbourne. I'm afraid I tend to tune out a bit when we get on to the English peerage. It never helps that they all seem to have the same name.'

'Quite,' Schofield said. 'Well, William Montagu was the illegitimate son of the fifth earl so there is a connection back to John Wilmot, Earl of Rochester.'

'OK.'

'Now, you may recall a famous painting of Wilmot which shows him with a monkey – in fact, I've got a copy of it,' and he opened up a black saddle-leather briefcase that was leaning against his seat. 'Here it is, or at least one of the versions of it – this one's in the National Portrait Gallery. You can see that he's holding a laurel crown over the monkey's head – the poet's laurels – but the monkey is tearing up a book and handing the crumpled pages to Wilmot who in turn holds a handful of pages of his own verse – a rather witty satire.'

'Is it?'

'Now,' Schofield placed the picture on the table, 'there were rumours at the time that when the monkey died he had it stuffed.'

'What?'

'Yes. Extraordinary, I know, but even stranger, I believe it was preserved in such a way that it could be used as a *dame de voyage* – a forerunner to today's blow-up doll.'

Max was seized by an almost uncontrollable urge to bellow with laughter but seeing that neither Schofield nor Sam seemed to find the notion as amusing as he did, he struggled to get his mirth under control.

'The *dame de voyage* is not without historical precedence,' Schofield continued. 'French and Spanish sailors constructed them out of sewn cloth or old clothes to comfort themselves during long sea voyages. However, this may be the first time an actual creature was used in such a way and I can only prove the validity of the rumour if I can find some allusion to it. The moment I came across a reference to Montagu's visit here, I realised that the inventory of the Dywenydd Collection may well hold the Holy Grail I have been searching for.'

'On what evidence – apart from the visit?'

'The tenth earl, of course.'

'Of Sandwich?'

'No, of Duntisbourne.'

Clarity dawned and Max said, 'Right. The Victorian prig who was crazy about taxidermy.'

'Precisely – and I suggest that he wasn't such a prig after all. I think that in his youth he had seen this extraordinary simulacrum and it spawned his fascination with preserving life.'

'It's all a bit tenuous, isn't it?'

'Perhaps, but if I can find some reference to it in the inventory here, I will know it existed. It would be an incredible breakthrough and would throw open a whole new chapter on the Earl of Rochester's merry gang, and your delightful colleague here–' Schofield leant forward and brushed a hand across Sam's knee – 'has promised to decipher as much as she can from the accounts of those extraordinary and debauched meetings of the eighteenth century.'

'As much as I can in my spare time,' Sam said.

Max wasn't sure whether his deep distrust of Schofield was building because he represented an eager rival for Sam's affections or whether something else was making him wary. As the years passed Max gave more credence to his hunches and there was something phony about this man.

'So,' Max said, 'written much then?'

'Yes.'

'Historical?'

'Of course. I try to fill the gaps left by other writers and eventually the Stuarts captured my imagination. However, I wanted to leave the Darnleys and the Charleses alone and hunt for the fascinating peripheral figures of the time.'

'Is the Earl of Rochester a peripheral figure?'

'Of course not, but his merry gang were and I'm focussing on them. My book on Captain Downs is doing rather well at the moment. The title's readily available – you should take a look. I think you'd enjoy it.'

'Perhaps I shall.'

'Good heavens,' Schofield said, getting to his feet. 'Is that the time? I hadn't realised. I must call a cab or I'll miss that train.'

'Would you like a lift?' Sam said.

'That's very kind of you. Well, yes, if I may – I am cutting it a bit fine.'

Max was on his feet. 'Let me take you,' he said. 'It's practically on my way.'

'Is it?' Sam said.

'Pretty much.'

'That's very decent of you, old fellow – but, do you know what?' and he turned to Sam. 'I've been toying with the idea of buying one of those little Mazdas that you drive and we could kill two birds with one stone by taking yours for a spin over to the station – if it's not too much trouble.'

'Not at all,' Sam said.

There was a deal of hunting for keys and fetching bags and Max found himself following the pair of them as they hurried down the stairs and into the courtyard.

'I'm through here,' Sam said. 'Night, Max. Really great to see you. Catch up tomorrow – yes?' and they disappeared round the corner towards the staff car park, Schofield's metal heel tips clicking a snappy tattoo as he escorted her away.

As a member of the seasonal staff, Max was obliged to park his Land Rover in the south car park. He was climbing into the driver's seat when he heard the toot of a horn. Sam's Mazda swept past him with the soft top down and he saw her raised hand wave at him as she sped off into the distance. The leonine head of Schofield was bent towards her, no doubt engaging her in more witty repartee. Max slammed his door shut and crunched the gear-stick forward, feeling a rising sense of irritation and disappointment.

'Isn't it ironic?' Schofield said as the car spun through the country lanes. 'We've lived within a stone's throw of one another for years – you in Chelsea, me in the King's Road – and yet I first make your acquaintance after you've moved down here, but I expect you'll be making frequent visits back to London.'

'I wasn't planning to,' Sam said.

'Really? Surely you haven't relocated completely?'

'No, not at all, but my daughter's using the flat at the moment and she's decided she needs a bit of space to sort herself out.'

'And so you've had to move out.' Sam heard a snuff of disbelief.

'It isn't like that. Duntisbourne Hall offered me the post and taking the job solved a couple of problems rather neatly. Claire and I are the best of friends but to be perfectly honest, when we live on top of one another we can get a bit irritable. Do you have children?'

'Good heavens no – but aren't you going to find it incredibly parochial stuck away down here in the Welsh Marches?'

'It's different, I'll grant you that.'

Schofield leant forward in his seat to fiddle with the audio system. 'Does it have a CD stacker?' He seemed inured to the beauty of the countryside that sped past them.

'Do you mind if we don't have music?' Sam said. 'I'm still enjoying the novelty of driving around with the roof down, hearing a snatch of birdsong here, the barking of a dog there. It's like being up in a hot air balloon, don't you think? Sounds and smells come at you in such volume on an evening like this.'

The road dipped into the heavy shade of an avenue of trees so thick they met above their heads like the nave of a vast green cathedral. The noise of the sports car echoed around the wood as if they were driving inside the building itself. The air surrounding them was redolent with the smell of moss and rich humus but as the car burst out of the shadow of the woods and into the evening sunshine, a gasp of summer air buffeted Sam's senses and surrounded her with the scent of new-mown grass, mixed with Schofield's expensive aftershave. Something unbidden vibrated deep in her thorax – that light purr of sexual attraction.

Schofield gazed around, his mane of hair tousling in the wind and she sensed he was finally in tune with her mood. As they continued on their journey, he lay back against the headrest and turned his face, eyes closed, towards the setting sun and she heard a barely perceptible sigh reverberate in his chest. A tiny finger of pink cloud slipped across the horizon, disrupting the fragile heat from the sun, and Schofield roused himself. Rolling his head as if he lay on a pillow beside her, he turned and looked at her and despite the brightness of the evening, the pupils of his eyes glistened black and wide like an opium user. 'I must admit,' he said, 'it is very beautiful around here.'

He smiled and let his head flop back as he closed his eyes once more. 'I'll just have to come down more often.'

– 6 –

As Max worked at the Hall every other day, the following morning he decided to do a little research at home into Hector Schofield's writing career. It didn't take him long to find him or the handful of historical titles attributed to him – *The Downfall of Downs*, *The Roaring Girl: The Life and Times of Moll Cutpurse* and *Fille d'Alliance: The First Feminist* – and he was heartily cheered to read a number of online reviews panning the validity of the research behind them, one reviewer caustically observing that the books should be in the fiction section of the website. Still chuckling to himself Max made his way into the kitchen and turned the kettle on. As he waited for it to boil, Monty trotted into the room and stood staring at the window.

'What's up, old chap?'

Max wandered across and looked out onto the quiet lane which ran past his front door and sure enough, an old Anglia had drawn up next to the verge and he could see the shadow of the passenger pulling bags forward from the back seat. A moment later the car door opened, emitting a noise of grinding metal, and his daughter tumbled out, a mobile phone and handbag spilling off her lap onto the ground. She retrieved them and said something laughingly to the driver as she hauled bag after bag out of the car and onto the ground before closing the door with a mighty slam and patting the roof as the vehicle drew away.

Monty rushed ahead as Max made his way to the front door.

'Daddy! My Daddy!' – and Charlotte hurled herself into his arms.

'Hi, sweetie. Goodness. However long are you staying?'

'Only two months.'

'But you decided to bring everything in your flat with you just in case.' Charlotte poked him playfully in the ribs and picked up some of the bags. 'Straight upstairs with that lot, please – I'll bring the rest. Monty! Get out of the way.'

Having settled her things upstairs Charlotte joined her father in the kitchen for a cup of tea. 'I had a really nice letter from the Hall,' she said. 'I've got to go in this afternoon for some sort of induction talk. Somewhere called the Siegfried Rooms. Why's it called that?'

'It's a family name going back hundreds of years, apparently. The first six earls were called Siegfried.'

'Easy to find?'

'As easy as any of the rooms in that rabbit warren of a place.'

'Come with me.'

'You don't need me there.'

'Please, Dad. I'd borrow your car but I hate driving that Land Rover. Bring Monty. We could go for a walk around the estate afterwards.' Max gave his daughter a disbelieving look. 'Go on. Say you will.'

'I'll tell you what – why don't I take you over and walk Monty around the estate while you have your meeting? How's that for a compromise?' Charlotte gave him a brief hug – that was exactly what she wanted him to do.

Having completed the perimeter of the Red Lake, Max lifted Monty into the back of the Land Rover and secured the lead inside to stop him jumping out. He flopped the tailgate down so that the dog wouldn't get hot and poured some bottled water into a bowl for him.

'Don't knock it over, old chap,' he said, pushing it along the floor towards him and ruffling the top of the dog's head. 'I won't be long.'

He had told Charlotte he would be waiting in the car for her but he knew the meeting rooms were below Sam's flat and hoped that if he hung around that part of the building he might run into her. He made his way across the great courtyard – the only pets allowed in here were the Earl's gun dogs – sauntered over to the Siegfried Rooms and peered in through the windows.

There were about ten people sitting in scattered groups around a projector, most of them students, and he spotted Charlotte's hectic hairstyle sticking up above the heads. Rosemary was giving out some sort of manual and her audience were shuffling in their seats and gathering their bags so he assumed the meeting was reaching a conclusion and he wouldn't have many more minutes to wait. He perched himself on a stone bollard and leant his back against the wall, warming himself in the sun. Half closing his eyes, he listened to the sound of the gravel crunching under the feet of the passing visitors, the murmur of voices, an occasional chuckle of laughter.

'You look comfy,' Sam said.

'Hello.' He roused himself. 'I was – I'd almost dropped off. Where did you come from?'

'I saw you sitting out here. I came to apologise.'

'What for?'

'Last night.'

'Oh, that. And what is the spry Hector Schocroft up to today I wonder?'

'Schofield – his name's Schofield.'

'Schofield, Schocroft. What does it matter? He's probably off buying a nice little Mazda just like yours?'

'Come on, Max. He's not that bad.'

'He's a type.'

'Aren't we all?'

'He's a scoke.'

'There's no such word.'

'There is now. It's a sort of roué but much more dangerous.'

'Why did you take such an instant dislike to him?'

'I've a feeling it'll save me a lot of time in the future.'

'You're impossible, Max. Hector isn't such a bad sort – I thought him rather charming. And this story about Lord Rochester's monkey has a certain validity to it. I'm happy to help out a bit – it would be a good piece of extra promotion for the Dywenydd Collection if it turns out to be true.'

'Of course it isn't true.'

'What?'

'A stuffed monkey from the eighteenth century? It's ludicrous. I'll grant you one thing – he does have his eye on a *dame de voyage* but make no mistake, she's very much twenty-first century.'

The doors to the Siegfried Room opened and the students spilled out into the sunshine, chatting among themselves.

'Charlotte,' Max said, 'come over here. This is Sam Westbrook, a colleague.'

'Dad's mentioned you,' Charlotte said. She didn't go forward to shake hands but instead slipped her fingers through her father's arm and held him affectionately by the elbow. 'Come on Dad, let's go home. I'm starving.'

'See you tomorrow I expect,' Max said as he was led away. A tall lad who had been in the meeting was walking in front of them and as soon as Charlotte had propelled her father towards the exit, she abandoned him and ran ahead to catch the young man up.

'Rufus,' she said, 'wait for us.' Max followed a few paces behind. He glanced back over his shoulder but Sam had disappeared. Charlotte and Rufus were waiting for him at the back of the Land Rover when he reached it and the lad was messing around with Monty.

'I wouldn't do that if I were you,' Max said. 'He's been in the lake. Smells like a shit-house midden.'

'I said we could give Rufus a lift over to Shobdon.'

'Did you?'

'Come on, Dad – it's not that far out of our way.'

'Only about ten miles.' Max laughed and patted the boy on the shoulder to reassure him that he was pulling his leg. 'Of course we can give you a lift. Hop in. We should all fit in the front seat.' He pushed up the tailgate and locked it into position. 'Sorry old stumper,' he said to Monty, 'you're going to have to stay there for a bit. Someone else has got your seat.' Monty flopped back down onto an old coat that was on the floor and sighed heavily before resting his jowls on his paws.

The Land Rover rattled along between the squared-off hawthorn hedges that rose up on either side of the road and the vegetation boiled along the verges in the slipstream of the vehicle. The modest slopes of Combe Wood rose up on their right as they headed towards the flatter land to the east of the county.

'Where are you at university?' Max said.

'Oxford.'

'Goodness. That's quite a long way away. Family nearby?'

'Shobdon.'

'Ah – the same as Charlotte then, a summer of home comforts. This'll be quite a trek in each day for you though, won't it?'

'I can cycle it in less than an hour.'

'Good man.'

Max was rather surprised that Charlotte had taken an interest in the fellow – he seemed a shallow, coltish, privileged sort of boy. She usually went for a rougher type and for several years he had lived with the dread certainty that she would end up with a boy who played an instrument very badly in some amateur rock band. Max acknowledged that judged by her former choices, Rufus ticked some of her boxes – he was dark, good-looking with luminous eyes and almost totally silent – but he was wearing a cheap black suit which must have seen him through sixth form. The fabric had the burnish of several years of hard-wearing and the trousers and jacket sleeves were too short. Rufus had obviously hit a recent growth spurt and he moved with that awkward gangle that suggested he was still trying to come to terms with these surprisingly long and ungainly limbs which eighteen months ago had been easier to control.

They dropped him off in front of a pretty timber-framed house on the edge of the village. 'Thank you very much, Mr Black,' he said.

'Call me Max, for goodness' sake – after all, we're going to be working together.'

'Bye, Charlotte,' he said.

'Facebook me.'

'OK.'

'Seems like a nice lad,' Max said as they set off back home. 'Bit posh for you though.'

'Stop it, Dad. We're not going to start seeing each other.'

'You'll see him at work.'

'You know what I mean. I felt sorry for him, that's all. He got a bit bullied.'

'Bullied? You were only there for a couple of hours. How on earth could he have found someone to bully him?'

'One of the Hall guides came over to talk about doing tours and she asked if anyone knew anything about the history of the earls. Poor old Rufus stuck up his hand and said he knew that the fifth earl fought at the Battle of Malplaquet and lost the tip of his nose, and this woman smacked him down like you wouldn't believe.'

'Because the nose was lost at Ramillies.'

'Evidently – but what's the bloody difference? She made him feel about two inches high. Poor chap went bright red. It was awful. I was pretty impressed Rufus knew anything at all and that he had the courage to speak and I told the silly old bag that's what I thought in no uncertain terms. She denied the whole thing – did a complete about-face in front of the whole room. Said she wouldn't dream of putting a young person down like that, I had misinterpreted what she said, she was just making sure he got the facts right.'

'Charlotte! I've told you, if you're going to survive here at the Hall keep your head below the parapet. You've got to rabbit crawl; don't draw attention to yourself.

'But she was horrid to him. I'm glad I won't be working as a guide.'

'Which old harridan was it?'

'I can't remember her name. Whippet-thin, lots of make-up, huge great panto head on a shrunken body.'

'Ah – I think I know who you mean. Edwina Lemon. She likes to be called Weenie – I suppose it smacks of the country set to use your nickname when you're a grown woman. She savaged me a few times when I first started. It's not pleasant but neither is it a good idea to make an enemy out of any of that old school of guides.' Max paused then added, 'That's not quite accurate actually. There are some very decent old-school guides there like Claude and Noel – and you know I'm a great champion of women but I have to admit that most of the trouble is caused by those old gals. I've never heard the old boys squabbling and backbiting. Why doesn't Rufus work outside instead?'

'He's good at languages – he speaks French and German, so he'd be wasted if he was out there with the rest of us. I think he said he gets a few pounds extra for doing language tours.'

'If they let him.'

'Why wouldn't they?'

'Let me think – because he's young, personable and enthusiastic for a start.'

'Stop it, Dad.'

'It's true – if Rufus was old enough to remember rationing he might be in with a chance, but otherwise . . . '

'You're pulling my leg.'

'You've got a lot to learn.'

– 7 –

As May moved into June, Weenie's mood continued to rise as if in concord with the daily arc of the sun. This particular Wednesday morning, she was standing in the indigo library waiting for the next tour to reach her so that she could go upstairs for a cup of tea. She wasn't wasting her time – she was working on her pelvic floor, pulling up and clenching the muscles as she stood. She had read that French women seldom suffered from stress incontinence in later life because they received specialist physiotherapy treatments after childbirth to re-educate their pelvic floor muscles and core body strength, and even though she had never had children, if it worked for the French, she felt sure it would work for her.

A group of visitors entered the china room and she narrowed her eyes to see if she could make out who was guiding them. Roger Hogg-Smythe was on the rota today and if he was taking the tour she intended spinning out her break so that she had the opportunity for a chat – he would be next up to the guides' room after her, but to her disappointment she recognised the delicate physique of Laurence Cooke. She sighed and wandered over to the French windows, pressing the handles down to check that the doors into the garden were locked before gazing out across the estate, wishing she was strolling down the river walk in this glorious sunshine, hand in hand with Roger.

'Weenie! You can't see the end of the room from there. Get back into position.' Bunty bustled up towards her. 'If one of the new recruits saw you they might follow suit.'

'I thought I heard someone trying to open the door,' Weenie lied.

'Did you? All right then.' Bunty went up to the window and

looked out. 'No one there. Perhaps it was the wind – it's blowing from the north today. Now, I was looking for you because I have been presented with a problem. Since Maureen Hindle left to join that revivalist crusade to India, the office have asked me to nominate a replacement for when I need cover.'

'A new head guide?' Weenie said.

'No, I don't think that's the right idea at all. I'm head guide – Maureen was there to deputise for me in the past, that was all. I'm not away that often. The office just want to feel that someone could step in at a moment's notice if by any chance I couldn't make it in – call it a duty guide.'

'I would be very happy to volunteer.'

'I thought you might – and you have been here such a very long time.'

'Not that long.'

'A very long time nonetheless. The only other person who has been here as long as you is Nerys Tingley and I will suggest that she is also nominated as duty guide.'

'Nerys? She couldn't possibly keep control of the Hall floor.'

'She'll have the support of the team, I'm sure of that.'

'She's far too fragile. She can only manage the door if I'm there to keep things under control and tell her what to do. She just isn't strong enough to do the job on her own. If she was let loose trying to organise tours the whole place would clog up in next to no time.'

'That can't be helped – it's not possible to put you forward and bypass Nerys. It's a matter of seniority, always has been. There's talk in the office that someone like Noel or Laurence could do it perfectly well. The other day I even heard them discussing Max as a possible candidate . . . '

'Noel Canterbury and Laurence Cooke? Preposterous. We've never had a man in charge – a man would take over immediately. And Max Black? He only started this season.'

'Precisely. But Rosemary has taken rather a shine to him. That's why it's vital we go down the route of years served and if I put your name forward, I have to put Nerys up to deputise too. I really can't see she'll ever be asked to actually do the job – we can make sure of that – but it'll quash any silly talk about having a man organising the floor.'

'I see. Well, I suppose it makes sense.'

'Go on then, go and have a cup of tea. I'll wait here until Laurence arrives. Not a word of this to anyone at the moment though. I need to speak to Nerys first and explain the situation.'

'Of course.'

As Weenie cut through the music room on her way to the statue corridor, she saw the dependable figure of Roger Hogg-Smythe coming towards her.

'Roger,' she trilled. He was looking exceedingly dapper – fairly tanned with his grey hair freshly cut into the short style that so suited men of his age.

'Weenie. Good morning. You're looking perky.'

'I'm feeling perky as a matter of fact. I've just had some rather good news.' She placed her hand on Roger's cuff and leaned in towards him. 'They're going to make me head guide.'

'Are they, by God? I've always thought one would have to be either very thick-skinned or stupid to accept that poisoned chalice.'

'Really?'

'And you're nothing if not thick-skinned, Weenie.'

'Thank you, Roger.' She continued on her way up to the guides' room feeling vaguely discomfited. Having made her cup of hot water, she sat down at Bunty's desk and started to read the selection of notices that had been stuck in position on its surface with blu-tack. One in particular began to lift her spirits – the date for the Summer Progress celebrations had been set for early August. It was during this Tudor extravaganza that Queen Elizabeth had first set eyes on the youthful Lord Siegfried, son of the first Earl of Duntisbourne, setting the family on a path to fame and fortune. As the original party thrown by Robert Dudley, Earl of Leicester, had run for three weeks in the summer of 1575 at Kenilworth Castle, the setting of the date for the Duntisbourne Hall celebration was a little like Easter – it was late some years and early others depending on whether the Earl was in the country or not and as Weenie had already identified it as the perfect opportunity to move in on Roger, the party could not come too soon.

Two hours later Max was staring at the same piece of paper and feeling diametrically opposite emotions. He loathed parties with a vengeance because they embodied many of the elements he had hated about his marriage. Every Friday and Saturday night he had been dragged round to the house of some vague acquaintance of his ex-wife where he would be stuck in the corner of the kitchen, stone cold sober because he always had to drive, with a group of people he hardly knew and couldn't talk to anyway because the music in the sitting room was too loud. He would watch a scattering of middle-aged people flailing around on the patterned carpet in the lounge like frogs nailed to the floorboards and long to be anywhere else on earth. All these years later he could still feel the exquisite joy of that first Saturday night after his wife had left. She had stripped the house of every decent piece of furniture but when he sank back onto the broken sofa in front of the black-and-white television with a beer in his hand he could only think, what bliss, I don't have to go out tonight.

'I'm not going to this,' he said.

'It's rather expected that you will,' Noel said.

'I hate parties.'

'Milk?'

'Thanks.'

'Thing is, old chap,' Noel said as he handed him his cup of tea, 'the Earl insists everyone attends. He maintains that he has never missed it himself, chiefly because they change the date to fit in with him, but he expects every member of staff to do the same.'

'No one will notice if I miss it.'

'I can assure you, they will. It's just one of those things we all have to do. But look on the bright side – the delightful Mrs Westbrook will be under the same obligation to attend.'

'Yes, I suppose she will.'

'It could be a fine opportunity to advance the friendship into something more serious.'

'Oh really, Noel.'

'And the young always enjoy it.'

'Bull shit.'

'What?'

'Charlotte will be there.'

'How's she settling in, by the way? Done your head in yet?'

'No, as a matter of fact I hardly see her. She seems to spend all her time out with the kiosk girls – and Rufus, of course. I catch a fleeting glimpse of her in the morning but that's about it.'

'They'll have a great old time at the party.'

'Supposing she makes a complete fool of herself.'

'The students usually do. I can't count the number of time I've seen Pugh out there the following morning with the rake, working the pools of vomit into the gravel.'

'For pity's sake.'

'Just high spirits and a free bar. It's all innocent fun really. I'm sure you'll enjoy it. Some of the oldies get a bit frisky too.'

'Can this get any worse?'

'Even Nerys has been known to let her hair – or should I say bun – down.'

'Nerys Tingley? Isn't she a fully paid-up member of the spinster aunts?'

'You'd be surprised. Fluttering underneath that twinset is a heart full of suppressed urges.'

'Noel!'

'Trust me – I'm not messing around. Come over here,' and Noel beckoned him to the corkboard where a number of group photographs had been pinned over the years. 'See this chap,' pointing to a picture of the guides' day out taken at the entrance of Stokesay Castle, 'that's Nigel Procter, the first IT man. When the trustees decided it was time to modernise, he arrived to link everyone up and get the Hall's website working, but he didn't last more than a couple of seasons – a couple of seasons too long in my opinion.'

'Really?'

'Oh, yes. He was a thoroughly unpleasant piece of work – short man, brutish temper, used to get right into your face and stab away at your shoulder with an offensive forefinger. Trouble was, the trustees were up a gum tree – no one really understood the system he'd installed and he'd been given free rein. He made himself unsackable within the year. Anyway, once stories started circulating of him hacking into people's private email accounts they shifted him pretty quick but it took a long time to sort out the mess. Anyway, unbeknownst to us, a rather unsavoury liaison was brewing up between him and Nerys.'

'Good heavens.'

'Yes – it caught us all a bit by surprise.'

'Whatever was the attraction?'

'It was rumoured that he was living in a Studebaker camper van parked up towards Nash Wood and was looking for a liaison that came with a permanent bed to sleep in. Nerys meanwhile had signed up to do an evening course in counselling and was looking for likely candidates to try her listening cure on. She certainly plucked a beaut when she settled on Procter. It all started to come out when, purely by chance, Bunty spotted Nerys parking up near the start of the long trail and standing on the hill with his arms open like the Spirit of the North ready to receive her was Procter. None of us believed Bunty until the Summer Progress party, where I'm afraid their behaviour left no one in any doubt whatsoever.'

Max peered at the photograph. The pale face of a balding man well into his fifties glared out at him and beside him Max recognised Nerys, although her hair was fuller and a little darker. 'I suppose that's quite nice for them, even if it wasn't such a pleasant thought for you,' he said.

'You old romantic,' Noel said. 'Who'd have thought – and I'd probably have agreed with you if it wasn't for the fact that after that evening Nerys had some sort of nervous breakdown.'

'Why?'

'No one really knows although Bunty – who can usually wheedle the most salacious pieces of information out of people – hinted darkly that he had done something appalling in the brown drawing room. This is the first season Nerys has been back since it all went off and Bunty has told us in no uncertain terms not to mention the events of that summer to Nerys under any circumstances in case she morphs from spinster aunt to raving loon again.'

'And Procter?'

'He went abroad. Last we heard of him he was living in the Czech Republic.'

'Czechoslovakia?'

'Well, it's not called that any more, but yes – Laurence and his partner visited the Sex Machines Museum in Prague a few years ago and there he was, working as a room warden.'

'You do talk a load of bollocks, Noel.'

'It's all true – ask Nerys's new best friend if you don't believe me.'

'Which is who?'

'Weenie, of course.'

'Really? You do surprise me.'

'Classic vain woman syndrome, isn't it? Weenie couldn't possibly have a meaningful friendship with someone like – I don't know – Sam, for instance. It would be far too challenging to be in the company of someone you think might be a rival for male attention, so you pick a plain friend. Nerys plays her part – she's about the only one here who can stand listening to Weenie puffing up her achievements and conquests. Nerys is a sweet old girl – I've even heard her complimenting Weenie on the way she looks and I'd rather eat my feet than do that.'

Max drained his cup and went over to the sink to rinse it. 'I will regard Nerys in a whole new light,' he said.

'And watch yourself at the summer party.'

Max was still toying with excuses to wriggle out of the August party when he arrived at the kiosk near the entrance to the great courtyard to collect Charlotte.

'Come on round to the back,' she said through the hatch. 'I'm almost done.'

He let himself into the portakabin which smelt of freshly sawn wood and raised a hand to Rufus who was sitting on a typist's chair, swivelling from side to side, watching Charlotte with a bovine regard. Charlotte was running through some papers with another girl a bit older than her. 'Goodness, it's rather smart in here,' Max said, 'a lot better than the guides' room. What that? A fridge? A kettle? A microwave?'

'Don't pretend you don't have those too.'

'Not the microwave. Noel said he tried to bring an old one in that had been left behind when his daughter moved out of her flat but Bunty sent him packing with it – she said the guides take far too long for their breaks as it is and if they were heating up food it would only be a matter of time before folk were flapping open damask tablecloths and settling down to a three-course lunch.'

'This is my dad,' Charlotte said. 'Dad – Robyn.' Robyn was a tall, athletic woman probably in her thirties. Without getting to her feet she tipped her finger against her eyebrow in a sort of welcoming salute. 'She's working upstairs in the Dywenydd Collection.'

'Humble room warden,' Robyn said before turning her attention back to Charlotte.

'Thing is,' Charlotte continued, 'you won't have to worry about anyone's age because if they've got a ticket you'll know that either me or Jess have vetted them out here.'

'Jess?' Robyn said.

'Jessica Williams.'

'Have I met her?'

'Don't know. She went early today but you'll meet her tomorrow. She's fun.'

'What about disabled access?'

'I've been told there isn't any.'

'That's not going to go down very well.'

'Just what I've been told.'

'If you're in a wheelchair, the collection isn't really for you,' Max said. All three young people turned to face him with expressions varying from amusement from Robyn to embarrassment from Charlotte.

'Dad!'

'What?'

'You can't go round saying things like that.'

'Why not?'

'Political hot potato,' Robyn said. 'I did a stint one year at a special needs summer retreat and they couldn't get enough of it. I was forever being called down to the sports field to get them back into their wheelchairs.'

'Stop it!'

'True.'

'Come on, Dad, it's time I got you home.'

'Need a lift again, Rufus?'

'No thank you, Mr Black. I've got my bike.'

'Robyn?'

'Oh – no thanks all the same – I'm running this evening.'

The four of them walked out to the car park together where Rufus unchained his bike and Robyn pulled her rucksack over her back and set off into the park at an easy jog.

'Does it worry you,' Max said, 'that you seem to have chummed up with two rather sporty members of staff?'

'They're not particularly sporty – and wait till you meet Jess.'

'Well, those two certainly make me feel like a couch potato,' he said, tooting his horn first at Robyn as they passed her and then at Rufus who was several hundred yards further on, pumping at the pedals of his bike, his shirt tail flapping in the wind behind him. 'I could always borrow a bike for you.'

'Please, I get plenty of exercise. Hey, but what about this party? Sounds like fun.'

Max groaned. 'Now for God's sake don't go making a fool of yourself – or of me.'

'Dad! Have a little faith.'

'There's a free bar.'

'Brilliant.'

Max shot her a disapproving look. 'Noel says the students have a bit of a reputation for overindulgence and I couldn't stand the embarrassment of the gateman having to rake your drunken offering into the gravel the following morning.'

'I've never been sick on drink.'

'Keep it that way.'

That evening, after Charlotte had eaten a cheese omelette and Max a steak, they settled down together in the sitting room. Max picked up the TV guide to see what was suitable for them to watch together but Charlotte moved over to the sofa and sat beside him with her laptop open.

'You know you think Rufus is a bit of a dork?'

'I do not. I said he was a bit posh, as a matter of fact.'

'I want to show you this.'

'It's not rude, is it?'

'No. It's funny.'

She clicked the playback arrow and a video started of a group of tourists shuffling around a stately home. 'Where is this?' Max asked. 'Should I know?'

'Somewhere in Oxford, I think, but that's not important. Wait . . . ' Charlotte was beginning to laugh. A couple of visitors at the front of the group half turned as the unmistakable sound of a fart momentarily rose over the voice of the guide, who continued with hardly a pause. The two visitors who had reacted were still trying to control their expressions when another longer noise rasped out and they leapt forward, their hands over their mouths, and the clip ended. Immediately a similar clip followed: this time a group appeared to be looking around a university building before they were distracted by several stentorian sounds ringing out, then it was the check-out queue of a supermarket, and so on for about two minutes.

'That's the stupidest thing I've ever seen,' Max said, removing his reading glasses to mop his eyes and blow his nose.

'It's Rufus.'

'What is?'

'He did it. He has a little remote control in his pocket that fires off the fart machine and a friend videos the group's reaction. Here – I'll run it back a bit for you. If I pause it here . . . ' and Max could make out a blurred face towards the back of one of the groups and recognised Rufus.

'How does he keep a straight face?'

'I don't know, but look,' Charlotte pointed to the number of viewings, 'he's had over sixty thousand hits on this one alone – and he's done others.'

'Not all farting.'

'No. Lots of different gags. He's beginning to make a bit of an income from them.'

'He's rather risen in my estimation, I must admit.' Then a thought struck Max and he turned in his seat to face his daughter. 'Now, hang on a minute – tell me you're not building up to say he's going to do that sort of thing around Duntisbourne Hall, or get you involved.'

'Come on, Dad. It's harmless.'

'Charlotte! Please. I beg you . . . '

She shut the laptop and planted a kiss on his cheek before standing up. 'You worry too much,' she said and tripped out to the kitchen to get herself a drink.

'By the way, I thought it was time I asked Sam Westbrook over for a meal,' he called through.

'OK.'

'What evening would suit you?'

'I don't mind. I'm out most evenings.'

Max couldn't work out if he was being particularly vague or if Charlotte was being intentionally difficult. 'I thought it would be nice if it was an evening when you were here.'

'Me? Why do want me here?'

'I'd like you to meet her.'

'I have met her. I see her around at work.'

'Properly. Get to know her.'

'If I must.' Charlotte stood by the kitchen worktop and sipped her juice.

Max frowned. 'Something bothering you, chick?'

'No,' she said turning to him. 'You do what you want but I'm only here for a couple of months, that's all.'

'Meaning what?'

'Meaning nothing.' She came through and sat down beside him again. 'I'm watching television. That all right?'

'Sure. I've got some work to catch up on.'

Max took his drink through to the study and turned on his computer. He checked a couple of emails but found his mind wandering, so he sat back in his chair and put his feet on the desk. Monty hadn't followed him through – he would be up on the sofa next to Charlotte – and Max began to puzzle over why her mood had changed from cheerful banter to monosyllabic. In the past he would have tried to winkle the reason out of her but he knew if he asked her to explain her motives for this sudden change of mood she might outline a problem that he had pushed to the sidelines because he hoped it didn't really exist. If they discussed the predicament they made it real, and Max sensed that he would be pressurised into making a simple choice – his family or his love life – and the latter would be the one he would have to forego.

After his wife had left he resolved never to bring another woman to the house until Charlotte had grown up, assuming, in his naivety, that when she reached maturity she wouldn't mind. Something in the back of his mind had already warned him that he had misjudged the situation – why else had he delayed his courtship of Sam for the last few weeks? Charlotte had had his undivided attention for over a decade, the two of them had been a team, and while she was in Bristol he had allowed his enthusiasm for Sam to convince him that the whole world would bless their union, including his daughter. He knew now that he had been fooling himself, hoping against hope that he was right but suspecting all the time he was wrong. Ironically the one person he could discuss this dilemma with was Sam herself. She had a difficult daughter, she would understand.

He sighed. Why did life never get any easier? He remembered struggling through his twenties in the certain knowledge that one day he would reach a kind of nirvana where he was financially stable and his life would be calm. Then he had careened into marriage and landed himself with another succession of seemingly impossible obstacles to happiness. Once free of that, worries about his daughter rushed in to vex him and after she had left home, that horrible bout of high blood pressure had landed him in hospital and skewed any harmony. His doctors had warned him that unless he changed his lifestyle, he would be on dialysis within the next couple of years, and taking the job at Duntisbourne Hall had been part of the plan – he had even managed to quit smoking, no mean feat for a man who had puffed through two packets a day since he was a teenager. Just forty-eight hours ago he had been walking around the Red Lake in glorious sunshine, with Monty questing in and out of the bushes in front of him, and he had felt bathed in happiness that Sam was back, his health was good and he was enjoying his job. He even felt glad that Charlotte was down for the summer because although she was high maintenance, he loved her very much. Yet here he was again, chewing over a hopeless dilemma.

'Bull shit!' he said.

– 8 –

'Good God, man,' Noel said the following week. 'If you don't pull yourself together I'm going to ask Bunty to swap you back onto the guiding floor and put someone on the door with me who isn't such dismal company. Whatever's got into you recently?'

'Life.'

'Oh that. Well, of course life's difficult – but compared to what?'

'Nothing like a metaphysical teaser to cheer a man up,' Max said.

'It's not metaphysics, it's common sense. Let me tell you, the moment you accept life's a bitch, things get a whole lot easier. Now, here's someone who never fails to bring a smile to your face. Good morning Walter, how's that organ of yours doing?'

Walter Willis was a retired music scholar who had taken responsibility for the mighty Wurlitzer organ in the indigo library. He gave Noel a watery smile. 'Struggling, I'm afraid to say. It's never really recovered from being ripped out of the Odeon in Cardigan Bay.'

'Probably had more to do with the cinema being blitzed by a bomb than anything else, don't you think?'

'Perhaps. We'll never know.' The little man sighed and looked out across the courtyard. 'I suppose I'd better get on back home. My wife thinks I spend too much time here fiddling with the organ as it is.' He turned to Max. 'How's it going? Enjoying it?'

'Generally – yes.'

'Walter wanted to be a guide here, you know – didn't you, Walter?' Noel said brightly. Max knew he was setting one of them up.

'I did, I did. I apply each year. I can't understand why they never take me on. I'm a Green Badge guide you know.'

'Are you?' Max said.

'Yes. I had the honour of receiving my Green Badge from the Mayor of Shrewsbury himself – ooh, must be five years ago now.'

'And what sort of area do you cover?'

'The whole of Shropshire. We were one of the first regions after London to have official tour guides, you know. I have a few regular tours up my sleeve – Charles Darwin, of course–'

'Naturally.'

'Brother Cadfael.'

'Really?'

'Oh yes. It doesn't have to be factual, you know, and those wonderful stories were all historically accurate. I take people on a tour following in the footsteps of that great twelfth-century sleuth from Chirk in the north right down to Ludlow in the south.'

'Goodness, quite a trek. Physically demanding then?'

'No – we go by car.' Max was determined not to catch Noel's eye. 'I do a tour of Shrewsbury in Tudor times and, of course, Dickens' *A Christmas Carol*.'

'That was set in Shropshire?'

'No, no, of course not, but the famous George C. Scott film was made here – one of the local boys played Tiny Tim.'

'Did he now?'

'Oh yes – and you can still visit the grave of Ebenezer Scrooge.'

'Surely not.'

Walter shot Max a look. 'The grave used for the film,' he said. 'Not a lot of people know that the very first reading that Dickens gave of the book was in Shrewsbury's Music Hall.'

'In the film.'

'No! In real life.'

'Well, I never. Sounds like you'd make the perfect guide here.'

'You'd think so, wouldn't you? I tried again this year but they gave the job to someone else who must have been even more qualified than me.'

'Evidently.'

'When was this, Walter?' Noel chipped in.

'About three months ago.'

'Oh dear,' Max said.

'Never mind,' said Walter. 'Perhaps next year. Who knows? I suppose I have to count myself lucky that the Earl is happy to let me come in whenever I want to tinker with the organ but I'd dearly love to have your job.' He smiled sadly at Max. 'Had you done much guiding before?'

'None.'

'Other skills then, I suppose.'

'Suppose so.'

Max and Noel stood side by side and watched the small figure make his way down the steps and out into the courtyard.

'Don't ever tell him,' Max said.

'I might.'

'It would break his heart.'

'Cheer up then and I won't.'

'Noel!' Turning round, Max saw Robyn from the exhibition hurrying across the hall towards them. 'Someone's hurt themselves, on the stairs. What do I do?'

'I'll go and tell the office,' Noel said, 'Frodders?' Major Frodsham, clad in his usual three-piece suit of tweed jacket, waistcoat and plus twos, was slumbering in the warmth of a ray of sun which shone through the window onto the desk in the hall. He was officially on the guiding team but in recent years, he preferred manning the bookstall in the hall where he had become accustomed to spending the day solving *The Times* crossword or slumbering. He came to with a snort and gazed around in some confusion. 'Major Frodsham! Get over here and look after the door will you? I've got to go and get Rosemary. Max, you go with Robyn and see what's happened.' Noel patted Robyn's elbow. 'Don't worry – these old folk go down like ninepins round here.'

Max hurried up the stairs to the minstrels' gallery and saw a small crowd of visitors gathered at the foot of the spiral stairs leading up to the Dywenydd Collection. He pushed through them and found a man sitting up against the wall making a weak attempt to fend off an elderly woman who was leaning over him and holding a pashmina scarf against the top of his bald head. Blood was dribbling down the bridge of his nose, brilliant red against the pallor of his skin, the fringe of the pashmina – too large for its new purpose – acting as a conduit for the flow, stippling his shirt with blood like a gory Jackson Pollock canvas.

'Off, woman!' the man said. 'It hurts.'

Max didn't know much about first aid but he knew the pashmina was probably not such a bad idea. He reached forward and gathered up some of the spare fabric from around the back of the man's head. 'Here, sir,' he said, taking the fellow by the wrist. 'Why don't you put pressure on the wound, you're more likely to get the right spot. Hold it firmly – that's great. Heads bleed an awful lot, don't they? It always looks a great deal more alarming than it really is.' Max got to his feet and said to Robyn. 'How on earth did it happen?'

She dropped her voice and turned away so that the patient couldn't hear her. 'It was only a little slip but as he went he cracked his skull on the spiral step above. Peeled a huge flap of skin off the top of his head–' she stretched her mouth down at the corners and shuddered.

'Horrid. Look – can you get these people to move along a bit?'

Robyn began to shift the crowd on, encouraging some people to continue up to the exhibition, others to make their way back downstairs. The elderly woman was obviously the wife and she stood beside her stricken husband holding her bloodied hands away from her clothes. Eventually Rosemary from the office arrived with a clipboard.

'Are you first aid trained, Max?' she said.

'No.'

'Robyn?'

'No. Sorry.'

'Oh dear. Well, I think I've lapsed too but never mind, we've called an ambulance, they'll soon be here. Robyn, get back upstairs – there are visitors up there with no room warden and Max, you'd better get back to the door. Right, sir,' she said, kneeling beside the victim, 'let's fill out this accident report, shall we?' From beneath the pashmina, a pair of jaundiced eyes rolled up to stare at her.

When Weenie came in the following morning she was sorry to have missed the excitement but once she understood the gist of what had happened she took it upon herself to make sure that everyone had the right story.

'Split his head open like a watermelon,' she announced during her lunch break in the guides' room.

'Not while I'm eating,' Noel said.

'He didn't exactly split it,' Robyn said.

'Yes he did. I've spoken to Nerys and heard all about it.'

'I was there,' Robyn said.

'Well – you're wrong.'

Robyn shook her head and went back to eating her lunch.

Weenie wafted around the room waiting for her tea to brew. She didn't like to stuff her face at lunchtime. Then she spotted a note on the head guide's desk and snatched it up.

'What's this?' she said, holding the sheet of paper at arm's length and squinting in an attempt to get the writing in focus.

'It's an invitation for volunteers to do a training day for first aid in a couple of weeks,' Roger said, then added in a fruity tone, 'I've put my name down. Perhaps you should too.'

'Do you know what? I think I shall,' and Weenie scribbled her name underneath Roger's. 'Anyone else?' she said.

By the end of the week the list had attracted nothing further except for a few rings of coffee so Rosemary came upstairs one afternoon to take charge.

'I have booked a day in the Siegfried Rooms during the first week in July for the first aid course. I'm very disappointed to see only two people have put their names down so far.'

'That's you and me, Roger,' Weenie said.

'I thought it would look rather good on my cv.' Roger winked at Weenie.

'Bunty, as head guide it is essential that you take part in the course,' Rosemary said. Weenie felt a flutter of disappointment. She would have preferred a one-to-one with Roger. 'Robyn, you will have to do it so that there's cover upstairs in the Dywenydd Exhibition and I would also like Major Frodsham to take the course.'

'Major Frodsham?' said Bunty. 'Why?'

'I'd like to see him pulling his weight a bit more and as I seldom find him out on tour these days, he would be in pole position should there be another incident. The front door is where the news is most likely to arrive – it was ridiculous that Max and Noel had to leave their posts the other week. You'll be joined by Jessica from the kiosk too. A paramedic called Andrew Stunt is conducting the course and he comes highly recommended.'

On the morning of the course Weenie rose early and spent longer than usual getting ready for her day. Her anticipation was high and she wanted to look her best if she was going to be in close proximity to Roger. It also crossed her mind that the paramedic might turn out to be a bit of a dish and she had always had a soft spot for men in uniform, particularly strong, capable men.

The course began with the first disappointment of the day when she walked into the room and found that Andrew Stunt reminded her of Tintin. He had a wiry body, a pale round face with a tiny nose and yellow hair cut close to his head. The only thing he lacked was the quiff and he wasn't even wearing a uniform.

Weenie settled herself at the U-shaped meeting desk and gazed at the disparate group as they arrived in the Siegfried Rooms, which had been renovated last season to further Lord Montagu's vision of the Hall as a promising corporate location. The room was dominated by three large paintings of battles from the War of the Spanish Succession, showing the fifth earl at the centre of each action including the Battle of Ramillies when he lost his nose (although the painting showed a scene a few hours before the incident). Stunt had placed a folder of information in front of each participant along with a folded oblong card to write their names on.

'No, Major Frodsham,' Weenie said quietly in his ear, 'you're meant to turn the name outwards so that Mr Stunt can see it. You know what your name is.'

Frodders chuckled. 'Depends how much port I've had the night before.'

'Let's introduce ourselves to the group,' Stunt said. 'I expect you all know each other but I don't, so just a brief description: name, job here at the Hall – that sort of thing.'

Weenie drew breath to speak first but Roger cut in. 'My name is Roger Hogg-Smythe. I have worked at the Hall for two seasons but it is only my love of history and the general public that brings me here. I am, in fact, a magistrate. I would also like to add that much of my time is spent working for the Sildchester Freechurch where I am a lay preacher. It is probably this experience that has helped me to be so successful at public speaking.'

'My name is Edwina Lemon but everyone knows me as Weenie and I have worked at the Hall for fourteen seasons – although I was very young when they offered me the post – and I like to think of myself as the international guide because I have a smattering of several languages which makes me very good with foreigners who love to hear the Queen's English spoken correctly – in fact, I have been mistaken for the Countess herself on many occasions.'

'Bunty Buchanan, head guide.'

'My name's Major Frodsham but I'll answer to anything – and I would just like to say that my sincerest hope is that no one goes down on my watch.'

'I'll second that,' Bunty said.

'Robyn Whitbread. I work up in the exhibition.'

'I'm Jessica Williams. I work in the kiosk.'

'Nice to meet you,' Frodders said. 'It's a pleasure to have a lovely young face among us.'

'Certainly is,' Roger seconded.

Weenie sniffed.

'Thank you, everyone – and welcome,' Stunt said. 'Now, you may feel that working here isn't going to expose you to anything more than someone feeling faint or being sick.'

'Sick!' Frodders said. 'I can't stand the sight of sick. It makes me feel terribly queasy. It's the smell, I think. Do you have any tips on dealing with that, Mr Stunt?'

'Cat litter,' intervened Bunty. 'The lumping kind is the best. Just scatter cat litter on it and then Sharon doesn't complain too much about clearing up the mess. Couldn't be easier – and I swear by bicarbonate of soda sprinkled on the patch afterwards – it takes the smell of stomach acid away in a jiffy. I always stock up before the grandchildren come.'

'Well, I understand your concerns,' Stunt said, 'but that's just housekeeping. We're here to learn what to do if someone is in real distress. Suppose a visitor falls down the front steps of the Hall and sustains a compound fracture of the leg – a bone has broken through the skin and the patient is in terrible pain. Would you know how to deal with that? Someone falls in the gardens. Have they broken their wrist? How can you tell? And – I'm sorry to say, the most likely of all – someone has a heart attack while they are on a visit. Would you be able to recognise it? How could you tell if the patient was having a faint, a heart attack or a stroke? It's vital that you can differentiate between them because obviously this will affect your choice of action.'

A hush had fallen on the cheery crowd in the room. 'Oh dear,' Frodders said quietly to Weenie. 'I'm not sure I'm cut out for this type of thing.'

'You have an observation to make, Major Frodsham?' Stunt said.

'No, not really. It's just that I'm terribly squeamish. I can't even stand Marigold paring down her verruca in the bathroom without feeling a little faint. I really don't think I should be here at all.'

'Come along Frodders,' Bunty said. 'You'll be fine. I've seen some simply horrible accidents with horses – and I have suffered from some exquisitely painful injuries. In fact –'

'I think you'll find,' Stunt continued over the top of her, 'that once you know what to do, a tremendous sense of confidence will take over and you won't find these things nearly as alarming as you imagine.' Frodders pulled a doubtful face at Weenie. 'Right, now, let's give you a scenario. It's a hot August day, the Hall is fairly crowded, someone in your group falls down onto the ground, quite suddenly. What do you do?'

'Run for this hills,' Frodders murmured to Weenie.

'Major Frodsham?'

'Run for the pills?'

'Well,' Bunty said, 'usually we put them in the cupboard in the music room until they start to feel better.'

'What?' Stunt said.

'It's a big cupboard and there's an old consulting couch in there. I think there's usually a bottle of Duntisbourne Hall water and a cup as well – and a bucket the last time I looked. They can lie down, a friend can sit with them – there's enough room for that – and once they feel better, off they pop.'

Stunt looked astonished. 'If they're unconscious, how are you going to get them into the cupboard?'

'Just load them onto a wheelchair and away we go. We don't want them lying around on the floor for everyone to step over. It's upsetting for the other visitors.'

'No, no, no,' Stunt said. 'You must never move the patient. The patient is your priority, not the other visitors.'

It was Roger's turn to intervene at this stage. 'My first season,' he said, 'some poor chap actually died in the great hall, so Rosemary had some screens put around him until the paramedics arrived.'

'Rather like they do at the races,' Bunty said. 'It was a marvellous idea.'

'If someone fainted we could do the same, Bunty,' Roger went on, not noticing Stunt's expression. 'I'm sure the screen's are still round the back somewhere. Why don't you . . . ?'

'Stop – now,' Stunt said. 'Let's try and get this back on track again. I want you all to write down "The Patient is the Priority". You do not move an unconscious patient. If the patient is in the way, you close the Hall.'

'We can't do that,' Bunty said. 'Whatever would the Earl say?'

'I don't care what the Earl would say. In the course of my job I have closed miles and miles of motorway in the rush hour to ensure the safety of just one patient. If I can do that, you can certainly close the Hall.'

'If you say so,' Bunty said, 'but he won't like it. You haven't seen the Earl when he's angry. He can be quite rude.'

'But,' chipped in Weenie, 'he can also be absolutely charming. In fact, when I was out in Germany for the tercentenary celebrations, he was charming in Ramillies.'

'The Earl? Charming? I find that hard to believe,' said the Major.

'Oh, but he was. Absolutely charming. I told him all about my weak ankles and he told me all about his hiatus hernia. I suggested he prop the head end of his bed up a little to relieve the symptoms at night, an trick an old boyfriend taught me – he was a doctor, you see – and the other morning, as I was coming in through the courtyard, he called out "Miss Lemon! Miss Lemon!" Just like that. He wanted to tell me that he had had the end of his bed propped up as I suggested but he thought Dean had raised it a little too high because he kept slipping down the mattress and out of the bottom. So funny. So charming.'

'Please,' Stunt said, 'can we get back on track? You will need to be able to tell the difference between someone who has fainted, someone who may have had a stroke and someone who may be having a heart attack.' Flipping over another sheet of paper on the display board, he began to write the symptoms of each in columns. Every time he added another symptom someone piped up, 'I've got that!'

The rest of the morning was spent listening to Stunt explaining the importance of the ABC system – Airway, Breathing and Circulation – and everyone had a go at inflating the chest of the rubber head and torso. Weenie had chosen to wear her short leather skirt which made kneeling on the floor difficult, but she was rewarded for her choice when she realised Roger was leaning back on the table behind her to watch. Frodders had a bit of trouble getting down to ground level and Stunt and Robyn had to come forward to help him up again. As the group began to concentrate, Weenie was glad to see that Stunt was starting to relax and seemed to be enjoying their progress, but just before lunch his confidence took another knock.

'Now, sometimes a patient will collapse and for a number of different reasons which we needn't go into, they may not actually be unconscious. It is important that you find out if they really are unconscious before you start hauling them around and jumping up and down on their chest. How are you going to make sure they're not faking it?'

Weenie puzzled the problem through in her head but before she could speak Bunty lit up with an idea. 'Stick a needle in them?'

'What?' Stunt said.

'Stick a needle in them.'

'Where? In their arm? Leg? Neck? How far are you going to shove it?'

Bunty put some careful thought to the problem. 'I wouldn't push it in very far and I suppose the thigh would be a good place.'

'Give me strength!' Stunt said. 'No, no, no. You do not go sticking needles into patients and shoving them into a cupboard in the music room.' He sighed heavily and walked back and forth a few times in front of the flip chart, rubbing his hand over his chin and down his neck. After a few moments of silence he clapped his palms together, turned to the room with a renewed expression of enthusiasm and said, 'I need a volunteer.'

'I'll do it,' Weenie said and sashayed between the table and chairs to the centre of the room to join Stunt. He placed his finger and thumb on either side of her shoulder muscle. She smiled at her audience and tried to turn her head so that she could include Stunt but he began to increase the pressure of the pinch and quite suddenly it was impossible to bear and she twisted away from his hand with a shriek. Some of the spectators laughed and – momentarily wrong-footed – Weenie glared at Stunt. She was furious with him. How dare he hurt her like that! Instead of apologising he strode back to his position by the display board. 'That is the way we recommend you find out if the person is unconscious or not. The Vulcan Grip. Try it gently on one another.' Weenie tossed her head as if she had a mane of hair down her back and made her way over to Roger, laughing lightly at the others to cover her irritation.

'Don't you like it rough?' Roger said.

'Let's see if you like it,' she said and began to squeeze his shoulder. He laughed and pulled away a little before getting to his feet and nipping at her shoulder with his large hand.

'Ouch!' Weenie cried. 'I've already had that done to me.'

'No one's done it to you yet, eh Jessica?' Roger said, sidling past Weenie and making his way over towards the back of the young girl's chair. She blushed and pushed her seat back in order to stand but Roger stood behind, blocking her before she had a chance to twist away, grasping both her shoulders from behind and rhythmically massaging the muscles at the base of her neck. 'Goodness,' he said, 'you're all knots. You must be feeling very tense. Just relax and let me –'

'No thanks,' Jessica said and tried to pull away.

'Playing hard to get, eh?' he said quietly. 'I rather like that in a girl.'

'Roger,' Weenie said, 'leave the poor thing alone. You're embarrassing her.'

'All right,' Stunt said. 'That'll do for this morning. We may as well break for lunch and then we'll crack on when everyone's had a bit of a break.' The group settled down around plates of sandwiches and poured themselves cups of coffee. Stunt disappeared outside for a cigarette.

'Seems funny,' Bunty said. 'That nice young man is medical and yet he smokes. Never could understand it. I had a sister who was a nurse and she was a terribly heavy smoker. So were most of her friends. Doesn't make any sense at all.'

'Oh, that's nothing,' Weenie said. 'What about all those obese health workers? Most of the nurses at our practice are absolutely huge. My GP thought I should have a general check-up the other day – a sort of ten-thousand-mile service, I suppose – and the woman who weighed me was the size of a mountain. She said

I was in the lower centile on the healthy weight chart and I felt like saying to her, "And shouldn't you be?" Imagine her telling a patient they had to lose weight.'

During the afternoon they embarked on getting someone into the recovery position.

'Provided you have ruled out any injury to the neck and you are certain the patient is breathing, the safest position to put them in is the recovery position. Does anyone know why?'

'Oh God, it's going to be about sick again, isn't it?' Frodders said.

'That's right, Major. An unconscious patient can quite often vomit and it is important that they don't inhale any of it.'

'I'm feeling a bit sick myself,' Frodders said. He was looking exceedingly pale.

'But what if it was someone as large as the Major?' Weenie said. 'I'd never be able to roll him over.'

'There's a knack to it,' Stunt said. 'A slight person can roll a heavy person over with ease. Now, let's have a large person – it's all right Major, I won't make you get down to ground level again. What about you, Roger? You're quite a tall fellow and Jessica here doesn't look strong enough to roll you but I am going to show you how to do it.'

'Let me do it,' Weenie said. 'I'm very small too.'

'No. Jessica, please.'

Jess came forward with apparent caution and stood beside Stunt twisting her fingers through one another as Roger lay down and smoothed his jacket. Stunt knelt on the floor and beckoned the girl to follow, but as Jess neared Roger, Weenie saw his eyes widen and heard him say, 'I do hope you're going to give me the kiss of life.'

'This is serious,' Stunt said. 'Now, Jessica, draw this leg up and across the other leg like this, bring his arm up and across his shoulder, but make sure that his head is protected as he rolls over,' and to Roger's surprise and indignation Stunt flipped him deftly over onto his side and Roger gasped. 'Now you try, Jessica.'

Jessica tried to follow the instructions. 'You've got to get closer to the victim – you'll never turn him at arm's length,' Stunt said. Weenie could see Roger watching Jessica intently and she was sure he was tensing his whole body to make it impossible for her to carry the manoeuvre. 'Come on, Roger,' Stunt said, 'you're meant to be unconscious. Go floppy.'

'Bloody difficult under the circumstances,' Roger said.

'For pity's sake,' Stunt said. 'OK, Jess, back to your seat. Come on, Robyn, you may as well have a go.'

Weenie held her breath as Robyn poised her athletic frame over Roger before starting to push and pull at him, but she needn't have worried – he rather crossly turned over under his own steam. 'Oh well,' said Stunt, 'you've got the basic idea, I suppose. Let's move on to choking.'

'Oh do let's,' Frodders said.

'Has anyone here ever choked?'

'I have,' said Weenie. 'I was once in this frightfully smart restaurant and I got a horrible little bone stuck in my throat and I choked and choked. It was absolutely terrible. And another time I choked on a glass of champagne and spat the whole lot all over the table. Terribly embarrassing.'

'That's not what we mean by choking,' Stunt said. 'Choking is when something gets lodged in your throat which completely seals off the air supply.'

'Yes, I thought so,' Weenie said.

'It's an extremely dangerous situation and the patient is in trouble within a matter of seconds. Women survive better than men because women wave and point and make a terrible scene–'

'I did that,' Weenie said.

– 'while men tend to shuffle away and go and die in the toilet. Bravery in this situation is lethal.'

'I'd be all right then,' the Major said.

The Major wasn't all right later on in the afternoon when Stunt began to talk about a number of ghastly injuries he had treated as a paramedic. He described compound fractures, painful and disfiguring dislocations, wounds bubbling with air or filled with the detritus of the roadside, burns and pendulous blisters, flail chests so painful that the patient preferred to die rather than try to breathe, and crush injuries which rendered the limbs unrecognisable. The Major's swift exit to the toilet at the bottom of the stairs put an end to this litany of horror and Stunt began to bring the day to a conclusion.

'So,' he said, 'have you all got it now? You understand the basic principles of first aid?'

'Yes,' Weenie said. 'We just sort of follow our instincts.'

Stunt stared at her, slowly and wearily moving his head from side to side. 'No, no, no,' he said. 'Absolutely not.'

'Really?'

'No!' Weenie jumped slightly in her chair. 'You follow ABC – Airway, Breathing, Circulation. Have you listened to a single thing I've said today?'

'Of course,' Weenie said. 'That's what I meant.' And she turned and pulled a face at Roger.

– 9 –

The start of the school summer holidays on the continent brought mixed reactions from the staff at Duntisbourne Hall. The management were delighted to see the car park in July jammed with French coach companies vomiting out hordes of rowdy French children, every one of whom was a paying visitor, but the guides and staff who had to deal with them were less enthusiastic.

Down at the wildlife centre to the north-west of the Hall the staff in the gift shop, suffering from battle fatigue after several weeks on the front, stood shoulder to shoulder behind the counter as yet another wave of French students rampaged towards them. Meanwhile, the students' progress through the centre was being monitored, not by the staff in the shop, nor by the teachers who had come with them, but by a figure in a full-length waxed coat who had been watching for some time now from the safety of the shrubbery beyond the plate glass windows. He had seen them poking at the compost which had trickled out from underneath the glass display in the wormery and one of them chasing a girl around pretending he had a worm in his hand. He followed the silhouettes of the school party as they passed through the moth house and again heard screams of terror from some of the students before they emerged from the other end of the single-storey building, swinging each other around by their rucksacks.

The two French teachers with them followed behind chatting to one another, unconcerned with the havoc their group was causing. The only time one of them reprimanded a child was when a particularly large handful of gravel peppered the ground at her feet, having missed its intended target.

Once inside the shop the students began to gather armfuls of souvenirs, pushing some of the smaller ones straight into their pockets. One of the French teachers made her way down towards the exit where there was a collection of postcards, placing her bag down beside the open door to leave both hands free. As she moved round the column of cards, picking them out one after the other and reading the backs, she did not notice a figure slip in through the exit and lift the bag off the floor. By the time she had chosen her cards and looked for her bag in order to pay, it was gone.

Sam Westbrook sat in the office above the music room. Through one of the circular windows she could see the last visitors of the day meandering across the great courtyard and she rested her chin in the palms of her hands and watched a dumb show play out in the distance: a couple stopped beside one of the great basins of summer bedding plants and paused, scanning the people who passed then waving a Chinese visitor over and handing him a camera. Smiling and nodding they moved back towards the flowers then embraced and turned towards their photographer. After a few moments their smiles faded and the young man peered and pointed, then released his girlfriend and hurried forward to take the camera back. The two men fumbled with it, the young man rushed back into position, the Chinese man was about to have another go, but just before he took the shot a figure in a long waxed coat barrelled between him and the couple and all three turned to watch the hunched figure hurry on. The couple shrugged and the Chinese man raised his hand with exasperation before aiming the camera for a second shot. It was a success. They parted, the man bowing, the couple nodding then turning away, heads bent towards one another, seeing how the picture had come out, springing apart in a silent mime of laughter. Sam smiled. It was a good place to work – people came here to have a nice time, they were happy, it was a beautiful summer's evening and two young lovers had a memento of their day.

Then she frowned. It was almost two months since her return to Duntisbourne Hall and apart from the occasional vague promise to get together some evening, she and Max hadn't actually managed to organise anything. She was partly to blame – her workload meant that she was seldom back in her flat much before nine o'clock at night, which seemed too late to telephone. She wondered if, despite his protestations to the contrary, Max had been hurt – angry even – when she was forced to let him down in the spring. This had never been her intention. She had been thoroughly looking forward to spending a weekend away with him and had her daughter Claire not turned up unexpectedly from New York in floods of tears with a suitcase and a broken marriage, she was certain the weekend would have been a great success. However, when people are no longer in the first flush of youth, modern courtship dictates a system of stages to follow and disrupting or missing one of those stages can throw confusion into the progression of a relationship.

She roused herself from her reverie – she was making her usual mistake, over-analysing a situation. What did it matter if it took them two weeks, two months or two years to finally get together? Max had said it himself – he was a grown man and had his own life, which was fine. It would be finer with her but he wouldn't be a broken reed without her.

She checked her watch – it was nearly closing time and Pugh the gateman would soon be locking up downstairs. She needed to catch him and tell him that she was going to be upstairs in the erotic exhibition for another hour. She had promised Hector that she would look through the inventory for him but she didn't like to do it during office hours. She made her way down the stairs into the indigo library and caught up with Pugh in the lower dining room.

'Good evening, Mr Pugh – and what a lovely evening it is.'

'It won't last. The wind will shift against the sun before it sets.'

'Will it?'

'Don't trust it, mind – it'll run back before dawn.'

'I'll bear that in mind.'

'Still, it should stay fine for the Summer Progress next week.'

'So soon?'

'Best party of the year.'

'I was actually looking for you because I have some work to do upstairs in the exhibition. I want to make sure I won't get locked in the Hall while I'm up there.' Pugh hesitated. 'Problem?' Sam said.

'I don't suppose so – there was a bit of trouble this afternoon is all I'm thinking. A visitor reported a bag stolen.'

'Really?'

'Mind you, it was down at the wildlife centre and it turned up later, handed in by someone who found it in a bush by the river walk, but it put Rosemary on high alert for a few hours. Tell you what, if I leave the deadbolt off the door to the music room and just lock it with the pass key, you can leave through that door when you've finished and I can lock it later in the evening.'

'Do I need to do anything about the alarm?'

'It's been decommissioned until they can get it serviced. They think too much dust got into the sensors when you had all that work done upstairs.'

'My fault then.'

'Pretty much.' Pugh chuckled then began to cough. He smote his breastbone with his fist and wheezed.

'I'm not taking the blame for that too,' Sam said.

'No.' He drew in a crackling breath. 'All my own work. Too late to quit now. I'll pop back when I've finished locking up outside – you should be done by then.'

He continued on his way into the main dining room and Sam watched him for a moment, his figure silhouetted against the light of the low summer sun which illuminated the motes of dust settling in the rooms along the west front.

She made her way up to the minstrels' gallery and along to an oak door studded in metal and pierced with woodworm. Pushed up against the wall beside the door were two notices, one guiding visitors to the Dywenydd Exhibition and the other warning them about it. She unlocked the door and, opening it towards her, stood at the foot of the spiral staircase, the stone of the treads buffed and dipped in the centre from centuries of traffic. She began to ascend, steadying herself on the central column with one hand as she climbed. About halfway up she stopped and turned, searching the underneath of the treads which spiralled away above her until she found a slick of blood already browned and dried from its exposure to the air. Climbing a little higher to bring herself nearer to the edge of the riser which had inflicted the wound on the visitor's head, she took out her mobile phone and photographed it. Back in the spring when she had curated the exhibition, access had not been part of her remit, but since accepting her new post she was responsible for the safety of the visitors. If the Hall wanted to keep the erotic exhibition open, something was going to have to be done and done soon.

Pocketing her phone she continued up and let herself into the room at the top, opening the central control panel by the door to turn on the lights. Although it was still a summer's evening outside, the exhibition was in perpetual darkness to reinforce its history as the sealed chamber. Light from the etched Victorian wall sconces honeyed the deep blue and rust acanthus leaf patterns running up the walls and in the centre of the room stood a trio of leather sofas, forming three sides of a rectangle.

Sam navigated her way between them and went over to a cabinet directly opposite the entrance to the exhibition. Inside lay a large book opened but resting on an angled lectern to lessen the stress on its spine. She found a smaller key on the bunch she carried and lifted the cover of the cabinet, laying it gently on the wall behind. A musty smell rose up towards her, the unmistakable scent of an old book deepened by the faintest hint of tobacco drifting off the ancient pages. Inspecting her hands, she brushed them together to make sure there was nothing on them to cause any damage – she believed wearing gloves to handle books limited dexterity, making damage more likely – then gently lifted the book and the lectern as one out of the cabinet, bearing them over to the table in the centre of the room where she seated herself to begin her study.

She had been doubtful that any reference to Hector's *dame de voyage* existed but a few days ago she had come across several passages containing the letters WAM, which could refer to William Augustus Montagu, the illegitimate son of the fifth Earl of Sandwich or could merely refer to an action. Sam had found quite a few of these vulgar idioms scattered through the smutty accounts, particularly as these young gentleman seemed far more interested in displaying their potency to their fellow guests by 'boxing the Jesuit' than pleasuring someone else which – considering the extraordinary collection of erotic paraphernalia which the ninth earl had acquired – was a bit of a shame, in her opinion.

She had been working for some time when a creak of metal moving on rust made her look up at the ceiling above her head. The mighty iron weather vane was turning on top of the chimney stack which towered above the west front – Pugh was seldom wrong – and she heard the sough of the rising wind and saw the tapestry on the wall move forward and sigh back in the draught. She stood up, stretched both arms above her head and, moving over to the cabinets along the wall, she opened one of the drawers and peered into the boxed display. The clitoral palpator lay beneath – that delicate creation of scrimshaw and soft suede – and an image sprang into her mind of an inamorato applying himself solely to bringing pleasure to his woman. And the face of that male lover was Hector Schofield.

Sam shoved the display drawer shut and swung round, her hands spread out along the top of the cabinet. From where had that image come? Like a blow on a mosquito bite long healed, an irritation welled up in her belly that was not wholly unpleasant nor unfamiliar, a craving that could not be completely satisfied. It was as if the poison still lay beneath her skin and the more she scratched to relieve the irritation, the stronger it became, impelling her to work away at it until it hurt.

She knew it would hurt – if she got involved with Hector Schofield, she would be hurt – and yet the desire she had seen in his eyes when they drove through the countryside into the setting sun was the drug she craved in its purest and most dangerous form. Damn Max – he was right. Schofield was a type, the type she was habitually attracted to – sophisticated and vain but with a careless bravado that hints of insecurity.

It would be disingenuous of her to pretend she hadn't been flattered by that look in his eyes but she also knew he had already, in a subtle way, criticised her ability when he cut in on her explanation to Max about the *dame de voyage* and that alone should be enough to warn her off. Max delighted in her achievements, he seemed to enjoy her superior knowledge in certain fields, secure in himself apparently that there were areas where he excelled which put them on an equal intellectual footing. The irony was that the comfort of her relationship with Max was the very thing that made it impossible to move on to the next stage and yet, although she hardly knew Schofield, she could already imagine embarking on a passionate liaison with him and it was a fantasy she wished she could expunge from her mind.

Exasperated with herself she returned to the book but the descriptions of levels of sexual excitement engendered by the artefacts that were all around her seemed to fill the room with the must of longing and desire. The weathervane creaked again above her head like the rasp of a huge bedspring and defeated she carried the volume back and laid it once more in the cabinet, locking it away until she could impose an essential detachment from the descriptions at some other time.

She walked back through the exhibition and as she passed through the dark and narrow passage from the eighteenth-century tavern to the Hellfire Club, her footsteps slowed and she recollected the time when she had finished creating the exhibition a few months ago and given Max his own private tour. She remembered the smell of vanilla from the chocolate he had been eating, she remembered his concentration, his extraordinary knack of seeming to follow every word she said and how disarming she had found it. His attention had seldom left her face – if he was not looking into her eyes, his gaze would drift no further than her mouth and then back up to engage with her once again – and she remembered how he had caught her hand and drawn her towards him and how she had longed for him to kiss her. Perhaps her longing had not been as exciting as the prospect of Hector or maybe it was this ruddy exhibition, it carnal magnetism creeping along the corridors and around the exhibits like wisps of fog that whispered to her to follow the path of danger and unhappiness instead of comfort and constancy. She needed grounding – she needed to see Max.

Locking the rooms behind her as she left, she sent him a cheery text saying she was popping in after work, then set out across the courtyard towards the staff car park. The breeze had freshened but she still put down the roof of the car so that she could enjoy the last of the sun, and driving round the perimeter road, with the Red Lake laid out on her left, she felt her spirits rise. She didn't want to ricochet down that old route of passion, disillusionment and pain all over again. Her feelings were conflicted – the pull towards the dark side was strong, but she knew Max was her easy hour, her confidante, the person with whom she didn't have to pretend she was someone she wasn't. Perhaps this was why when she imagined a physical encounter with him – and she had on many occasions imagined it – she felt more exposed than if she had been swept away with a gut-wrenching passion. She had an uneasy feeling that all that past groaning and sighing that accompanied sex was an act, a deceit to keep her real self hidden, and without it she would feel stripped bare right down to her inner soul.

As she drew near the visitors' car park on the south of the Hall something caught her attention. A car was parked in the shadows of a large horse chestnut tree and the figure on the driver's side seemed to shrink as her car approached as if the man was slithering down in the seat to hide himself. She wondered if he was waiting for someone and his behaviour made her think it must be a clandestine meeting. As her car passed, a pale moon face turned and watched her. She felt a strange apprehension and looked away swiftly to avoid catching the man's eye.

By the time she reached Max's cottage the incident had gone from her mind. Max was at his kitchen window bent on some task in the sink but he looked up as she was parking, peered then waved at her. He was at the door by the time she made it up the path. Monty hopped and circled around her heels and she rubbed the top of his head.

'Hello. This is a nice surprise.'

'Didn't you get my text?'

'No. I hardly ever read texts. The only person who ever texts me is Charlotte and she's here.'

'I thought I'd pop in for a drink.'

'Perfect. Come on through.'

'Hello, Charlotte. How are you getting on?'

The girl was sitting on the sofa with her legs curled up underneath her and without looking up from her laptop she said, 'Fine.'

'Good.' Max had gone through to the kitchen and Sam stood in the sitting room for a moment wondering if Charlotte was going to say anything else. Realising she wasn't she walked through and joined Max. 'Look, if it's not convenient ...'

'Course it is. What can I get you? Beer? Or I think I've got an open bottle of Zinfandel here.'

'Pink would be lovely.'

'Tell you what. It's a great evening – let's take these outside,' and he led her back through the sitting room and out of the French windows into the garden.

'The last time I saw this it was covered in snow,' Sam said.

'Heavens. Was that the last time you were here, the night I rescued you?'

'Now it's covered in plants.'

'Tends to happen in the summer. I just let it do its own thing.' The evening sun flooded the small terrace where Max put the drinks and as Sam walked across the plants that sprouted from the gaps between the paving stones, gasps of resinous herbs rose up into the air.

'It's pretty.'

'So – to what do I owe this visit?'

Before she could answer Charlotte appeared at the French windows. 'Dad. I need to get over to Shobdon.'

'OK.' Max thought for a moment. 'I don't need the car. Take it.'

'I'm not driving that thing.'

'Well, lovey – I'm busy.' Max gestured towards Sam and frowned at his daughter but an insouciant smile softened his look.

'I can't get over there any other way and I promised Rufus I'd go over because he's working on another film and I said I'd help him edit it.' She stared at her father, who shrugged and shook his head.

'I could give you a lift in about half an hour on my way back,' Sam said.

Charlotte ignored her and continued talking at her father, never once catching Sam's eye even though she had stepped out onto the terrace and was standing facing both of them. 'Half an hour is no good at all because Rufus has got to go out later and if he doesn't get this one finished and posted up there tonight all his followers who log on for the new clip won't see a new one and they won't bother to log on next week.'

'I wasn't going to stay long,' Sam said.

'No, stop. This is ridiculous, Charlotte . . . '

'It may be ridiculous to you but it's not ridiculous to me and I'm stuck down here all summer and all my friends are up in Bristol and just about the only friends I've managed to make are all over at Rufus's tonight and the only way I can get over there is if you take me and you said you weren't doing anything this evening so it's not exactly unreasonable of me to tell them it was fine, I could get over, and now you're saying I can't.'

'I'm not saying you can't. Just not right now.'

'For God's sake . . . ' and she disappeared back into the house.

Max stared out across the garden. A single wren chirruped in the hedge at the end of the lawn and the sound of a mower drifted over from next door. He sighed.

'I've got one of those,' Sam said.

'I know you have.'

Sam reached for her drink and took several long gulps before standing up. 'I think you'd better take her.'

'Come with us. We can chat on the way.'

'I don't think that's a good idea.'

'Wait here then, finish your drink. Monty can entertain you. I'll only be half an hour.'

'I don't think so.'

'Bull shit! This is ridiculous.'

'It doesn't matter,' Sam said, although what she actually wanted to do was thump into the house after his daughter and tell her not to be such a spoiled little madam, but if Max had done that to Claire she would never have forgiven him. 'I'll catch up with you some other time. I should have rung before coming over. It was silly of me. I've put you in an awkward position.'

'You haven't. What was it about anyway?' Max said over his shoulder as he carried the glasses back into the kitchen.

'Nothing important – it can wait.'

Max was watching the football when Charlotte got home – she had rung to say that Robyn would bring her back – and she dropped her laptop down on the table and snuggled up against him on the sofa.

'Sorry,' she said.

'What for, chick?'

'Being rude.'

Max looked down at the top of her head. He knew it took a lot for her to apologise and he wasn't going to use it as a cue to berate her for her behaviour earlier in the evening – instead he planted a kiss on her hair. Relieved she sat up and reached for her laptop and asked, 'Do you want to see what we've been doing?'

'I don't know. Do I?'

'It's funny.' She scrolled through some photographs and clicked to make one full-screen before handing the computer over to him and leaning up against his shoulder, a little smile of anticipation on her face.

'Where's that? Oh – it's the suit of armour at the Hall, isn't it?'

'Yes.'

'Why is that funny?'

'Look.'

'Well, it does look a bit different, but I can't see . . . hang on. What that?' The suit of armour had something balanced on its right hand and the left hand reached across the chest and pointed an articulated metal finger towards it.

'It's a tablet computer. The suit of armour is using a tablet.'

'Why?'

'It's just funny. I'll show you another,' and Max was looking at the Lumpen Oak, the most renowned tree on the estate, the chimneys of the Hall clearly visible in the background but as he examined it more closely he saw that three of the ancient holes which made the tree famous now boasted a front door perfect in every detail with decorative knockers and brass handles. Then it was the Venus Specchi on the river walk wearing a bikini, and then the Buddha in the arboretum gazing down at an open copy of the King James Bible on his lap.

'Don't be cross,' Charlotte said, probably sensing his reaction was less than enthusiastic. 'We put everything back exactly the way it was once the picture's taken.'

'We?'

'Rufus comes up with the ideas but he needs our help. There's no harm done.'

'Charlotte, Charlotte,' Max laid the computer back down with a heavy heart. 'You're going to get into such hot water if this goes on. The Earl isn't exactly renowned for having a sparkling sense of humour and all this is on the internet – out there where thousands of people can go and look at it and trace it back to you.'

'Oh, come on, Dad, none of those old folks are on the internet.'

'That is such an arrogant assumption. Of course they are.' He sighed and stood to take a few paces around the sitting room. He didn't want to spend the whole summer criticising his daughter and arguing with her, nor did he want her to start hiding things from him. His disapproval was unlikely to make her stop but it would make her secretive. 'Look, darling,' he said, 'how can I set out my worries in a more appealing context for you? I'm just concerned that some people could quite reasonably regard this as common vandalism and if it turned out that all of you were involved, you'd be out of here without a day's notice.'

'It's not vandalism. Vandalism is doing something that harms a shared social space and sort of implies a kind of obscenity, but what Rufus is doing isn't malicious. It's subversive, a dig at elitism, but fundamentally he does it because he wants to make people think, to communicate an idea, and the ideas have charm. Didn't the Lumpen Tree make you wonder what sort of little home is beyond that door?'

'Yes, irritatingly it did,' Max said. He shook his head and took another deep breath of resignation. 'I'm not happy about it,' he said.

'You worry too much.'

– 10 –

Earlier in the year Sam had met Arthur Matthews several times. The local architect had been invaluable during negotiations with the council when planning the Dywenydd Exhibition in the sealed chamber above the minstrels' gallery. He had expressed his concerns back in the spring about the safety of the access and warned her that the Hall would be in breach of a number of fire regulations if they did not create a secondary exit from the room. She had passed his warning on to her predecessor, BS Moreton, but nothing further had been done about it. Back then she believed she had satisfied her brief simply by passing the information on, but now that she was in charge she needed to reopen negotiations and find a solution.

She led the young architect down a narrow passage and through a room in the exhibition which had been laid out like an eighteenth-century tavern. They passed underneath a portrait of Philip, Earl of Wharton, the man credited for starting the Hellfire Club, the intention of which was to mock religion and indulge in a prodigious amount of drinking. Finally they stood in the recreation of the caves underneath West Wycombe where the Hellfire Club had their meetings. Matthews gazed at the artificial rock walls with professional concentration but Sam suspected it was to save him from having to look at the dining room table which had been set out as it might have been in Francis Dashwood's day – dishes of food fashioned to represent the breasts of Venus and the Devil's loin, napkins folded to replicate erect phalluses, plates adorned with scenes of monks spanking or fornicating with nuns.

'I believe that behind here,' Matthews said, tapping the artificial wall, 'there is a space large enough to bring people through.'

'How large?'

'The size of a master bedroom.'

'Really? What did it use to be?'

'I don't really know.'

'A master bedroom?'

'Possibly. I don't know.'

'Look, Art, I'm not prying but–'

'I know.' Matthews held up a hand of submission. 'I didn't want to put you in an awkward position with your new bosses.'

'Why would you do that?'

'Because I went to see BS Moreton.'

'Oh – I see.'

'It was off the record – and he thinks that on the other side of this wall is the room that was used for the lying in state of the third Earl of Duntisbourne.'

'OK. Meaning?'

'That it's quite a big space – a proper room in fact – and we can bring people through the room and then down an external spiral staircase which will be obscured by one of the columns on the west terrace.'

'Do you think the council would approve that?'

'As a solution it causes minimal disruption to the fabric of the building and I am confident that visually the impact would be negligible. I know that your CEO has a number of contacts on the council and if we could perhaps prevail upon him to open up the discussions in theory with the planning officer I think we would stand quite a good chance of them considering the application favourably.'

'We would need to limit the disruption to all this.' Sam gestured around her.

'Most of the work could be carried out on the outside first, then the exhibition wouldn't have to close for more than a couple of days to make good on this side. We may even find a contractor who is willing to work out of hours, perhaps through the night.' The architect tapped round the edge of the artificial wall of the Hellfire cave. 'What's this made of?'

'Gypsum.'

'Oh, so quite light – that's ideal. I need to get into the room as soon as possible to have a look and make accurate measurements before I can draw up the plans for the council but I think we may be able to shift this section of wall temporarily – break through one evening and just slide the gypsum back in position to cover the hole.'

'That would be brilliant.'

'We don't need planning consent to do that.'

'Let's book it.' Matthews began to stow his papers in his brief-case and Sam watched him, aware that his earlier revelation still hung in the air. 'How is he, by the way?'

Matthews looked up and smiled. 'His usual self – charming, engaging.'

'I am glad.'

Matthews pressed the locks of his briefcase home and pulled an expression of resignation. 'He's bored,' he said, picking up the case and preparing to leave. 'I think he's bored and bitter – and I think he's deeply depressed.'

'There's a French teacher in the Hall without a ticket,' Noel said. 'She's come to collect a bag that was handed in yesterday. I said it was OK for her to go straight down to the office.'

'Fine,' Max said.

Sharon, who never seemed to finish the routine cleaning before the front door opened to visitors, was standing behind them with a bucket in one hand and her mop in the other resting on the floor like the rifle of a soldier standing at ease. Max had noticed that throughout each day she moved systematically around the Hall and the estate as if following the Stations of the Cross, but unlike the faithful making their pilgrimage of faith, she moved between the people who were content to spend a few minutes chatting to her or listening to gossip.

'Those French,' she said, 'they'll run me ragged. The amount of damage they do here – I'm surprised they aren't banned from places like this.'

'Can't do that, Sharon,' Noel said as he continued checking tickets and directing visitors. 'They bring in plenty of money.'

'They were down in that moth house tearing the wings off, they were.'

'Were they?' Max said.

'Tearing them off. They're out of control. I had to go down to the wildlife centre three times yesterday because they'd broken the toilets, and one of them got hold of my radio and flung it down the pan. Flung it right into the pot and flushed it.'

Noel caught Max's eye and twitched an eyebrow at him.

'And those teachers – they just tag along behind, jawing away and stopping for a coffee and a meal and a glass of wine and a bit of shopping. They couldn't care less about what their students are up to.'

'Someone told me they have a different system over there,' Noel said. 'The class teachers aren't responsible for pastoral care but they're the ones who come over on the trips and they aren't trained to discipline the students.'

Sharon sucked her teeth and shook her head. 'How difficult is it to tell kids to stop behaving like animals? They should be ashamed of themselves, dirty little tykes. The Earl doesn't like them neither – he was out in the courtyard yesterday yelling at them to get off the gates – they were climbing all over them like monkeys. Wish one of them had slipped and got a spike up the jacksie – that would have learned them. And they can't keep their hands off each other – snogging, fiddling – how old are they meant to be?'

'Yesterday's group? About fifteen, I think.'

'I suppose it's a blessing they're banned from . . . ' and she dropped her voice, '. . . up there.'

'Up where?'

'There,' and she pointed her mop in the direction of the minstrels' gallery.

'Have you not been up there yet?' Noel said.

'I'm never going up there again. Rosemary sent me up to clean when it all started and they'd cleared everything out, but I saw what was written on those boxes and it was disgusting. So was the room. I said to Rosemary, "I can't clean up here – it's filthy." Never been up since.'

At that moment Max heard the slam of the office door in the statue corridor and a woman emerged holding a bag away from herself at arm's length. As she approached the group on the door Max thought he heard her mutter '*Merde!*' in a shocked tone as she passed.

'*Merci, madame,*' Noel said.

She hurried down the outside steps to where a friend was waiting. She pushed the bag towards her companion, chattering and gesticulating, shaking her head.

'Another satisfied customer?' Max said.

'That's right – there goes the French teacher.'

'Bloody French,' Sharon said.

'These continentals always look like they're having an argument,' Noel said, 'even if they're just discussing what time the next bus is due.'

Max was fairly certain they were not discussing the bus times because just before they turned to make their way back towards the exit, the teacher raised her voice and he heard her say, *'Non! Non! Mais ça sent mauvais!'*

'C'est pas vrai! De la merde?'

House martins screamed and swerved around the great courtyard as Sam walked out into the sun, the gravel as white as bone in the glare. The trees in the park beyond the boundary were in full leaf, oaks and elms padding out the horizon, a glade of copper beech shot through with dark terracotta where they were reflected in the lake, the water in their shadow the colour of chocolate.

Today she was lunching with Hector Schofield and she was looking forward to it. He had rung that morning because he was over in Boscobel researching John Wilmot's father. She thought it was a thin excuse for him to be in Shropshire again but in a way that was what made her agree to lunch instead of suggesting he drop by and have their meeting at the Hall. However unreasonably, she had felt irritated by the scene at Max's house the evening before, not so much because he put his daughter first – she would have done the same – but because he hadn't bothered to ring her later in the evening once he had dropped Charlotte off at Shobdon. He must have had the evening to himself but instead of wondering if Sam was all right, or being sufficiently interested in what she had come over to chat about, she had obviously slipped right out of his mind. He had probably got home, poured himself a drink and settled down with Monty without giving her another thought. She was an old-fashioned girl and didn't believe in pursuing a man. Last night, she had offered Max the perfect opportunity to develop the relationship and he had chosen to ignore it.

When Sam arrived at the hotel Hector was waiting for her in reception and came forward to kiss her on the cheek – not an unusual ritual for two Londoners – but instead of escorting her into the dining room, he motioned to the concierge who disappeared through a door. Hector touched her on her elbow to turn her towards the front door.

'I thought we were eating,' she said.

'We are but it's such a beautiful summer's day I thought a picnic would be nice. Have you got the keys to your boot?' He held out his hand and his expression of pleasure and anticipation increased her curiosity.

She followed him out into the sunshine and he hailed two waiters who were coming across the baking gravel from the side of the hotel, their long white aprons bumping on their feet as they walked. One carried a wicker hamper, holding it with both hands, a plaid rug draped over a forearm, the other carried a compartmented basket of glasses and a black insulating bag emblazoned with the crest of the hotel group. Hector moved a few things aside in Sam's boot, peering momentarily inside both the hamper and the black bag as they were laid inside, then palmed a folded note to one of the waiters. 'Many thanks,' he said. 'Excellent job.' As they walked away he shut the boot and looked up at her with a broad smile. 'Tell you what – as I know the way, I'll drive,' and before Sam had a chance to comment he was in the driver's side feeling around the seat to adjust the driving position.

'Where are we going?' she said, getting in beside him.

Having leaned over towards her to fasten his seat belt he looked up from under his brows and said, 'I have a plan.'

The elegant bow of the river boat glided over the surface of the water, pushing up a miniature bow-wave which sent light dancing and rippling across the hull. Sam was glad of the glass of champagne that Hector had handed to her because it was calming the nerves she had felt building over the last hour. They had begun the moment Hector turned out onto the road and opened up the engine but Sam, who was always a nervous passenger, thought it stemmed from being driven in her own car. To calm herself she tried not to watch the road ahead but to gaze out to her left across the countryside which lay panting in the heat. The wind buffeted around her, cooling a line of perspiration that had sprung up along her hairline. Hector made some complimentary remark about the handling of the car and when she turned towards him she felt a wave of anxiety – or excitement – blight her appetite and dry her mouth. By the time they arrived at the quay to pick up the boat she was feeling as uncomfortable as a teenager.

Hector must have sensed her unease because he organised things – paying for the boat hire, stowing the picnic, helping her to step over the gunwale and seat herself comfortably – with a sort of brio which brooked no argument from her about the appropriateness of the plan. Before setting out onto the river he blew the champagne cork across the water with a self-conscious cheer before pressing a glass into her hand. She sat in a kind of stupor as the rich red water passed beneath the boat and the mineral smells rose up from the glittering surface in warm gasps.

Eventually Hector – who had been standing at the wheel with his hair fluttering from his forehead – slowed the craft and navigated towards the bank where a shingle beach pushed out from the shore. There was a deeper lagoon which had been carved from the banks of clay by the winter eddies and here Hector brought the boat in and hopped over the side onto the shingle with practised ease. He tethered the boat and came back to the side.

'Hand down the basket,' he said, as if they had been chattering merrily for the whole voyage. 'Now the drink – and eventually you. So – what do you think?'

Sam looked out across the river, the water beyond the shingle running smooth and deep, combing the vast beds of river weed speckled in tiny white flowers which dipped and rose in the current.

'I'm stunned,' she managed to say.

Hector's swagger seemed to flag. 'Where's the best place for the rug?' he said but there was uncertainty in his voice. He cleared his throat and strolled away from her across the shingle until he reached a flatter area where tufts of grass sprouted and began pushing the larger pebbles aside with his shoe. He turned round to say something else but when he realised she was still standing on the spot where he had left her, he slumped ever so slightly. 'Have I made a terrible mistake?' he said.

It was this humility that saved him. Sam forgot her anxiety, her sense of mild affront, the inappropriateness of his campaign and smiling, she picked the folded rug up from the ground and went over to join him.

'Not at all,' she said. 'It's lovely here.'

'Thank God,' he said and like a scolded dog who has finally been forgiven, he rushed around finding flat stones for the glasses, flapping open the rug and sitting down first to check his choice of spot for comfort before opening the hamper and peering in.

'I wasn't exactly sure what you might like,' he said. 'Come and sit down – see what I've got.'

Nestled among crisp damask linen were boxes and covered plates. Sam sat down beside Hector and joined him in unwrapping foil and arranging the food within arm's reach. There were lobster and brown shrimp timbales with a pot of wobbling mayonnaise, a delicate raised pie of chicken flavoured with tarragon, a terrine of pressed game and a pudding of salted caramel tarts. Hector had chosen two different wines as well as a small bottle of Tokay for the pudding. He refilled their glasses before taking the bottles down to the river's edge and scrunching them into the gravel to keep them upright in the cool water.

Dropping down again onto the rug he turned to her, his forearm, tanned and freckled, lying across his raised knee as he tipped his champagne glass towards her.

'What shall we drink to?' he said.

'I don't know – the summer? This beautiful day?'

'Why don't we drink to the success of the quest?'

With little desire to know to which quest he referred, Sam chinked the rim of her glass on his. What other choice did she have after he had put so much thought, so much effort, into his scheme? The least she could do in return was to drink and eat and enjoy spending a hot summer's afternoon down on the shore of a lazy river.

Towards the end of the afternoon a storm began to bubble up over the Black Mountains. The breeze strengthened, mild and damp, and drove waves through the fields of barley on the hill slopes across the valley from the Hall. The poplars along the water's edge fluttered, semaphoring the approach of the cold front by flashing the white down on the underside of their leaves. The afternoon sun lit the vegetation acid green against the indigo sky but as the storm approached it faded to monochrome. As the first few spots of rain darkened the tarmac, a figure hunched beneath a full-length waxed coat which he held over the top of his head made his way along the edge of the stable yard. A car swung out into the quadrangle, its automatic headlights responding to the encroaching darkness of the storm, and the figure pressed himself into the beech hedge and turned his face away towards the shadows. The moment the car had disappeared around the corner, he stealthily continued his way towards the stables and the back entrance of the music room.

Once inside the music room he slid the waxed coat off the top of his head and draped it in the style of a cape across his shoulders revealing the bald pate of a short man in his sixties. Flattening himself against the mighty Wurlitzer organ, he crept around it until he could see along the full length of the library. No one was in sight – the gathering storm had encouraged the small handful of late-afternoon visitors to make their way to the buttery.

In a flash, he was through the door and into the well of the spiral staircase leading up to Sam's office. As he climbed, the waxed coat swished against the stone walls and his shoes clicked sharply on each step. By the time he reached the upper door his chest was heaving and he placed a hand on the cool stone, resting for a moment, before cautiously turning the rattling brass handle and entering the empty office.

The room was hot and stuffy, a computer hummed in the corner, and he could smell old coffee and stationery. He scanned the room and his eyes alighted on the large leather bucket bag that Sam used to bring in her lunch. Still panting slightly, he crossed the room towards it. He could see it was expensive, it was undoubtedly Italian leather, and it sat on a chair beside her desk full square, stable. He could slip his hand inside without even rocking it. He pushed the waxed coat off his shoulders and let it fall in a heap behind him as he stepped forward. Crouching down to the level of the chair he reached towards the sturdy clasp and drew in a deep breath as he heard the catch release under the pressure of his fingers. He rocked forward gently into a kneeling position and brought his nose level with the rim of the open bag. Hovering over the dark abyss he flared his nostrils to catch the musky scent of leather.

The telephone shrilled next to his ear and in his confusion he pushed his hand downwards to propel himself to his feet and sent the bag flying with a great clatter of plastic boxes and the ping of falling cutlery. The phone rang just three times before the answering service clicked on but by now the moment was gone. He stared around, flustered, and then, through the small circular window which overlooked the stable courtyard, he spotted Sam Westbrook hurrying towards the Hall beneath an umbrella and crossing over to the outer door of the music room below him.

Grabbing his coat from the floor, he dropped it to collect up the scattered contents of the bag and cram them back inside, then picked up the coat again. He flew towards the door and began to crump down the spiral staircase. He almost fell, catching his foot on the trailing wax coat, and his left heel drummed over three consecutive stone steps without stopping but he slapped a hand onto the slit windowsill halfway down to steady himself and paused for a moment to catch his breath. He heard the clunk of the outer door into the music room and flew down the remaining few steps, making it into the indigo library a split second before Sam Westbrook glanced casually over on her way up to the office.

All that she saw was a short man with a waxed coat over his arm making his way up the library, but her afternoon by the river had filled her mind with more pressing matters and she did not give it a second thought.

- 11 -

The following afternoon the Hall closed early to prepare for the annual Marilyn Monroe dinner. This glamorous event had become increasingly popular and therefore more elaborate year on year, and this season the organisers were laying pink carpet across the dining room and setting up the subway blower in the centre of the hall. They hadn't asked to have any of the state rooms opened for the evening which meant only two guides were needed. Weenie always volunteered, convinced that she looked more like Marilyn Monroe than any of the guests, and she persuaded Nerys to put her name down too because she was the only guide who agreed with her. The evening was likely to be a late one – by the time each guest had mingled, eaten and tottered onto the subway blower it was usually well past midnight.

Weenie had offered Nerys her spare room for the night because her friend lived half an hour away and didn't like driving after dark. Weenie certainly wasn't going to admit that night-driving had become a bit tricky for her too in recent years and besides, her bungalow was barely a mile away from the Hall. When the doors shut at five, the two women went back to Discoed for a cup of tea and to change into their evening wear. Weenie unloaded the car and handed Nerys her large tote bag.

'Goodness me,' she said, 'this weighs a ton. Whatever have you got in there?'

Nerys took it off her with a laugh and they made their way up to the front door. Once in the kitchen, Nerys burrowed into her tote, pulled out her empty lunch box and went over to the kitchen sink to wash it.

'Come on,' Weenie said, 'what else have you got in here?'

'My night things, of course, and my soap bag.'

'What's all that?' said Weenie, leaning over and peering into the bag.

Nerys looked over her shoulder. 'Oh, just bottled water – the water in the taps at the Hall comes straight out of the lake, you know, and I don't like to drink that; and there's a book to read, and the guides' notes, and another jumper in case I get cold, and a pair of comfortable shoes in case I have to walk into town and catch the bus . . . '

'I thought I carried a lot.'

'It's taken me ages to get back to having a big roomy bag and it makes so much sense when you have to spend a whole day away from home – or a night for that matter.'

'I always think of you lugging around a huge bag.'

'Do you? How odd. I couldn't face it when I was ill.'

Weenie moved across the kitchen and busied herself making the tea because she wanted her friend to talk and didn't want to disrupt her flow.

'The strangest thing happened after I had that little breakdown – I couldn't stand having anything more than a tiny little clutch.'

'Was that something to do with getting rid of the clutter in your life, do you think?' Weenie said as she searched the cupboards for the packet of biscuits she had bought at the beginning of the week in readiness for her friend's visit.

'Oh, my GP had all sorts of theories about it and she felt it was terribly important to my recovery to start using a big bag again. At first, every time my counsellor confronted me with one, I couldn't even bring myself to open it. I found it terrifying, a real phobia.'

'Really?' Weenie was beginning to feel a bit bored.

'Well, it was. I resorted to carrying everything I needed in a carrier bag, then I was referred to a psychiatrist who suggested I try a canvas bag the same shape as a carrier bag and that worked until I eventually got over the phobia and I'm happy to say that recently I've started using big bags again – this is the biggest I've had for a long while. Now, instead of feeling afraid, it takes me back to my governess days when I had to have quantities of hankies and crayons and all the children's spare clothes and shoes.'

'And now it's just your spare clothes and shoes.'

'I suppose so.'

After their tea they both went off to change into their evening things – Nerys into simple black, Weenie into a gold lamé halter-neck dress.

'Do you really need to bring that great big bag with you?' Weenie said when they met in the kitchen.

'Yes, I do.' Nerys could be rather stubborn when she chose. 'It's not that heavy now – I've unpacked my night things and just put a few essentials in.' She looked Weenie up and down. 'It's chilly in the Hall in the evenings. Won't you be awfully cold in that?'

'You must suffer to be beautiful,' Weenie replied, wrapping a faux fur stole across her shoulders and heading for the door.

'Wait a minute,' Nerys called after her, 'you've got a blob of mascara on your cheek, dear.'

Weenie glanced in the hall mirror and then turned to her friend and frowned. 'It's not mascara – it's Marilyn's famous beauty spot.'

Weenie milled around the guests bobbing and smiling, confident that the reason no one was making an effort to talk to her was because she eclipsed their lookalike status. The men who accompanied their Marilyns looked debonair in dinner jackets and Weenie was surprised that they didn't strike up a conversation with her because their partners were a different kettle of fish – Marilyn may well have been famous for her curves but frankly most of the guests there should never have had that much flesh on display.

The majority of them had turned up in a version of the iconic dress in *The Seven Year Itch*, itching – no doubt – for their moment on the subway blower, and once the meal was over out they flowed, glasses tipping and spilling in their hands, to clamber into position and stagger and shriek and reveal hideous underwear to the shouts and whoops of the audience. One particular Marilyn was packing quite a lot of luggage in the underwear department which made Weenie very suspicious indeed.

Finally the judging was over, the victor was crowned and Rosemary came out of the office and told Weenie that she and Nerys might as well get off home early, thanking them for their help throughout the evening.

They had almost reached the car park when Weenie clutched Nerys by the wrist and said, 'I'm awfully sorry, I really must go to the loo – all that fizzy water's gone straight through me. You go on – I won't be a sec.'

She was away for some time, however. To create the iconic line to the lamé dress, Weenie had begun the evening's preparations by hauling on her all-in-one strapless body shaper, and in order to have a pee she had to disrobe and peel the whole thing down. By the time she had pulled everything back on she was exhausted and hot. Irritated, she hurried out into the darkness. The noise of the revellers came across the courtyard and her shoes crunched on the gravel but she stopped and listened again because the echo of her feet didn't seem to match her steps.

'Nerys?' she called, but when no reply came she continued on towards the car park, which was deserted. She made her way past the coaches towards her car, expecting to find Nerys, but her friend was nowhere to be seen.

It was a beautiful evening and the sky over the Black Mountains still glowed from the setting sun, bathing the estate in a crepuscular light. Bewildered she looked out across the park and over the lake but there wasn't a soul in sight. She walked around to the passenger side of the car and to her surprise she saw Nerys's tote propped up against the hub of the wheel, the zip firmly closed across the top but the contents of the bag scattered over the gravel. Perplexed she gathered up a lipstick, a wallet, a plastic rain hat, a small powder compact and a scarf before picking up the bag. She unlocked her car and put the bag on the passenger's seat, placing the handful of items in the storage tray of the centre console. Walking away from the car, she scanned the park one more time. In the far distance, on the opposite shore of the lake, she thought she saw a small figure moving at speed away from her. She recognised the gait. It was Nerys.

'What on earth . . . ?' she said to herself, hurrying back to her car as fast as her strappy sandals would allow.

The engine coughed into life and she turned the car away from the Hall and down the road that led towards the lake – a road not open to the public. No one was on duty to stop her and as the dusk deepened, she drove on around the perimeter of the water, the small figure now lost against the brighter light of the headlamps. Coming up a small rise, the beam caught the figure again and Weenie saw that her friend was running. She limped as she ran

– she had lost a shoe – her hair had come loose from its pins and trailed out behind her, her skirt was torn and the wrap that she had worn over her shoulders for the evening was hooked around one elbow and swept the ground behind her. Weenie flicked the automatic window on the passenger side down as she approached and, leaning across as she slowed the car, she called, 'Nerys! It's me, it's Weenie. What on earth are you doing?'

Her friend turned towards the car, her eyes staring before she stumbled off the road and into the rough grass, moving away from Weenie. Weenie came to a halt and leaving the engine still running, set off on foot in pursuit of her friend, her kitten heels sinking into the soft turf. She caught up with her within minutes and grabbed her by her shoulders. 'Nerys!' she said. 'Nerys! It's me, it's Weenie. Where are you going?'

Nerys tried to shake her off but she caught her again and swung her round. Her flowing hair poured across her face and Weenie reached up to sweep it to one side. Nerys stared through her and tried to shake her off again. Weenie gripped her by the shoulder and she stopped struggling and stood, panting in short sharp breaths.

'Nerys! Speak to me. What are you doing?'

'I thought he was robbing me.'

'Who?'

'He was crouching – that face, that horrible moon face – it's happening all over again.'

'Who? What's happening again?'

She didn't reply and although her breath came out as shallow pants, Weenie sensed the old woman's shoulders relax beneath her grip and she lightened her hold and came around beside her, putting her arm around her waist. 'Let's get you back to the car,' she said, and like a sleepwalker Nerys was suddenly compliant. Together they walked slowly up the slope of grass and Weenie opened the passenger door to help her in.

The tote was on the seat and as Weenie reached forward to move it to one side, Nerys suddenly stiffened again and began to wail. She struggled and tried to run off but Weenie held her tightly by the elbow and firmly guided her into the car. She took the bag and put it on the back seat, made her way around to the driver's side and drove out of the park.

Once they were on the open road, the increasing warmth seemed to soothe her friend and after a few miles Nerys's head slumped to her chest as if exhausted. Weenie drove on in silence but as the car continued to heat up, the interior began to fill with an extremely unpleasant odour. At first she thought she must have trodden in excrement in the park but the smell became so powerful she was forced to open a window, beginning to fear that Nerys had soiled herself. The old lady seemed to be asleep and Weenie knew the best thing was to get her back home, clean her up and put her to bed.

Weenie poured herself another stiff drink and sunk down on the sofa. She had changed into her lounge wear and, kicking off her mules, she gazed across the room, deep in thought.

She had failed to get any sense out of poor Nerys but she was relieved that her initial assumption about the source of the smell had been wrong – when she helped her friend into the night things she had laid out in the spare room at the beginning of the evening there was no evidence that Nerys had accidentally taken a little turf.

Deeply worried about her state of mind, Weenie wracked her

brains to see if anything had been mentioned during the first aid course that might help her care for her friend. Nerys's mood was unstable, swinging from long, brooding silences to tears and moans and back again. Weenie wondered who she could telephone at this late hour – Roger would be furious if she called him at home. Eventually she decided to be guided by her instincts, found some old sleeping pills in her bathroom cupboard, and insisted Nerys take a couple with a glass of brandy and hot water. Within ten minutes her friend became more relaxed and eventually fell into a deep sleep.

Weenie drained her glass and then remembered that in all the excitement, she had left Nerys's bag in the back of her car. Teetering on her mules, she unlocked the front door once again and clicked her way across the concrete drive to where the car was parked. When she opened the door, the smell assailed her nostrils more strongly than ever and reaching into the back, she breathed through her mouth as she retrieved the tote. She wondered if a forgotten fish sandwich nestled somewhere inside but she distinctly remembered her friend washing up her lunch things earlier in the evening.

She carried the tote into the kitchen and as she lifted it onto the surface of the table, the smell in the room became overpowering. She took a scented handkerchief from her sleeve and pressed it against her nose. The zip of the bag was closed and the light in the kitchen glistened on a thin line of mucous that ran down the side. Weenie recoiled once more but then, with the handkerchief pressed firmly over her nose, she reached out, drew the zipper carefully along the top and edged forward to look into the base of the bag.

Resting snugly against the pretty cotton lining on the inside were three perfectly formed pieces of conker brown human excrement.

'She was calmer this morning,' Weenie said, 'and when I dropped her off at home she made a solemn promise that she would ring her GP the moment the surgery opened and tell her everything that had happened.'

'It sounds as if you took very good care of her,' Roger said from the other side of the guides' room as he stirred his coffee.

'It was a simply horrible night, I must admit.' Weenie was conflicted. She longed to share the full story of the night's adventure and catapult herself to the forefront of the room's attention but she didn't want to add to her friend's humiliation by describing her vile discovery. Nerys's behaviour last night and this morning was sufficiently odd for Weenie to question who had defiled the handbag. She hadn't felt like making a close study of the evidence, emptying the contents into the flower bed before bunging the whole bag into the washing machine. The following morning she draped it over the back of a chair with the lining prolapsed out to dry but when she helped Nerys downstairs, the old lady cried out as it came into view and turned away, shielding her eyes with a raised forearm. Weenie couldn't tell whether this reaction was caused by guilt or fear so she put Nerys's things into a carrier bag and resolved to throw the tote into the bin when she got home that evening.

'Should we do a card, Bunty?' Roger said.

'Anything but that,' Noel said. 'A card from Duntisbourne Hall with the words "Get Well" is the kiss of death.'

'Does she have family?'

'There's a niece somewhere,' Weenie said, 'she keeps in touch with Nerys. I'll pop in on my way home this evening to see how

Nerys is and suggest she contact her.'

'Try and get an idea of when we can expect her back at work, will you? The diary's all sixes and sevens without her.'

'Bunty! I don't think you have the foggiest idea how bad poor Nerys is – she was like a raving loon last night. There's no way she'll be back at work in the near future.'

'She needs to pull herself together,' Bunty said.

– 12 –

Under the August sun, the countryside was losing its freshness. The grass on the verges was beginning to lighten, the seed heads ripening in concord with the fields of wheat. Although the longest day had passed, the summer evenings were still poised at the top of their parabola, the decline in their duration imperceptible, the acceleration of shortening days towards winter months away.

To his great surprise Max found he was looking forward to the party. He had dropped Charlotte off in Shobdon during the afternoon so that she could get ready with her friends and now, freed from the constraints she wordlessly imposed, he thought the evening could turn into a fine opportunity to advance the friendship with Sam into something more serious. The weather was balmy and pleasant, there would be wine and good food, everyone would be in the mood for celebration. This could be his moment.

He managed to fill the early part of his evening at home with extensive preparations. He laid his clothes out on the bed in a series of different combinations then showered, flossed vigorously, shaved and trimmed errant whiskers from his nose – he even pared his toenails although he acknowledged that this was probably an unnecessary precaution. Monty lay on the bed watching him with a despondent air as if he knew Max was going out for the evening and a walk was not part of the plan. Max cast a final glance in his full-length mirror and rubbed Monty's head before leaving the room. The dog dropped onto the floor and followed him to the top of the stairs but instead of accompanying him to the front door, he lay down again with his chin on his paws and sighed. Max stepped out into the light of the early evening and waved to his neighbour who was mowing his front lawn, and taking a deep breath of freshly mown grass he climbed into his Land Rover and set off for the Hall. He arrived a comfortable ten minutes after proceedings had begun.

When he entered the Siegfried Rooms his spirits sank momentarily as that familiar feeling of ennui and awkwardness set in, but one of the caterers was at his elbow with a tray of drinks and among the group of thirty or so people from all over the estate who Max had never seen before, he spotted Laurence talking to Noel by a large ice-bowl of lumpfish caviar. As he approached Laurence was loading up a finger of toast, the shiny black eggs trembling on the tip.

'My toast's gone terribly limp,' Laurence said juggling with the flailing end in an attempt to get it into his mouth without flicking the contents down his front.

'You put too much lemon juice on it, old chap,' Noel said. 'Hello Max.'

'Max,' Laurence said, 'can I load up a piece of toast for you?'

'Not for the moment.'

'Can I say that I think you look absolutely magnificent this evening. Is that jacket new?'

'Well, thank you Laurence. As a matter of fact it is.'

'But I don't think he's wearing it for your benefit,' Noel said, nodding towards the door through which Sam had entered. 'Now that's what I call magnificent.'

Max turned and felt a hot pinch underneath his rib cage. She was wearing a tailored dress, gas blue, and he had never seen her more beautiful, but the look she returned was apologetic as the figure behind her emerged from the muted light of the landing and stepped into the room to take his place at her side – it was Hector Schofield.

A few hours earlier Weenie had been waiting at the foot of the drive up to her modest bungalow in the village of Discoed. Like Max, she too had spent the early part of her evening getting ready for the party and, also like Max, she was full of eager anticipation following a difficult few weeks.

Roger's behaviour at the first aid day had irritated her spectacularly and afterwards she made certain he felt the full force of her disapproval by flouncing out of any room he entered and refusing to make eye contact when it was impossible to avoid him. At first he responded to these slights by blustering to his colleagues on some unconnected subject but by the end of the week Weenie sensed this bravado was waning, and when she stalked over to the opposite side of the dining room to sit and wait her turn for the next tour she felt his mournful gaze tracking her across the room. It was late in the afternoon with not a single visitor in sight.

She sat staring at the bronze of Perseus that stood on the chimneypiece opposite, wondering why he had a foreskin – she thought circumcision started in ancient Egypt and couldn't work out if Perseus was before or after that – when she realised Roger had taken the huge risk of leaving his position and making his way over to speak to her. If Bunty happened to come into the dining room at that particular moment he would be in terrible trouble.

'It's no good old girl,' he said. 'I can't bear having those blue peepers turned away from me any longer. What have I done to upset you so much?'

He got the full blast of her blue peepers then but as she snapped her gimlet gaze onto him she was struck by his hangdog demeanour which rather took the wind out of her sails and instead of giving him both barrels all she managed to say was 'I think you know,' but she said it with great dignity.

'I don't know. I'm floundering.'

'Much the same as when that young girl was trying to get you into the recovery position then?'

Roger's face simultaneously registered comprehension and chagrin, but the latter he quickly dismissed. 'Oh, that. You can't take that seriously. I was just having a bit of fun, putting the new girl at her ease.'

'She didn't look very comfortable to me.'

'Nonsense. She loved it. I wouldn't fool around like that in front of everyone if I was serious.' Roger waited for a reply but Weenie lifted her chin and turned away from him again. 'Come on, old thing – don't be haughty with me any more. I've managed to get a free pass for Friday night – wifey's out playing Lady Bountiful. I can pick you up and take you to the Summer Progress party if you like.'

Weenie tipped her head slightly and stole a sly look at him. This really was a turn-up for the books – walking into the party on the arm of Roger Hogg-Smythe instead of steeling herself to walk in on her own again. That would show her colleagues she was still in the game.

'Really?'

'Of course. Do say yes. We'll have a great old time together.'

So here she was, exfoliated and scented, waxed and plucked, waiting at the foot of the drive with the fur collar of her coat pulled up under her chin to keep out the chill of that cunning east wind.

'Who the hell's that?' Noel said.

Sam came straight across the room towards them, Hector following a few paces behind. 'I don't think you know Hector Schofield,' she said to Noel and Laurence. 'He happened to be down from London this evening. Max of course you know.'

'Good evening, Max,' he said. 'How pleasant to see you again and what luck to find myself down here this evening of all evenings. Sam had kindly allowed me to spend some time browsing through the inventory of the Dywenydd Collection after the Hall had closed and when I asked her for a local recommendation of somewhere half decent down here where I could tuck into a grim little artisan dinner she absolutely insisted I join your celebrations.'

'What are you researching?' Laurence asked, and as Schofield began to explain, Sam touched Max on the sleeve and turned away from the group. 'I'm so sorry,' she said. 'I had no idea he was turning up today.'

Max shrugged and took a gulp of wine. The room was filling fast. He spotted the Major sporting a magnificent brocade waistcoat and Bunty who didn't look radically different although she was wearing a bit of lipstick and he couldn't see any ladders in her tights. Even Claude – who was chatting to himself in a corner – had scrubbed up reasonably well and was wearing a double-breasted chalk-stripe suit. At that moment Max's daughter arrived with her friends and he thought she was about to come over and say hello, but she glanced at Sam and immediately appeared to instigate an unseemly rush to bag a table in the far corner of the room before the meal started. It didn't go unnoticed.

'Have I done something to offend Charlotte again?' Sam said. Whether it was a hint of criticism in her tone or her sanctioning of Schofield's blatant intrusion into an evening that had held such promise, he replied more sharply than he intended.

'Why don't you leave Charlotte alone? Ignore her. Go and enjoy your evening. Come on Noel, Laurence – we'd better grab a seat before we get stuck sitting with the Earl and the CEO,' and he walked away from her towards an empty table.

He settled himself down with his back towards the room and Laurence and Noel took the seats to his left and right. Max twisted the stem of his wine glass – he was aware he had behaved poorly but she had hijacked him, caught him off his guard.

'Do you mind if Roger and I join you?'

He glanced up and Weenie was leaning on the back of one of the chairs. She looked spectacular but not in a good way. She was wearing a pair of red leather trousers which were slightly too short in the leg and high on the waist. The seat of the trousers may once have hugged her buttocks but whether it was the loss of muscle definition around her skinny backside or the many years of stretching that the leather had taken, the trousers hung in loose folds like the skin on the arms of an ancient crone. She had topped the outfit with a cropped jacket in shocking pink which she must have owned for well over twenty years because it had shoulder pads so enormous she looked like an American footballer. Underneath was the same strappy leopard print blouse she had worn the other night and Max jerked his gaze away to avoid another flash of her chest.

'Join us? Why not?' he said, watching Roger struggle his large frame through the chairs to sit beside her.

'Can I pour you a wine, my dear?' Roger said, splashing a generous helping into Weenie's glass.

'Thank you, Roger. It's always so much nicer from a man's hand.'

By the time the disco music started to boom from the room next door Max was feeling wretched. The table was scattered with paper streamers oozing dye into the leftover cream on the pudding plates and the tannin in the Duntisbourne wine seemed to be coating his teeth, making them feel as if he'd been eating rhubarb all night. He turned round to see if there was a bottle of water on the table behind and saw Sam sitting a few tables away, her chin in the palms of her hands, listening intently to Schofield who had removed his jacket and was leaning in towards her to make himself heard over the sound of the music, his legs splayed mannishly either side of the corner of her chair.

'Oh – oh,' said Noel. 'She's off.'

'What?'

'Weenie. There she goes, off to the dance floor with Hoggers. He could be in trouble – I saw a nasty look creep into her eyes a moment ago rather like a cat who had just seen a crippled vole appear on the horizon,' and Weenie and Roger disappeared into the boiling crowd of younger employees. 'I think I should ask the DJ if he could play *Enjoy Yourself – It's Later Than You Think.*'

'I hate parties,' Max said. 'I think I'll call it a night. Have you seen my daughter?'

'She's probably out on the dance floor.'

Max made his way over to the table where Charlotte and her friends had been sitting. Robyn and Jess were still there, talking with great intensity to three lads Max recognised from around the estate. 'Hi, Robyn,' he said, and to his surprise she leapt to her feet and seemed to place herself between him and the others at the table, flinging her arms around his neck and landing a noisy kiss on his cheek.

'Whoa!' he said. 'What was that for?'

'We love you, Max. All of us love you.'

Drunk as a skunk, he thought. 'And I'm very fond of all of you too but I was looking for Charlotte. I'm off soon and I wanted to make sure she was OK for getting back. Any idea where she is?'

One of the lads stood up and shuffled away, and the other two stared down at the table, one of them starting to move a pool of spilt beer around with his finger. Robyn had woven her arm around Max's waist and was gazing down at Jess, who stared back at him. He wondered if they were all drunk but with a rising sense of prescient doom he realised something was terribly wrong. Pulling a chair away from the table he sat down with caution, as if by holding himself firm he could minimise the shock.

'What on earth's happened?' he said.

His expression must have conveyed his fear because Robyn put an arm around his shoulders and gave him a comforting shake, saying, 'She's fine. Nothing's happened. Charlotte's fine. She's outside with Rufus.'

'Oh God.'

'No. No. It's not what you think. She's trying to help. Rufus has got himself in a bit of a fix, that's all.'

'What sort of fix?'

Robyn shook her head and Jess put her hands up to her mouth – Max was sure one of the lads snickered – but then Jess reached up and pulled at Robyn's hand, pointing across the darkened room to the door. 'They're back,' she said, and Max turned to see his daughter looking white and anxious, making her way towards them with Rufus trailing behind her. When she spotted her father she slowed and hesitated but then relief seemed to take over and she hurried on. The music boomed away behind them.

'Well?' Robyn said.

'Hopeless,' Charlotte replied. Rufus slumped down beside her and grasped two handfuls of his hair as his head sank towards the table.

'For God's sake will someone tell me what's going on?' Max said, unwinding Robyn's arm from around his shoulders.

In reply Charlotte held a hand out towards Rufus who, without raising his head, drew his mobile from his pocket and passed it over to her. She navigated to a photograph and handed the phone to her father.

At first he couldn't work out what he was looking at and twisted in his seat to get the screen into a better light. He recognised a room in the Dywenydd Exhibition, the Boulle-work on the brass-bound buggery box. Charlotte reached across and tapped the screen and the picture enlarged. It was only then he realised that something was sticking out of the orifice in the box, and when he peered more closely he saw it was the Golden Hand of Jerusalem.

'What the hell's that doing in there?' he said, his voice loud over the music. Everyone around the table shushed at him, the lads looking around nervously. 'Rufus?'

'It's for one of his projects,' Charlotte cut in.

'One of your projects?' Max said to Rufus, who turned his head fractionally and rolled an anguished eye towards him. Max stared at him, fury building in his chest, until Rufus blinked and looked away. 'You mean to tell me that you've unhooked a priceless artefact from the chains in the dining room, taken it upstairs to the exhibition and stuffed it, finger first, into the business end of the brass-bound buggery box?' Rufus raised his head once more and looked back at him, slack-jawed and remorseful. 'And what were you going to do then? Put the blasted picture on the internet or something? Have you gone stark staring mad?'

'No.'

'No what?'

'I've had second thoughts about publishing it.'

'Well, thank God for that.' With relief Max dropped the phone onto the table and looked around the group. They were motionless as if each one of them was holding their breath. 'That's all right then,' Max said. 'Get rid of the picture and make sure no one blabs that you've been very, very stupid. Jesus Christ, kids – don't any of you value your jobs?'

'It's not as simple as that,' Charlotte said.

Max dropped back in his chair and sighed. 'Why am I not surprised?' he said. 'Come on then – what's really going on here? Did someone see you doing it? Charlotte?'

'No, Rufus did it all by himself this time – he wanted to try it out as an idea. No one saw him. Rufus – you've got to explain.'

'Yes, Rufus,' Max said, folding his arms across his chest. 'Why don't you do just that?'

'It came to me on the spur of the moment,' Rufus said. 'I realised that the exhibition had been left unlocked –'

'Because Sam Westbrook's date was working up there when I left,' Robyn said, 'and Sam told me she would come in later and lock up when he was finished.'

'Anyway,' Rufus had stopped sighing and slumping and become rather more animated as he recounted his adventure. 'Pugh was also late because he was called away to sort something out over here for the party. It was sort of like the perfect storm – the shutters were all closed in the dining room when I looked in to see if Bunty was still around to ask whether it was all right if I left. She wasn't there, the dining room was empty, so I shinnied up onto the dining-room table and unhooked the hand . . . ' Max groaned and pressed his fingers into his eye sockets. 'It came away quite easily but it was a lot heavier than I expected it to be – I lost my footing and nearly knocked over the flower arrangement.' He guffawed at his audience but then he looked at Max and pulled himself together. 'Anyway, I waited under the minstrels' gallery until I heard that man leave and then I slipped upstairs and popped the finger into the hole, took the picture and was going to send it to this lot –' he gestured to his audience, '– to see if someone had a better idea for the gag but I couldn't get a signal. So, realising I was probably a bit short of time – I popped back downstairs and outside through the music room door to get a signal. And I did. I sent the picture off and waited – and Charlotte texted back to suggest it might look funnier if the Hand was inside the box and the finger was appearing out of the hole, so back I went, in through the music room – that was all right – and then I saw Sam coming along the statue corridor so I nipped into the library bedroom until she went past, back through the state rooms – still no Pugh – and up to the exhibition and . . . '

'Well, come on. The tension's killing me,' Max said.

'The door was locked.'

One of the youths suppressed a laugh and his companion thumped him on the back. Jess tried to glare at them but shot her hand up to her face and pinched the corners of her mouth to stop herself from laughing. Even Charlotte's expression was one of illicit mirth, as if she had just witnessed someone take a ludicrous but wounding tumble.

Max gawped from one to the other in complete astonishment, a thousand catastrophes tumbling through his mind – police, prison sentences, criminal convictions that would blight the futures of these bright young things – and all they could do was laugh.

'You idiot,' he said to Rufus. 'You moron. Have you any idea what you've done? It won't seem so funny tomorrow morning when they open the place up and find the Hand is missing and the police are called and you're all taken away and questioned. You think they'll see a well-spoken, well-educated middle-class lad and think – what the hell, it was just high spirits? Well, they won't. If you were a morbidly obese one-legged scrofulous youth from a sink estate with a conviction record as long as your arm you'd be in with a chance, but the moment they hear your well-modulated Oxford accents ringing out across the court they'll squash you like a bug.'

He looked into the faces of each of the young people sitting around the table and was reassured to see that his tirade had driven all merriment out of them, although he wasn't completely sure it was contrition that made them look so glum. His daughter was the first to speak.

'Look, Dad, we can either sit here for the rest of the evening bollocking Rufus or we can come up with a plan.'

As Weenie had hoped, the effect of the alcohol, the pulsating music and the low light levels in the room was stoking Roger's libido and he pressed his sweating cheek against hers and shouted over the music, 'Weenie, you minx. You're driving me wild.'

Buoyed by his compliment and eager to keep anticipation high she broke away from him to execute some extravagant thrusts of her groin but she was wearing a pair of stiletto boots which hadn't seen the light of day since New Year's Eve a decade ago and she was a little tipsy so couldn't get balanced to execute the move with confidence. Instead she lifted her hair from the nape of her neck and pouted provocatively across the two metres of floor between them as she tried a stiff shimmy but her heel slithered sideways and sent her ricocheting back into Roger's midriff with an animal grunt which luckily was muffled by the loud music.

Roger grasped her under the arms and pulled her back into an upright position. 'Stop it!' he shouted playfully, 'I'm in pain,' and he pressed himself against her so that she could feel the reassuring bulge in his trousers.

'Roger! We're going to have to do something about that.'

'But where?' he said, his voice rasping a little either because of the strength of his desire or from the effort of shouting.

'I've got an idea – follow me,' she replied and, zigzagging ahead of him, she made her way towards the dining room where she had left her bag. She was relieved to see that the rest of the people who had dined with them had dispersed. She grabbed her handbag and scrabbled around in it until she located a key on a large brass fob. Roger was at her side with his hot, damp hand on her waist and she opened the mouth of the bag and showed him the contents, raising an eyebrow coquettishly. He looked quizzically at her.

'I had to cover for Bunty last Sunday,' she said. 'There wasn't a spare pass key so she gave me this – it's for the front door.'

'Weenie, whatever can you mean? Not in the Hall, surely?'

'Why ever not?'

'The alarm system,' he hissed at her. 'You'll set the whole thing off.'

'It's been temporarily decommissioned. It got full of dust when all that building work was done and kept going off in the middle of the night and waking up the private side. The Earl won't have it back on until it's been completely overhauled.'

Roger began to smirk. Tightening his grip on her waist, he pulled her over towards him. 'You're a very resourceful woman, Weenie,' he said, 'but at your age I expect you have to be.'

- 13 -

'You've done what?' Noel said and then, much to Max's surprise and considerable annoyance, he threw his head back and roared with laughter. 'That's capital news. Wish I'd thought of it myself – let me pour each and every one of you a drink. That silly old fart thoroughly deserves it.'

'Noel! For God's sake, man,' Max said.

'I knew this daughter of yours was a bright girl the moment I set eyes on her and as for you, young man,' Noel flung an arm around Rufus's shoulder, 'you are a genius. What an inspired notion, utterly brilliant. Oh, to be young again! The whole world is in a conspiracy to give you everything you want.'

'You're drunk, Noel.'

'I most certainly am not – I'm delighted, overjoyed. What a capital lark!'

'Pull yourself together. This is serious. There could be dire consequences for everyone around this table.'

'Don't be such a sourpuss Max. Lighten up. These people here,' and he swept his hand towards the revellers in the room around them, 'have given that ruddy man years of loyal service and all he does is complain and grumble and criticise us. Look at the way he spoke to Nerys the other day – and you've not been immune, have you? You felt the smack of his insolence a few months ago for doing nothing more than leaning on a table. And what did you do about it? Exactly the same thing all of us do. You turned the other cheek and took another stunning blow across it from his exquisitely expensive kid glove. Serves him bloody well right – you can't treat people like that and expect loyalty or respect.' He raised his glass to his audience. 'A toast to every single one of you. Best thing to have happened at the Hall since – I don't know – since the second Earl of Duntisbourne bedded good Queen Bess.' He took a large mouthful of wine and sucked a little air through it over his tongue, swallowing it and smacking his lips with relish. 'Just wait until I tell Laurence and the Major.'

The moon had thrown a black moat around the Hall and using this as cover Weenie and Roger flitted along like a couple of drunken vampires until they made it up the steps and stood at the front door of the Hall, hidden in the shadows thrown by the mighty portico. Before using her key, Weenie pressed herself against the door and turned her pale face up towards Roger. 'Are you sure about this, tiger?' she said. He answered by grabbing her hand and pressing it into his crotch. Weenie wasn't sure she felt much more than the folds of his trousers but she gave it an encouraging squeeze anyway before rolling herself round and feeling for the keyhole with her free hand.

The lock turned with an echoing clunk and they both froze, listening, then began to giggle and splutter with excitement. They pushed against the heavy door until it opened enough to admit them and pulling back on the inner handle to make sure the door closed as softly as possible, Roger eased it back into position until the latch clicked into place.

'Out of the way,' Weenie said. 'I need to lock it again. '

'No, don't do that, ' Roger said, 'we may have to make a quick exit. No one else is going to come in tonight.' He took her by the hand and they made their way to the right, guided by the light that shone across the courtyard from the dance. They had become dark-adapted by now and were able to navigate around the grey shapes of familiar objects towards the library bedroom where, by wordless agreement, they knew they could get horizontal on the four-poster bed designed by William Chambers which had stood in the room for the past two centuries.

Roger hovered in the doorway, his hand resting nonchalantly on the architrave and said, 'Come into my boudoir,' pulling Weenie into the room. He pushed her up against the wall and started kissing her earnestly, groping her all over and bumping her head on the wall behind. He broke away with a pant and began to draw her across the room towards the bed. Forgetting the heavy red rope that dissuaded visitors from venturing too far into the room, Roger caught his knee and sent the two wooden supporting stanchions crashing to the floor. 'Oops!' he said and they both started giggling again.

Weenie had never stood right next to the famous bed and was surprised to find it higher from the floor than she expected. After a couple of abortive attempts to haul herself up, she rolled over with a chortle and began to crawl inelegantly on all fours up the slippery counterpane, Roger pushing her leather-clad buttocks with his hands. Finally on the top of the bed, she rolled onto her back and received Roger into her arms.

Roger had discarded his jacket and undone his tie and Weenie worked away feverishly at the buttons of his shirt, which proved extremely stubborn. Roger was having an equal amount of difficulty with the trouser stud beneath Weenie's belt and after a minute or two of fruitless struggling, they both sat up and undid the fasteners to their own clothes.

Although the half-light of the room was seductive, the air was chilly and the ardour and heat generated on the dance floor had cooled during their flight across the courtyard. Weenie was relieved not to have to discard every article of clothing, reassuring herself that in recent years men had often found her more alluring in a state of semi-undress than completely nude. Pulling her top off over her head, she pushed Roger's shirt open and let his skin press against hers. His flesh felt dank and cold from the sweat of dancing. He slipped his leg across her body and she began to work the top of his trousers down. This seemed to cause an unparalleled surge of excitement in the man and Roger began to push his large white buttocks up towards Weenie's hand. She moved it away and towards his left hip but he began to manoeuvre his buttocks again, forcing her to move her hand away for a second time.

Eventually Roger stopped this intricate dance of the buttocks and attempted to assuage Weenie's concern by imparting a vital piece of information. 'I've depilated my arsehole,' he murmured huskily in her ear.

Weenie liked to think of herself as experienced in the language of eroticism but this enlightenment left her a little baffled and she felt it wiser to respond with nothing more than a smouldering and knowing glance through the darkness from beneath her savagely plucked eyebrows.

Max stood in the deep shadow cast by the topiaried yew and waited. All of them – Laurence, Noel, the Major and himself – had contrived to slip away from the party at intervals so as not to arouse suspicion but he knew Sam had spotted his departure. He had felt her eyes on him when he was plotting with Robyn and it probably hadn't been wise to leave with her but she had a torch in the car which they were going to need.

Standing in that dry and pine-scented vault, Max tried to analyse what had goaded him into agreeing to this foolhardy escapade

– alcohol, the thrill of adventure or simply a paternal conceit that he could protect his daughter from the consequences of her boyfriend's rash behaviour. It was the curse of his generation, the baby boomers – a determination never to clip a wing or stifle a dream, to protect his child from unhappiness and disappointment at all costs, to sort things out, make things go away, and in the process rob her of the opportunity to make her own mistakes and allow the pain of regret to forge her adult self.

He was roused from his gloomy censure by the snap of a dry twig close by and turning he saw the liquorice gleam of a human eye deep in the vegetation. 'Robyn?' he whispered but with a sound little louder than a quilt being drawn from a bed, the glint was no more. He heard a crunch of gravel in front.

'Max?'

'In here, Robyn.' She dipped in under the yew and handed him the torch. 'You were behind me a second ago.'

'No. I came straight across the courtyard.'

'That's curious.' Max looked back into the shadows. 'Never mind. You'd better get back inside.'

'You sure you old boys are going to manage?'

'Enough of the old. Go on – get out of here.'

He made his way out of the courtyard and round the back of the stables to avoid going near the private apartments. The conspirators were waiting for him, their silhouettes grey against the monotone of the twilight: Laurence, who knew how to open the window of the watercolour room, Noel, who had deputised for the previous archivist, BS Moreton in the past and had keys to the exhibition and the Major, who had persuaded them he would make a good look-out while they were inside, returning the Hand to its rightful place. Wordlessly they crept along the side of the

Hall to the west front until Laurence held up his hand and beckoned them over to a window.

'This is it,' he whispered. 'You can push the sash up easily from outside.'

'But the shutters are closed.'

'The locking bar on that shutter gave up the ghost years ago – push on it and you can slide a finger into the gap and flip up the temporary catch.'

'How do you know all this?'

'I had a heady liaison with a footman on the private side a few seasons ago.'

Max removed his jacket and handed it to the Major. He stepped up onto the ledge which ran along the west front and, with Noel and Laurence supporting his lower legs, braced himself against the window and pushed. It moved with ease and he felt a breeze of warmer air scented with wax polish brush across his face. He twisted to raise his shoulder so that he could locate the latch across the shutter but he was at full stretch and couldn't reach.

'I need to get a bit higher,' he said. He could already feel a tremor in Noel's grip on his leg and, pushing the toe of his shoe into an indentation in the rough stone, he extended his knee in an ungainly hop and stabbed the latch free before tumbling back onto his friends in a jumble of arms and clutching hands.

They brushed themselves down, laughing weakly. Bending forwards, his hands braced on his knees to get his breath back, Max looked up and said, 'We're too old for this.'

'Rubbish,' said Noel.

'Fancy a bit of tuck?' the Major said, holding out a handful of chocolates from the party. 'Might give you a boost of energy.'

Max's second attempt was more successful and he managed

to get his elbows over the window sill. Hanging there for a few moments, he heaved himself up, swinging a leg onto the sill and rolling his body over and into the Hall. He landed lightly on the Savonnerie carpet and strained his ears into the darkness. He sensed a kind of rhythmic movement like the pulse of an ancient piece of machinery but as he began to isolate the sound, it quickened and died.

Hearing a 'Psst!' from outside the window, he turned and saw Laurence dangling on the sill. He rushed forward to help but Laurence was past the point of no return and tumbled in with a guffaw onto the floor at Max's feet. He began to pull himself up Max's legs whispering, 'Sorry. Really sorry. Shh!'

Noel followed with great difficulty, Laurence hauling away at one arm, Max pulling on the belt at the back of his trousers. As they composed themselves Max looked down from the window onto the Major, who stood like a cricket umpire bedecked with their discarded jackets. He saw him put his hand into his pocket and draw out another chocolate which he popped into his mouth before settling his back against the stones of the Hall and scanning the last glow of light along the horizon with his rheumy eyes.

After a great deal of struggling Roger had finally navigated his way around Weenie's underwear and entered her, although the initial experience fell short, in every way, of her expectations. Trapped beneath his large frame, she had tried to maintain an encouraging groan of excitement but his thrusting was shallow and fast and it was difficult to catch her breath. He shuddered and began to breathe laboriously in her ear.

'What's the matter, Roger?'

'Don't you know?' he said irritably. Weenie started to wriggle from underneath him. 'I couldn't help it,' he said.

'Shut up, you fool,' she whispered. 'I thought I heard something.' She sat up like a skinny meerkat and listened – Roger was struggling to retrieve his pants and trousers from around his ankles and his loose change spilled across the slippery counterpane and rattled onto the floor. He cursed.

'Shut up!' she hissed again, and then she heard a soft thud in the room next door followed by hushed voices. 'There's someone in the watercolour room,' she said. 'Get dressed.'

She felt around the bed for her top and jacket and slithered down onto the floor where she stood buttoning her clothes and listening. She patting her hair back into shape she turned to Roger, who had managed to pull one of his trouser legs inside out and was flapping the garment irritably to rectify the situation. 'Will you hurry up – we're going to get caught.'

With a great deal of hopping, he eventually managed to get them on, but stopped again. 'I can't find my tie,' he whispered. 'I think it's gone down the back of my trousers.'

Weenie moved cautiously towards the door and opened it. She could see the entrance to the watercolour room because someone was shining a torch on the carpet. She heard a murmur of voices and after a few moments the light moved and faded away. Moving back into the room she crashed straight into the looming form of Roger, who had soundlessly crept up behind her. 'Roger!'

'Who's out there? Is it Pugh?'

'I don't know.'

'Has someone raised the alarm? Oh, Christ – we were seen coming in here by someone in the private apartments. They have a clear view of the courtyard. Is it Dean out there?'

'I don't know who it is but they're not looking for us. We need to find out what's going on.'

'What? Are you mad? We've to get out of here.'

'Don't be so spineless, Roger.' She paused for a moment, conscious of her hectoring tone – she imagined that his pride had taken a serious knock from the premature end to their night of passion. Had they not been disturbed she might have found the patience to soothe him by suggesting that they had probably drunk rather too much or given him the opportunity to regroup and exonerate his manliness but surely the thought of thwarting a plot in the Hall would blunt his sense of failure. 'There are intruders in the Hall and if we are useful witnesses the Earl is bound to reward us.'

In the half-light she saw him draw himself up to his full height. 'I'm getting your drift,' he said gravely. 'I'll lead the way.' He pushed past her and beckoned her to follow, silently indicating the open window of the watercolour room as they passed the door.

They crept along until, from the safety of the unlit room, they saw three men beside the Earl's chair at the head of the dining room table. One of them was shining a light upwards until the beam caught a glint of a chain which moved and twisted almost imperceptibly. Weenie drew in a breath and clapped her hand over her mouth to stifle the gasp. She pulled at Roger's shoulder until his ear was next to her lips and whispered, 'They've stolen the Golden Hand.'

Roger caught her by the wrist and drew her away from the dining room.

'We've got to raise the alarm,' he whispered.

'No. Let's get nearer. We may need to identify them later,' and huddling together they slipped back towards the dining room – but the group were gone.

'My God,' Weenie said, 'we've got to find them.'

'They could be dangerous – gypsies, mountebanks, violent criminals.'

'We'll stay out of sight.' She grabbed Roger by the hand and led him on through the state rooms. As they turned the corner into the brown drawing room they saw torchlight flickering on the carpet ahead, silhouetting the figures as they moved through the Hall. Creeping along between the plinths of the statues, Weenie was aware that Roger was lagging behind but she knew that the windows in the great hall were too large for shutters and hoped that the light from the party across the courtyard would illuminate the intruders sufficiently for her to remember them for identification. She was – as the three men made their way up the stairs to the minstrels' gallery she saw exactly what they looked like.

Roger came up behind her and grabbed her by the shoulders. 'Weenie. Stop. We can't do anything about this.'

'Did you see who it was?'

'No. I was back there – guarding you from behind.'

'Oh, we're in no danger, Roger – that wasn't a group of mountebanks, it was Max Black, Noel Canterbury and Laurence Cooke.'

'You can't be serious.'

'I most certainly am. Imagine what the Earl is going to say when he discovers three of his employees have stolen the Golden Hand. Hush – what's that noise?' She tipped her head to one side and squinted with concentration. 'They're unlocking the door up to the exhibition.'

'Are they stealing from there too?'

'I have no idea.'

'Please Weenie, I beg you – we've got to call it a night. We shouldn't be in here anyway. I don't know what they're doing – I don't care what they're doing. But I do care what we were doing and if we say anything, we'll have to explain.'

'Explain what? Why we were in the library bedroom for such a short time?'

'That's spiteful.'

'Stop feeling sorry for yourself. Tonight may do both of us a great deal of good. These are the men that management want running the floor – they won't feel so kindly towards them when this comes out.'

With a final glance up towards the minstrels' gallery to check the group had not re-emerged, Weenie grabbed hold of Roger's hand and pulled him across the hall towards the front door, but when she turned the handle and pulled it didn't move. She pulled again and then grabbed at the wrought-iron ring with both hands and leaned her body weight against it, which made it rattle.

'Shh! They'll hear us,' Roger said.

'It's locked. I didn't lock it.'

'You must have.'

'I didn't.'

'What does it matter?' Roger's whisper cracked with exasperation. 'You've got the bloody key – unlock it, for pity's sake.'

'Who locked it?'

'I don't care. Probably Pugh or someone. Please Weenie, for the love of God will you unlock the damned thing and get us out of here.'

The moment Max opened the upper door and entered the exhibition something in the air stimulated the hair follicles across the back of his shoulders and he shivered.

'Strange smell,' Noel said.

'Like someone's just mixed one of those horrible cup soups that Nerys has for lunch,' Laurence said. 'Does it always smell like that up here?'

'It never has – not even when the weather's hot.'

'Armpits – it's definitely armpits.'

'Perhaps it's the gypsum on the walls.'

'Never mind,' Noel said, 'we'd better hurry. Put the lights on. No one will see from the outside – no windows up here.'

The cabinets flickered on and they weaved their way through the twists and turns of artificial corridors – the tavern room, the Hellfire Cave, the Beggar's Benison with a replica of the ceremonial frigging platter next to the pudenda display trays from the collection – until they reached the room where the brass-bound buggery box stood, bathed in an amber light which coruscated off the facets and lines worked by the engraver three centuries earlier. They gazed at the raised and ornate gilded woodwork which surrounded the deep dark hole that disappeared into the depths of the box – a hole unobstructed by the Golden Hand of Jerusalem.

'Where's the Hand?' Noel said, stepping over the ropes and making his way around the back of the box, ducking down to peer underneath.

'Inside the box maybe?' Laurence suggested. 'How the hell do you get it open?'

'There's a concealed latch under here,' and reaching down Noel released the lock and raised the lid of the box. Both men stood on tiptoe to get a view of the interior.

'No,' Laurence said, 'it's not in there.' He reached into the interior and patted around the lining to make absolutely sure but swiftly pulled his hand out and stared at the palm. 'Heavens!'

'Caught yourself on something?'

'No. There's some exudate inside – give me the torch, it's difficult to make out what it is.' He looked in over the edge again. 'Yes, I can see it glistening on the fabric there – like a slug or something's had a wander around.'

'Probably all part of this irritating prank,' Max said.

Laurence straightened up again and took a handkerchief from his pocket to wipe his palm. 'Absolutely no sign of the Hand though.'

'What on earth did they mean then?' Noel said, turning to Max.

Max pushed both his hands into his hair and paced up and down the floor a few times. 'That bloody stupid child. Is this all part of his elaborate hoax? What's he doing, filming us?' Max turned and shouted at the ceiling, 'You filming us right now? Are we going to be the next internet sensation? A hundred thousand hits on three old crocks breaking into Duntisbourne Hall on a wild goose chase?'

'Max, calm yourself.'

'Well, where the bloody hell is it? It's not hanging above the Earl's chair in the dining room.'

'You don't think by any chance . . . ' Laurence stopped and stared at his companions with an expression of emerging and horrified enlightenment.

'What?'

'That Rufus has stolen the damned thing and tricked us into breaking in so that we'd get the blame.'

'Jesus!'

'Would he do something like that?' Laurence said. 'Come on, Max, you know the lad. Is he capable of stealing?'

'I don't know him – I hardly know him and I've no idea if he's capable of theft. I wouldn't have thought so but then I can't begin to understand this obsession with putting stuff up on the internet. Who knows? It's possible if it's part of his hoax, but I really can't imagine that getting the father of his girlfriend arrested is part of the plan.'

Noel closed the top with great care and turned to Max. 'Look, old chap,' he said, 'I think maybe this has gone far enough. When it was just a matter of putting the thing back I was all for it, but if the lad really has done something with the Hand, it would be reckless of us to get involved.'

'We are involved.'

'Further involved then. I think the most prudent course of action is to leave things exactly as they are, clean up any fingerprints we may have left and get out of here before we get dragged further under the wheels of whatever disaster this lad has thundering towards him.'

– 14 –

It was dawn and for a few moments Sam watched Hector with the voyeuristic sense of spying on the unaware, thinking how much younger he looked as he lay sleeping, his face cradled on his forearm, his hair in disarray. He was curled up in the foetal position on the sofa in her sitting room, his clothes from the evening before carefully folded on the floor beside him, his dinner jacket hung over the back of a chair. She moved around the flat as quietly as possible so as not to wake him – she had to meet the clerk of works in the exhibition just after half past seven. Creeping back from the kitchen with a hot cup of tea in her hand she had paused to look down on him. He would have looked the same if she had woken to find him asleep in bed with her but it would not be the same – she would not feel the same.

She had lived her early adult life in the slipstream of the sexual revolution, believing that if she found a man attractive and available, there was little point in delaying gratification as all the downside had been eliminated – pregnancy could be prevented and if by any unlucky chance you picked up something unpleasant, it could be cured by a dose of antibiotics and a week off alcohol. When her marriage ended and she had sexual freedom once again the world had changed but it was not these real consequences of casual sex that troubled her – something else about that way of life was costing her dear. It may have been a deep-seated sense of failure that dogged her after her husband left or simply a greater maturity and understanding of her own nature but she came to accept that sex was never just sex for her – it generated powerful feelings. This would have been a risk worth taking if she could trust her choice of men but more often than not she would know with a sickening certainty within a few months of that first night of dramatic physical passion that the man she imagined her lover to be was someone else entirely and she would have to tear the relationship asunder and suffer. If Hector really wanted to have a relationship with her, he would have to wait.

The clerk of works was standing outside the music room door. When he saw her approaching he rolled the burning ember of his cigarette off on the wall behind, blew down the filter and tucked the stub behind his ear.

'Morning, Mr Jenkins,' she said.

'Mrs Westbrook. Did you enjoy yourself last night?'

'Very much indeed. And you?'

'I'm not much of a party person myself but I like to show willing. I slipped away once the Earl had given his talk.'

They were making their way up the main staircase to the minstrels' gallery when Dean the butler appeared in the Hall and called up to them. 'Jenkins. We need a ladder in the dining room – a tall one.'

'I'll come and find you when I've finished upstairs,' Jenkins said.

'Now. The Earl wants this done now.'

'Wants what done now?'

Dean glanced at Sam and seemed to hesitate but then went on, 'We've been cleaning the Golden Hand and we want to get it back in position before we open – I need you to get the ladder immediately.' Jenkins looked at Sam with an exasperated expression and turned to make his way back down the stairs.

'Let me come with you,' Sam said. 'I've always wanted to see the Golden Hand at close quarters.'

'Not necessary. That will take up even more of Jenkins' time. Wait for him upstairs – I won't keep him more than ten minutes,' and in order to impede further discussion the butler stalked off towards the morning room as Jenkins disappeared in the opposite direction to collect a ladder.

'Sorry it took so long,' Jenkins said when he finally made it up to the exhibition. 'It was a devil of a job to get it back up – the damned clasp wouldn't lock around the wrist at all. It's the trouble with these old things: they're held together with rust and dirt and when you dismantle them, it's a job to get them back up. Talk about fitting a square peg into a round hole. Looks good though – they've done a fine job cleaning it up; it looks brand new.'

They went through to the Hellfire Club, Jenkins loosening the plates which secured the gypsum cave walls while Sam moved things out of the way and unfolded some dust covers for the floor. 'Is two hours enough time?' she said.

'It should be.' He folded the false wall back and began tapping along the plasterwork before laying into the wall with a claw hammer.

'I'll be back in half an hour,' Sam shouted over the noise and left him to it.

She made her way down into the hall and along to the dining room, eager to see the Golden Hand. Just as Jenkins had described it, there it hung ten feet above the Earl's chair, glinting with the freshness of meticulously cleaned giltware – so clean in fact that it looked almost vulgar, the nails as bright as silver, the pearls around the wrist larger and more luminous than she had remembered. It was ever thus with familiar things here at the

Hall – now she was studying it she couldn't completely recall what it had looked like before it was cleaned.

'Will you ring the office for me and say I'm not coming in today? Tell them I'm sick.'

'What's wrong with you?'

'Nothing.'

'Then ring them yourself.'

'Dad!'

'I'm not covering for you, Charlotte.'

'You did last night.'

'And look where that's got us – absolutely nowhere thanks to that wretched boyfriend of yours.'

'He didn't take it. I wish you'd believe me.'

Lassitude at the tedium of the conversation they had been having most of the night swept over him and he stopped trying to knot his tie and leaned on the architrave of Charlotte's bedroom door. 'You do what you think's best – I'm going in to work. If you're not, make your own excuses. I put myself in grave danger last night.'

'Dad. Don't exaggerate.'

'In danger of losing a job I enjoy and want to keep.' He pulled his tie out through his collar and looked down at it, irritated. 'When you came up with this hare-brained scheme of spending the summer down here, what was the one thing I asked you not to do? Can you remember?'

'Not to embarrass you.' Charlotte, who had propped herself up on her pillows, looked down at Monty who was sprawled on the covers and fiddled with his ears. Max hoped he was witnessing a fleeting moment of remorse.

'Exactly – and let me tell you, I am embarrassed.'

Charlotte pushed her covers slowly back from her legs and swung them round onto the floor, searching with her toes until she located her slippers. She hadn't looked her father in the eye but she pulled her dressing gown on and slipped past him towards the bathroom. Without turning she said, 'If I'm ready in twenty minutes, can I have a lift?'

Sam was already on her way back to the exhibition when the radio hissed and she heard Jenkins' voice say, 'Mrs Westbrook? I think you need to see this.'

She increased her speed, taking the steps two at a time, and when she reached the top of the spiral staircase up to the Dywenydd Collection she was out of breath. Motes of dust floated around the spotlights in the ceiling and she could smell brick and plaster. Inside the Hellfire Club Jenkins had done a fairly good job of keeping the mess in the exhibition area to a minimum but as he held back the blue plastic for Sam to enter his small place of work, she saw he was as white as a miller. The dust formed a rime on his eyebrows and hair but in stark contrast his eyes blazed with excitement. 'You are not going to believe what I've found.'

He bent to pick up a torch which was standing on the ground and shone it through the jagged hole in the plasterwork. The dust swirled around the beam of light as it penetrated the cloud and as Sam strained to see beyond the particles, her eyes drew out odd shapes, strange structures.

'What is it?' she said.

'I don't rightly know. It looks like some sort of bed, a four-poster bed.' Jenkins played the light over a thick dark shape that rose up towards the ceiling and in the gloom she began to piece together an enormous structure.

'It's too big to be a bed.' She looked down at the rubble at her feet, gauging whether she could step over the jagged sill and into the room.

'I wouldn't go in yet,' Jenkins said. 'The floor might not be sound. I've called Darren – he's bringing over a couple of site lights. He'll be here in a minute and we can get a better idea of what's going on in there.'

When his assistant arrived, Sam stood back and let them pull away at the base of the partition to make a narrow walkway. The lad inched in along the wall carrying the site lamp on its stand, the wire snaking back through the hole. He called out from the darkness to tell Jenkins to flick the switch and with a clunk the thousand-watt bulb buzzed and blinked, filling the room with a blue glare.

'Christ on a bicycle!' Jenkins said.

The beams of the structure were made of black oak carved with elaborate patterns, twisting broad-hipped bodies, high-breasted nymphs interlocked with sinuous male limbs, animals mounted one on top of the other, bodies clutched together in exotic and impossible positions cascading down every post, across every frieze, licking and stroking, stripping and embracing, grooming and caressing, a huge undulating mass of fleshy mammals. This extraordinary construction framed what at first glance appeared to be some kind of machine with a forged arc of metal like a giant sextant from which hung a complicated system of chains and shafts supporting an elaborate harness. The leather on this was padded and had deteriorated with age, a filigree of cracks running over the folds where the leather had dried, but the upholstery was overstuffed and buttoned with great attention to detail. In the shadows below this mighty pendulum stood another piece of upholstered furniture which looked like a tilting couch but had armrests curling upwards from it carved in rhythmic undulating tentacles that reminded Sam powerfully of Hokusai's most famous shunga, the erotic depiction of a diving girl being ravished by octopuses.

'What on earth is it?' Jenkins said. Cautiously Sam stepped over the rubble and moved across the room. 'Watch the floor,' Jenkins warned. 'It's holding a great deal of weight and we don't know how strong it is.'

'Can you shine the lamps over here?' she said. As the lad lowered the beam of light she could see that the couch bifurcated and spread out before folding downwards towards the floor where the leather gave way to extravagant carvings of the haunches of an animal finished with cloven hooves which seemed to crouch over the base of the piece, similarly upholstered in the form of a companion couch. 'It looks very much like the *fauteuil d'amour*,' she said.

'What?'

'A high-class brothel in Paris had a chair like this made for Edward VII. It came up for auction at the end of the war when Le Chabanais closed down but these armrests echo the much earlier influence of Japanese erotic fantasy in art.'

'Oh – I see.' Jenkins moved a piece of plaster around the floor with his foot and Sam thought she heard the lad snigger. Testing the floorboards she inched forward and saw that some kind of leather bolster was strapped between the armrests. 'I have no idea what this is though,' she said, kneeling down to peer more closely.

'That's odd,' Jenkins said in a breezy voice from the other side of the room where he had crept. 'There's a chain running through the wall here,' he played the beam of his torch along it until it disappeared into the wall. 'There must be something on the other side, perhaps another room – no, hang on, it's a free-standing partition, I can get round it here,' and he disappeared into the shadows. He called out, his voice muffled, 'The chain comes through on this side with a grab handle. This is all very rum.'

Sam wasn't listening. As she moved around to the head of the couch she realised she was not looking at a leather bolster but at something else altogether. 'Can I have your torch, Mr Jenkins?' she said, but she also needed space to study this without Jenkins' embarrassment or the lad's simpering amusement. She walked around the edge of the room to meet him and added, 'I need some time on my own in here now. I'll contact you on the radio when I've finished.'

'The Hall opens in an hour.'

'I know – I'll take responsibility for any mess up here if there's not enough time to make good. In the meantime I want you both to see if you can find some more lamps for in here.' Jenkins didn't move. 'Go on, both of you – and by the way, not a word about this to anyone for the moment. I need to work out how to handle it before news spreads and we have everyone trooping up here to take a look. Can I count on you?'

Reluctantly the workmen left the exhibition and Sam returned to the couch. When she shone the torch on the end of the bolster she recoiled – two glass eyes glinted up at her from a small leathery head and a row of spiked and yellowed teeth was framed by lips petrified into a perpetual snarl – she had found Lord Rochester's monkey.

Weenie was woken by sunlight as bright as a laser beam boring through her eyelids. She turned away from the window with a groan and tried to open her eyes but the lashes pulled and her lids fluttered with the effort – she should have taken her make-up off last night. She reached out and felt around for the glass of water which stood on her bedside table. Wetting her index finger, she began to ease the rheum which clung to her lashes, picking at her lids and rolling the crystals down her face. Hanging her head she hauled herself into a sitting position and paused, waiting for the room to steady before tentatively lifting her chin and looking around for her wrap. She needed to fetch some painkillers from the bathroom because it felt as if someone had plunged an ice pick into her temples, and she needed fizzy water to rehydrate her skin which was tight and itchy and dry. She also wanted strong black coffee but as her heart was still thudding under her rib cage from the alcohol, a caffeine overload might not be the best idea.

She made her way down the corridor feeling a bit unsteady on her mules. She peered into the sitting room which was in disarray from the night before – the whisky bottle lay on its side near the fireplace where she had thrown it over her shoulder with carefree abandon when she and Roger finished it, and her boots stuck out from beneath the sofa as if there was a body underneath. She went in and sat down heavily before reaching forward and picking up the cut-glass tumblers, one in each hand. She turned them, inspecting the rims, then placed the one smeared with lipstick back on the table. The other glass – Roger's glass – she held up to the light until she located the misting on the edge and the dribbles of whisky down the side where his lips had been and she ran her tongue over the deposits as she had lapped up his kisses last night.

Sinking back onto the cushions, she sighed. What a night it had been – romance, passion, the excitement of witnessing a real crime while it was happening. After leaving the Hall, Roger discouraged her from returning to the party and persuaded her to collect her coat and let him drive her back to Discoed. Despite his clear agitation he did not forget his manners, rushing ahead of her as she approached the passenger door in order to open it for her. As he scurried round to the driver's side she took the opportunity of taking her atomiser from her purse and giving her throat a quick spritz, making sure that a liberal quantity sprayed onto the seat belt where it ran across her left shoulder. That should give little wifey something to think about next time she climbed into her husband's car.

Once inside Weenie's house they drank and snogged and plotted until his blasted mobile rang and she had the humiliation of listening to him weaving some complicated story about having a flat tyre and flagging down a motorist in a forlorn attempt to find a garage open and realising the nearest was in Leominster – and on and on while she sat as quiet as fish unable to even sip her whisky in case Harriet Hogg-Smythe heard.

Throughout the conversation he kept her clamped underneath his armpit, making no attempt to speak to his wife privately by leaving the room. It pleased Weenie on one level but also worried her that he could lie so readily in front of a witness. She wondered why men seemed to think that the more elaborate the falsehood, the more likely it was to be believed because the opposite was true – instead of concocting this convoluted sequence of implausible events Roger could just as well have said he was having a nightcap with a woman he had just shagged on an eighteenth-century bed in Duntisbourne Hall – his wife would immediately think he was joking.

Roger tossed the phone down and turned to kiss her. 'I really should be going,' he said, 'but I shan't.'

'Won't you be in awful trouble when you get home?'

'Won't be the first time. Let's polish off that whisky – it's nearly spent.'

'We need to decide what to do tomorrow.'

'About what?'

'About what we saw.'

'Oh, that. Does it really matter? They'll get caught anyway.'

'Of course it matters – how drunk are you?'

'Not too drunk to have another go,' and he leaned his body weight across in an attempt to push her full-length across the cushions.

'Roger! Stop it.' Weenie shoved him away and moved to the end of the sofa, pulling the shoulder strap of her top up as she went. 'When they find out the Hand is gone, there's going to be an investigation and we will be in pole position to shop the culprits and bask in the gratitude of not only the management but also the Earl.'

Roger straightened himself up and reached forward to pour two more drinks. He handed one to Weenie and – although his eyes had a hooded look and he seemed to be concentrating hard not to slur his words – he turned towards her and said, 'Weenie, you've got to drop this scheme. You can't possibly admit that we were in the Hall tonight because we shouldn't have been, and we left that bedroom in the most God awful state so it won't take them long to put two and two together and guess that you had been high on the Hogg in there.' Weenie shrieked with laughter and thumped him on the shoulder. 'I'm being serious. It's all very well for you, you're not married, but I've got my reputation to consider – and apropos of that, so have you. Do you really want all your colleagues knowing you're carrying on with a married man?'

Weenie, who had been listening to him with an expression of mock solemnity, felt the muscles of her face begin to droop. She was delighted for her colleagues to see her with Roger – he was an attractive and cultivated man, a real catch. She didn't care about gossip, in fact she hoped people were talking and speculating about the relationship and if they had their suspicions before this evening, they must have had them confirmed tonight particularly when Roger chose the darkness of the dance floor to work his hands down the back of her leather trousers and twang the top of her pants.

It was all very well for people like Noel to mock her when she regaled her work colleagues with stories of yet another male conquest or admirer. Admittedly she had embellished some of the remarks made to her by visitors on her tour but a man had once asked for her phone number and only this year one fellow had returned after taking her tour to find her in the dining room specifically to ask if she ever came up to London because he would love to take her out to dinner. It didn't take her long to tell everyone at work that day how keen this fellow had been, how complimentary, how charming – she omitted to add that the poor chap was well into his seventies and must have had a stroke because he dragged his foot when he walked and had a lazy arm – but he had asked her to dinner in London. Some of her stories were more a sort of wish than the truth – the fan mail she promised to bring in and show everyone and the boyfriend who wanted to take photographs of her naked, for example – but this evening she had proved to everyone that she was still irresistible to men, that she couldn't possibly be as old as Noel kept hinting at with his irritating digs about using her bus pass or getting a concession price on theatre tickets – she would rather pay double than admit to some spotty youth at the cinema that he was right to offer her a discount.

'Why shouldn't the people I work with know about us?' she said.

'Because they'll think less of you.'

'Are you saying you think less of me? Is that it?'

'Of course not, old thing.'

'What?'

'Not when it's between you and me – but if you go blabbing to the whole world that we were having it off tonight, what may be forgiven for drunken fumbling could be rather frowned on.'

'Did you really think I was going to march into the office tomorrow morning and say, "Oh, by the way, because Roger turned out to be a quarter-pump chump I had plenty of time to follow three felons around the Hall and see them steal the Golden Hand"? Of course I wasn't. I was going to show amazement that the Hand had gone and then tell them that we had left the party during the evening for a breath of fresh air and seen the three of them breaking into the Hall.'

'But we didn't.'

'I know we didn't – but we'll say we did.'

'Where? Where did they break in?'

'Through that open window, obviously.'

'How? Are you going to say we saw them climbing in? Did they have a ladder? What exactly are you going to say you saw?'

Weenie waved her hands around in the air as if she was trying to swat away a fly. 'I don't know. Does it matter?'

Roger moved up the sofa, grasped her by the shoulders and gave her a couple of shakes. 'Weenie, stop this nonsense – I beg you. We can't make up some crackpot story like that and hope to get away with it. We'll get the blame – we may even get the blame for the burglary if you go flapping your loose mouth around the place about this.'

Like a viper striking its prey, Weenie's hand shot out and caught Roger a smarting blow across his cheek. Momentarily stunned he leant back against the scatter cushions and stared at her then he puckered his mouth, stroked his cheek like a child and said in a baby voice, 'Whatever made you do that to poor little old Roger?'

Weenie snorted with irritation and struggled to her feet. 'I think you ought to get back to little wifey, don't you?' She suspected he was too drunk to drive and there was a part of her that would have liked to cause further trouble in the Hogg-Smythe household by making him stay the night but he had nettled her – particularly as there was a certain logic in his argument that they couldn't point the finger without implicating themselves – so she gathered up his coat and pushed it into the centre of his back as she propelled him down the corridor towards the front door. He made a final lunge at her and pressed his damp lips over hers before stepping into the night and threading his way carefully down her garden path.

This morning she felt galled by the whole situation – she was burning to tell the world what she had seen. If gossip was the illegal trade in hunch and hearsay, for the first time in her life she was holding the golden key and there was absolutely no way she could use it.

– 15 –

As Max parked the Land Rover he saw Rufus hurrying over the gravel towards them. 'What's that ruddy boy want now?' he said. Charlotte shot him a look but must have thought better of commenting. Besides, Rufus was already at the driver's door and, tugging it open by the handle, he reached in and clasped Max's hand in both of his.

'I can't thank you enough,' he said. 'I know I've been stupid – really stupid, but thank you. Thank you.'

Max pushed the door open and got out of the car, backing away because Rufus was rushing once more into his personal space. He held a hand forward to keep him away but Rufus gripped it anew and began to pump it up and down. Max shook his hand free.

'Will you leave off. Whatever's the matter with you?'

'The Hand. You put the Hand back.'

'I did not.'

Rufus guffawed and nodded merrily towards Charlotte, who was walking around the side of the vehicle to join them. 'What's going on?' she said.

'The Hand's back,' he said to her.

'Really?' she looked at her father.

'Yes – really. Jess texted me. It's back. You did it, Max. You did it.'

Max glared at the lad and took a deep breath to steady himself. When he spoke his voice was quiet but his tone grave. 'If I say I didn't put it back, I didn't. If it's back, thank God. If you put it back yourself and this is yet another of your convoluted and irritating deceptions, I don't care. I don't want to hear any more about that ruddy Hand and to be perfectly frank, I don't particularly want to hear any more about you. I'm now going to work. Good morning.'

He stalked away from them both and strode across the court-yard in a fury. He heard a voice behind him call his name but he didn't turn, and when someone clutched at his elbow he clenched his fist, tightening his mouth ready to bellow his message once again, but it was Laurence who had caught up with him.

'That's a bit of a relief then,' he panted.

'I don't want to hear any more about it,' Max said without slow-ing his pace.

'I ran into Robyn on my way in and she told me the good news. It's all a bit of a mystery, isn't it?'

Max stopped and turned to Laurence, but looking at his good-humoured expression seemed to deflect his anger and he patted him on the shoulder and said, 'It is – but let's put the whole thing behind us and try to forget it, eh?'

'OK. But it was rather fun.'

The clunk of the front door unlocking echoed around the courtyard and they hurried up the steps, knowing they were late. Bunty stepped out of the door and looked down on them as they approached, arms akimbo. 'Hurry up,' she rallied. 'We've got a busy day ahead. Max, you're on the door with Noel. The Dywenydd Exhibition is closed for the morning so make sure the visitors know it'll be open from one o'clock and absolutely no refunds on tickets. The girls from the booth are coming up to the Hall to help out this morning.'

'Doing what?'

'Security – or they can help Rosemary in the office stuffing envelopes. If they stay in the booth the public will keep pestering them for a refund, so it's better if they're up here. Laurence, wait upstairs – you're not supposed to be in until eleven. You're on a late.'

'Am I? Again?'

'Take my stuff upstairs,' Max said handing his lunch bag to Laurence who gave Noel a thumbs-up as he passed.

'Why's Laurence so chirpy this morning?' Noel said once Bunty had bustled off down the corridor.

'Because the Hand's miraculously reappeared, of course.'

'In a way it has but we're not out of the woods, yet old man – if that Hand's giltware, my cock's a kipper.'

'What?'

'Go and look for yourself – they've put the resin replica back.'

'The resin one?'

Noel beckoned Max to join him on his side of the door so that he didn't have to talk across the stream of visitors that filed in between them. He lowered his voice and said, 'You must remember – when our venerable ex-archivist was arrested they found the giltware Hand in his house.'

'I remember.'

'And it came out that the Earl had had a resin one made years ago to hang in the dining room in its stead, assuming – quite correctly – that no one would know the difference.'

'But I thought the giltware Hand went back on display in the dining room after the trial.'

'Clearly it did – Rufus commented on how heavy it was. He definitely unhooked the giltware Hand, I have no doubt about that – but I tell you, the Hand hanging above the chair now is not that Hand.'

'Has anyone else noticed?'

'No idea – Bunty was squinting at it earlier.'

'Why haven't we heard anything then?'

'The private side aren't going tell us what's going on, are they? They couldn't care less about our opinion and they certainly don't see any point in keeping us informed. I keep telling you, the guides are the lowest of the low.'

'So all sorts of dangers could be brewing over there.'

'Precisely.'

'Oh, God – I'm so fed up with hearing about the ruddy Hand.'

'Something else is going on which'll make you wish you only had the Hand to worry about and it concerns Schofield.'

'What about Schofield?'

'Jenkins was saying they've found some sort of enormous sex machine behind a wall but he isn't meant to tell anyone. Sam obviously told Schofield because he went rushing up there before the Hall opened and – brace yourself for this old boy – he was wearing his dress shirt underneath his overcoat.'

'Meaning?'

'Meaning he didn't make it back to his hotel last night.'

'Daddy, my Daddy,' and Charlotte ran up the steps towards the front door with Jess at her side. 'We're over here for the morning. Can I help you on the door?'

Max tried to jolt his attention onto his daughter but Noel's news had emotionally hijacked him. He didn't want Charlotte on the door – he wanted to stare into the middle distance and rock slowly from foot to foot to soothe himself, to push images of Sam and the Scoke gripped torso to torso, limbs twining and curling around one another, caressing, exploring, connecting.

'Come on Dad – stop worrying. The Hand's back, you're a hero, everything's right with the world.'

Sam picked up Hector's overcoat from the floor where he had

dropped it in the dust in his hurry to enter the room.

'What on earth is this?' he said, gazing up at the mighty construction. 'Is it a siege weapon of some sort? A trebuchet?' He ran his eyes along and down until they alighted on the couch towards which he moved, trance-like as though in a dream. He was now crouched down at its head with the torch in his hand and an expression of rapture on his face.

'Well, hello to you – you ugly little brute. You don't look like the poet laureate now, do you?' He gazed up at Sam, his eyes shining. 'It's pretty incredible, isn't it? Scholars have been writing about the significance of that painting of Rochester for years and yet here he is – not a consummate example of Rochesterian self-representation, satire and irony but an early sex doll. The condition isn't all that bad – the skin on the paws has dried and cracked badly but the rest of the body seems OK – bit bare in places but that's not surprising.'

'What's it doing here?'

Hector straightened up and walked around the edge of the couch, playing the torch along the monkey. 'He seems to be on some kind of frame which has been clicked into position on the chair. Perhaps there were other types of dolls that could be fitted here.'

'I can't believe this whole elaborate structure was designed around the monkey. This must have originally been designed for something altogether different. These great swirling tentacles that curl up and become footrests for the upper seat are a fairly sound indication of what its occupant would expect once ensconced there.'

'Really?'

'The design is so similar to a Hokusai woodblock – *The Dream of the Fisherman's Wife*.'

'I don't know it.'

Sam paused for a moment – if she was talking to Max she would have had no problem explaining but she shied away from discussing details of the print with Hector. 'Look it up,' she said. 'You'll find it on the internet, I'm certain of that.'

'And the couch at the base?'

'Two more footrests at the top of the slope and a cushioned area for kneeling on? I would imagine the earl could pleasure two women at the same time – but quite how this huge machine was involved I have no idea.'

'There's one way to find out.' Sam frowned across at him but he moved the beam of light up and along the top of the frame before putting his hand on one of the pillars and trying to rock it. 'It seems fairly stable. Shall we have a go?'

'I beg your pardon?'

'No, no. I mean, let's see if we can get the mechanism working and it may give us a better idea of its purpose.'

'It's got to be for lowering him into position, hasn't it? The earl is strapped into the upholstered harness and swung into position over the armchair of love. The ninth earl was an exceedingly heavy man towards the end of his life – it would need to be strong – and perhaps when the comely wenches of earlier days stopped enjoying the room he turned to more reliable receptacles of pleasure, such as the monkey.'

'I can't picture in my mind how swinging a huge peer of the realm backwards and forwards on that sextant's arc could possibly result in a satisfactory trajectory for entry. I think I'll go behind the wall and give the chains a gentle pull.'

Sam had a vision of catastrophe as oak and metal clattered to the floor. 'For God's sake, Hector, I can't let you do that. This thing hasn't moved for nearly two hundred years, it's been sealed in here away from light and probably humidity, all the pulley wheels and joints could be fused with rust. You'll bring the whole structure crashing down.'

'Just one little pull?'

'No.'

'The metalwork doesn't look rusty – in fact, it's extraordinarily bright. It must be really dry up here, possibly the heat coming up from the rest of the house.' Hector put his hand on the sextant arc and without taking his eyes off Sam, pushed his fingers through the filigree metalwork and eased the pendulum slightly to the left. A gentle moan sounded from the top of the structure and a few flakes of dust fluttered down.

'Hector! I can't let you stay if you do that again.'

'Sorry. I can go round and have a look at the chains though,' and he disappeared behind the partition wall.

'Don't touch anything.'

Hector's voice, muffled by the partition, said, 'Someone must have stood in here to operate the machine without compromising the earl's dignity – if he had any left. Who do you think that would have been? The butler?'

'One of the other members of the club I would imagine.'

Hector reappeared. 'If you look on this side there's a continuous chain running beside the harness so I wonder if someone got him underway and then retired, leaving him to operate the machine himself. There must be some mechanism for lowering the harness.'

'Or raising the chair as the swing reaches the lower part its trajectory.'

'Yes, maybe that too.'

'Poor old monkey – imagine that spinning towards your nether regions like a giant *deus ex machina*.'

'God, I wish we could get it going.'

'Absolutely not. We must leave everything exactly as it is until I've spoken to the Earl.'

'Shouldn't we notify the British Museum or English Heritage or something?'

'Of course not. This belongs to the Earl. What happens next is up to him.'

'But it's of great historical interest.'

'I agree – but it doesn't belong to the nation any more than the Hall does.'

'You mean he could brick this place up again and do nothing about it – just let it rot?'

'I suppose so, but I'm sure he won't do that. I would imagine in time this will take over as the centrepiece of the exhibition, and if that's the proposal I will contact the British Museum and get someone down here to value it and work out a conservation plan.'

Hector was staring down at the monkey, a disconsolate expression on his face, but then a thought must have struck him. Smiling, he said, 'The monkey doesn't belong to him. It belongs to the descendants of John Wilmot.'

'Come on, Hector – in the circumstances it's likely to be considered lost and therefore belonging to the Earl. It's all academic anyway, isn't it?'

Hector sighed heavily but Sam thought there was something cunning about his expression.

Down in the hall below Max moved through his tasks like an automaton, thankful that Rosemary had whipped Jess and Charlotte away to help her in the office with a mailshot. Twenty-four hours earlier he had been looking forward to a party for the first time in his life because it meant spending time with Sam. Now, as he apologised to people who wanted to go and see the erotic collection, he seethed at the thought of Hector Schofield. It was a bitter enough blow that he had stayed the night with Sam but a week ago a discovery such as the machine upstairs would have had her flying down to the front door to share her excitement with Max. One night of passion and it was Schofield she called to her side, Schofield who rushed up to be in on it with her.

He shouldn't have been surprised – of course she would be attracted to that shallow sort of Londoner – but he was disappointed in her. He had admired her reluctance to leap straight into bed with him when their relationship seemed to be getting more serious, allowing them a deeper understanding of one another. He likened his knowledge of her to swimming in the ocean, the glitter on the water dazzling his eyes so he could not see beneath the surface, but as they got to know one another it was if he had swum into the shadow of the cliffs and without the shimmer of the sunlight he had been able to look deeper into the water, down into the depths of her essence, and truly understand her.

Now he mocked himself for this poetic analogy – if he had been more pushy she clearly would have been happy to sleep with him on the second date, and had he been bold enough to push for that, as Schofield clearly had, he would have put their relationship on a more serious footing before his rival appeared on the scene. She and Max had made such a good team during the spring when they investigated the missing treasures from the collection and unfrocked BS Moreton – that rogue of Falstaffian proportions who had been feathering his nest with the spoils of the Dywenydd

Collection – that Max thought his position as her confidante was impregnable. Instead she had wilfully reinforced her betrayal by calling Schofield to assist her.

There was a lull in the flow of visitors arriving at the front door and Max walked out under the portico and stared across the park feeling dejected. His eye was drawn to a tangle of twigs clinging to the top of one of the stone columns and this abandoned nest made him huff ironically as he remembered an incident back in those heady spring days of hope and romance when he first began his subtle courtship.

Sam had only been at the Hall for a few weeks and he had pointed out the pigeon that was building the nest. 'Here he comes,' he said to her as the bird flew in across the park with a beakful of twigs and branches. The pigeon swooped under the portico and onto the ledge where he busily installed the new material into his construction. Little bits of dirt dropped onto the paving stones in front of them, then the bird was off again, flying low over their heads before turning sharp right and into the blue sky. As he soared upwards, wings outstretched, for a moment he paused, seeming to stall at the top of the climb like an Olympic diver, before dropping and flying away to fetch more building material.

'He did that out of pure joy,' Max had said. Sam had smiled her warmest smile at him, touched, he assumed, by his observation.

The morning had worn on and the pigeon came and went over the heads of the visitors but as the lunchtime lull began there was a shout from the Major on the bookstall inside the hall. The pigeon had made a terrible mistake – instead of dropping from the nest and taking a right into the park, he had taken a sharp left and flown straight in through the front door.

He flapped about high in the ceiling disturbing dust on the old hangings before perching on the railing of the minstrels' gallery. Someone tried to shoo him back towards the door but he flew higher and settled on a lofty beam, peering down at Max, shifting uneasily from foot to foot. Throughout the afternoon the guides tried a series of hopeless exercises to coax him back out, desperate to succeed because Bunty had said when the Hall closed, they were going to have to call the bird man. Max had no idea who the bird man was but it didn't sound good. 'I'm sure he'll use a net,' Sam suggested to him the next time she passed through the hall. Max wanted to hug her – she was such a townie.

When the final visitors left and the door was closed and locked, Max crept back to watch the end of the story. The bird man arrived and, tethered to the safety rail high above the hall, it took him three shots from his air rifle to down the pigeon. The final shot caught the bird full in the chest and – with hardly a feather loose – that brave bird closed his wings tightly to his side and pitched off the beam in a final fall to earth. This time his wings never opened, he didn't soar and stall, he plummeted like a dead weight and landed with a plop on the cold tiles.

The summer winds tugged and pulled at the twigs the pigeon had so diligently gathered and woven into the nest above the front door. No other creature had invaded his territory and his plight seemed to resonate with Max's deep sadness. That little pigeon, so full of hope, made one wrong turn and all his dreams and hopes had been smashed to the floor.

He was abruptly plucked from his absorption by Robyn, who bounded up the steps to the front door and flung herself at him. In his surprise he raised his arms to lessen the impact but as a result succeeded in embracing her wiry body. She planted a kiss on his cheek and, gripping him by the shoulders, she whispered in his ear, 'You are a saviour – our bloody saviour. Thank you,' kissing him again.

Max, who still had his hands on her waist, moved her away, flustered by the vigour and suddenness of their contact. Behind her he saw Sam and Schofield coming down the stairs from the minstrels' gallery – Sam had slowed her step and was watching the interchange with an unsettled expression. Max caught her eye over Robyn's shoulder but Sam looked away and shook her head before hurrying her steps to catch up with Schofield.

'Control yourself, Robyn,' Max said. 'We're in a public place. And besides, I didn't do anything.'

'Oh, stop it Max – I don't care. You're my hero,' and with a cheerful pinch at the seat of his trousers she laughed and continued her ascent to the minstrels' gallery.

'What's going on over there?' Noel said. A group of elderly visitors were gathering in the courtyard, milling around something on the ground. 'Oh Lord, someone's gone down. Frodders?' he called over his shoulder to the Major who was manning the bookstall.

The Major looked up from *The Times* crossword with a merry smile on his face. 'What was that, old chap?'

'Someone's fallen in the courtyard. They're flat out.'

The Major's expression froze. 'Why are you telling me?'

'First Aid Officer, Frodders,' Noel reminded him.

The Major came out from behind his desk and stood beside Max looking out across the courtyard. 'Call Robyn back,' he said. 'She'll be much better than me.'

'She's upstairs stopping people going into the exhibition. She can't leave her post.'

'Weenie – get Weenie.'

'She's out on a tour.'

'Roger – what about Roger? See if you can raise him on the radio.'

'Come on – you can do this. Take a wheelchair down there and try to help.'

'They haven't been sick, have they?'

'I can't see from here but I don't think so.'

'OK. I'll go and see what I can do.'

Like a condemned man the Major set off down the ramps with one of the Hall's wheelchairs. Max had never seen a man move more slowly. For some unfathomable reason the Major had decided to traverse the courtyard along the drainage channels, avoiding the gravel altogether but increasing the length of his journey considerably. His strategy worked because by the time he had reached the group, the woman who had collapsed was sitting up supported by one of her friends who helped to get her into the wheelchair and accompanied the Major down to the buttery. The Major returned ten minutes later and walked up the steps towards Max with a swagger of success.

'That didn't go too badly at all,' he said, 'even if they had rather more faith in my abilities than I did myself – as I approached I heard one of her companions say, "It's all right dear, the man's here." She didn't want any fuss so I settled her down with her friend over in the buttery. I think all she needs is a bit of tuck and a strong cup of tea. Sweet old dear – she gave me a rather generous tip.' Major opened his hand and showed Max and Noel a crumpled ten-pound note.

'Keep that to yourself if I were you,' Noel said. 'If Weenie gets to hear about it she'll have no compunction reporting you.'

'We're allowed to accept tips,' the Major said.

'Not since 1998.'

'I know they took the tip box away then but I can't remember anyone saying we couldn't importune for a few extra funds every now and then.'

'I wouldn't put it to the test if I were you – keep it quiet.'

'The exhibition is closed until further notice,' Bunty said as she bustled up towards the front door followed by Charlotte and Jess.

'We've told everyone they can come back at one o'clock,' Max said.

'Well, they can't. The Earl is going up there late in the afternoon and he doesn't want to see any of the general public.'

'There'll be a lot of angry people.'

'Can't be helped. Send them back to the booth – the girls are going back now to organise refunds.'

'See you later,' Charlotte said.

'I don't suppose the visitors will mind too much,' Noel said after Bunty had gone.

'Really?'

'You know what they're like – if they think it'll help out his nibs they're happy to do it. Celebrity is a powerful tool. If they only knew how much he resented them.'

– 16 –

Weenie was thankful not to be working the day after the party because it took her a full twenty-four hours to recover from the after-effects of too much wine and whisky. She detoxed for the whole of Saturday, starting the day with a cup of hot water and the juice of half a lemon and eating nothing more than a peeled apple for lunch and a handful of raw almonds for supper. She supplemented this with several litres of water into which she mixed a splash of cayenne pepper and a few sweeteners. She knew she should be using maple syrup if she was following the detox correctly but there were calories in maple syrup. She spent the day relaxing in front of the television and visiting the loo and went to bed early after a glass or two of slimline tonic with some gin in it to help her sleep.

She was woken at about nine-thirty the same evening by Bunty, who seemed astonished she had turned in for the night when really she should have been apologising for ringing so late but Weenie couldn't stay cross for very long because Bunty had rung to tell her she was taking tomorrow off and wanted Weenie to deputise for her.

'As head guide?'

'No – I'm head guide, whether I'm there or not. You'll be the duty guide. You need to be in by nine to get the ropes up and the lights turned on. I've left a list upstairs on the desk about which windows the Earl likes to have open.'

'Is it going to be hot tomorrow, then?'

'Doesn't matter. He likes the rooms to be kept as chilled as possible. Stops the smell of body odour if the visitors are cold.'

'Righto.'

Weenie turned over in bed and tried to get back to sleep but it didn't work. Instead she thought about Roger. He always did a Sunday and as head guide she would have plenty of opportunity to spend time chatting to him and crystallise the progress she had made at the party. She hoped that by agreeing to his stipulation that no one must know what happened the night before he would realise she really was the woman for him. This led her into a glorious world of make-believe.

She knew he lived in a rather imposing stone house near Knill about fifteen minutes' drive away because one afternoon she had spotted him getting into his car outside the pharmacy in Presteigne and followed him out of interest. Unfortunately the bulk of the house was set at right angles to the road and she wasn't able to get a good look at it from the open gateway when she passed but she imagined it having the most beautiful views out across the Lugg Valley, perhaps with a stone terrace facing south. She could see Roger wandering out from the large kitchen carrying two glasses of chilled white wine and settling down to watch evening fall over the still countryside as they talked through their day together. She knew the house would suit her – lots of extra space for entertaining and enough room upstairs for her to have a walk-in wardrobe. It wasn't a complete fantasy – she was certain his marriage was in trouble. Why else had he been so eager to court her, to come to the party on his own, to consummate their relationship?

She had no intention of making the same mistake she had made with Edgar all those years ago. Early on in their affair a close friend of hers had said, 'You've got to get him to leave his wife before the year's up or he'll never do it,' but Weenie didn't take the advice. As Edgar's wife became more difficult Weenie became sweeter and never forced him to choose – neither, it seemed, did his wife and the long cold war began. This time was going to be different.

Sunday dawned dry and sunny and Weenie decided she would take the opportunity to walk into work by taking the footpath up through the estate. As she neared the visitors' car park, she heard the toot of a horn and turned to see Roger's Discovery cruising along the drive to intercept her. When he drew level with her, the window on the passenger side slid open and he leaned across and said, 'Get in.'

'Good morning, Roger. You're awfully early.'

'Get in – I need to tell you something.'

Feeling mildly taken aback by the abruptness of his manner she opened the door and hauled herself up into the high seat, struggling to stow her bag at her feet.

'Well,' she said, 'you're in a rather disagreeable mood for such a lovely summer's day.'

'Quite the reverse,' Roger said as he accelerated towards the Hall, 'but I had to see you before you got in this morning.'

'That's nice, Roger. And I very much wanted to see you.'

'Yes, of course, but I wanted to make doubly sure you're weren't going to say anything about what we saw on Friday.'

'We've been through all this, Roger. I told you I wouldn't but it's going to be rather awkward keeping my mouth shut when every-one else is squawking about the theft.'

'That's the whole point – they won't be.'

'Of course they will, you know what this place is like.'

They had reached the car park and Roger spun the vehicle over to the copse of trees at the far end and parked in the shade. He turned the engine off, undid his seat belt and pulled himself round to face her. 'It's back,' he said.

'What is?'

'The Hand.'

'How do you know?'

'I popped in yesterday to see the lie of the land.'

'You did what?'

'I pretended I hadn't filled in my time sheet and after I'd been into the office I had a stroll around. It's back, hanging over the Earl's chair just like it always did. Bunty said it had been taken away for cleaning so whatever you think you saw on Friday, it wasn't a theft.'

'But I saw them – Max, Noel and Laurence.'

'Did you actually see them take the Hand?'

Weenie thought for a moment. 'No – I suppose I didn't.'

'There you go then. You've done what you always do – put two and two together and made five.'

Weenie shot him a cussed look. 'What were they doing then?'

'I don't know – and I don't care – but the Hand was over on the private side being cleaned on Friday night. It couldn't have been stolen.'

'But they'd broken in – they were up to something.'

'And so were we.'

Weenie sighed heavily. She felt bitterly disappointed and her defeated demeanour prompted Roger to reach across and take her by the hand. 'So you see, old thing, it's vital we keep Friday night to ourselves.'

'I suppose so. But I'm not happy about it.'

'I know, I know.'

Weenie shook her head as if tossing her hair and said, 'Well, I can't sit here talking to you all morning – I'm head guide today.'

'Are you, by Jove? That'll be fun. I like being under a powerful woman.'

Despite herself Weenie laughed and settled herself back in the seat, Roger's return to flirting banter dulcifying her.

'Was everything all right when you got home on Friday?' she asked.

'More like Saturday by the time I got home – and I wouldn't exactly say all right.'

'Why? What happened?'

'To tell the truth I can't remember much about it, but when I left your village I was feeling a bit squiffy so I pulled into a lay-by to have a rest.'

'Oh Roger, you should have stayed at mine.'

'I know I should have but I vaguely remember getting the impression that I had displeased you towards the end of the evening only I don't know how.'

'It was nothing.'

'So I did displease you?'

'A bit.'

'How?'

'It doesn't matter now.' The promise of a spectacular marital row was more important. 'Go on – what time did you get home?'

'Ah – there's the rub. I didn't wake up until about five in the morning and I drove on home but thought it might not be such a good idea to stumble into bed at that time so I dropped off to sleep again in the drive and the next thing I knew I was rolling out onto the gravel because Harriet had yanked open the driver's door.'

'Oh dear.'

'Oh dear indeed.'

'What happened next?'

'The usual chiding and sulking – a lip so tight you could have twanged it like a Jew's harp. She's certain I spent the night with someone else – I was able, in all honesty, to tell her I hadn't. I said I didn't think I was sober enough to drive and slept in a lay-by which is completely true.'

'Did she believe you?'

'Probably not.'

Weenie reached out and placed a hand on his forearm. 'How horrid for you.'

Roger sighed and patted the top of her hand, a look of brave resignation on his face. 'Never mind,' he said, 'it'll pass.' He drew himself forward and began to tighten the knot of his tie in the driver's mirror. 'You'd better get going – I'm off to the buttery for a coffee and to see if Judy has any scraps left over from yesterday.'

'Scraps?'

'Yes. She saves the date-expired sandwiches for me.'

'And you get them for free?'

'Of course. I'm staff.'

'When are we going to see each other again?'

Roger turned to face her and frowned. 'Well . . . today.'

'I'm not talking about here. When can we get together again, just you and me?'

'Oh, I don't know, old thing. I'm going to have to tread a bit carefully for the next few weeks, concentrate on a bit of Harriet maintenance.'

'What's that supposed to mean?'

'Keeping things quiet on the home front – you know the sort of thing.'

'What was Friday night all about then?'

Roger sighed heavily. 'Honestly old girl, this is worse than being at home – you firing one question after another at me. Friday night was jolly good fun and I very much hope to repeat it but I have to be careful – we both have to be careful.' He glanced down at his wristwatch. 'And as I said a few minutes ago, you'd better get going – it's gone nine. I'll give you a head start so that no one sees us walking in together.'

Weenie set off across the courtyard fuming with rage. She never imagined that a night of passion would send Roger scuttling back to his wife for a bit of 'Harriet maintenance'. What sort of woman was this wife of his? Clearly he had behaved extremely badly on Friday night and even though he hadn't spent the night with her, surely his wife assumed he had been unfaithful. Weenie was astounded how much humiliation some women were willing to accept in a marriage.

Her bad mood was mollified somewhat once she started organising the floor for the working day. She spent a few minutes in the office with some sticky tape getting the words Head Guide attached to her name badge before striding through the state rooms hailing the cleaners with a dismissive waft of her hand. Pausing frequently to catch sight of herself in the pier glass mirrors that ran the full length of the Hall she was heartened to see that her boucle Chanel-style suit struck the perfect balance between femininity and power.

She was upstairs in the guides' room as the staff began to filter in. Noel put his briefcase on the desk and Weenie looked up at him, irritated because she was trying to work out the guide allocation for the day. Noel caught her eye and raised the corner of his mouth in a sardonic smile.

'Just unpacking my lunch,' he said. 'I won't be a tick.'

She knew he was mocking her. If Noel disapproved of her behaviour on Friday night with Roger he had better think again – he couldn't take the moral high ground with her after what she had seen. She was on the verge of making an aside which would have left him in little doubt of her meaning when Roger himself strode into the room with a hearty 'Morning, everyone.' She felt a flash of irritation and returned to writing her lists of which guides should be allocated which groups.

'Noel, I want you and Max on the door today,' she said.

'Max doesn't work Sundays.'

'Doesn't he?' She peered at the rota. 'Oh, I thought you boys liked to do everything together.'

Noel frowned. 'I'm sorry?'

'Have I got that wrong?' she said. 'I thought you and Laurence and Max were like the Three Musketeers.'

'Want to borrow my reading glasses, sweetie?' Roger boomed from across the other side of the room but the endearment smacked of sarcasm, not affection, and the look he was giving her was thunderous.

'I could do the front door with Noel,' Rufus piped up. 'I've brought my cardigan in.'

'Certainly not!' Weenie said. She was determined to adopt Bunty's principle of those who ask don't get. 'You can be upstairs covering the exhibition.'

'There are quite a few French groups coming in later in the morning – I could take them round. I still haven't had a chance to do my French tour and I learnt it weeks ago.'

Weenie dropped her pencil on the table and leant forward towards him. 'I'm the head guide today and I will decide where you go and what you do. Roger, I want you to take the French round this morning.'

'I can't speak French.'

'Slow English – they want slow English.'

'You know I'm not that fond of doing students.'

'If you wouldn't mind – all the same,' she said and gave him her sickliest smile. As she looked away she could have sworn she saw him catch Noel's eye and make a face.

The first hour of the morning ran smoothly but at midday Laurence came back from the library and said, 'There's a terrible log-jam in the state rooms, Weenie. Roger's been with that French group for over an hour and they've only just made it to the china room. Nerves are fraying.'

'I thought you had nerves of steel,' she said with an arch lift of the eyebrow.

Laurence laughed unconvincingly. 'I don't think anyone would accuse me of that.'

'What could they accuse you of then?'

'I really don't know,' pausing and scanning her face, 'but I think you need to sort out the log-jam.'

She swept away from him, raising her chin as if the weight of a huge ponytail, heavy with water, was pulling her head back. She pushed her way through the group that were stuck in the dining room, visitors shuffling from foot to foot and fanning themselves, their guide, Claude Hipkiss, at the entrance to the next room chatting to himself as he waited for the group in front to move. She could see Roger clearly above the heads of his tour and she caught his eye and gestured to him to get a move on, but he ignored her and embarked on another anecdote in the slowest English she had ever heard. There was nothing for it – she was going to have to break with a time-honoured agreement never to embarrass a guide in front of their group.

'Roger!' she called. 'You need to move.'

'I will when I've finished.'

'No – move now. You've brought the Hall to a standstill.'

Roger stared at her, his mouth pursing with fury, then turned slowly back to his group and said, 'I would like to draw your attention to the ravishing hard-paste porcelain in the cabinet because it was made in a French city not a million miles from your university. Now who would like to tell me what it's called . . . ?'

Weenie felt a tap on her shoulder and turned to see Rosemary standing behind her. 'A word please,' she said, leading her back out through the dining room and into the corridor. 'Look,' she said, 'we've had complaints in the office from the leader of a group of disabled three rooms back – they've been stuck there for over an hour. They're hot, they're cross, and they've got a coach to catch. If you can't get your team under control we're going to have to go over to free flow – we can't offer guided tours if you let them take this long. I thought you knew how to deputise – you've been here long enough.'

As dusk was falling Weenie left her house and climbed into her car. The day had been a disaster – Rosemary had insisted on going over to free flow and to add to her humiliation, Noel had been pulled off the front door to get the floor moving again. The stand-off between her and Roger had made the day extremely uncomfortable and by the afternoon she was regretting taking such a bombastic line with him. She resolved to explain her reasons to him after the Hall closed and apologise to him for being snappish. She had tried to catch him before he left but despite trotting after him and calling out a couple of times, he had climbed into his car and swept off down the drive, leaving her standing in the middle of the gravel out of breath and hot, with aching feet and the prospect of a half-hour walk home.

She resolved to pour herself a stiff drink the moment she got in through her front door but as she trudged along the footpath wondering how she would get through the evening without speaking to Roger and making amends, an idea began to form in her mind.

When she arrived home she didn't fix herself a stiff drink. Instead she changed into a pair of comfortable slacks and driving shoes, took the car out of the garage and set off in the gloaming towards Presteigne. When she neared Knill she parked in a lane several yards down the road from the entrance to Roger's drive and headed back on foot. The sun had dropped behind the slopes of Upper Radnor Wood and the thick yew hedge which flanked the drive provided plenty of cover. The surface was tarmac not gravel, so her shoes made no sound. She had been walking up the long approach for several minutes when she heard the rattling of a diesel engine behind her and realised that Roger was not in the house but coming up the drive. Her plan had been to let him know she was here so that he could find an excuse to stroll out into the summer night garden and speak with her, but she realised his wife might be in the car with him. She pushed herself between two great yew bushes seconds before the headlamps swept by in an arc and the Discovery drove past her and on up the sloping drive. She heard the engine stop and a single door slam – he had been on his own.

Cautiously rounding the corner, she saw the house ahead of her and cut across the shrubbery onto the lawn. Most of the downstairs lights were on and she saw Roger in the hall window before he moved out of view. She made her way round the house until she came to a terrace, much as she had imagined it, the light from a conservatory dining room spilling out onto the grass. In the room beyond she could see Roger heaving carrier bags up onto a kitchen island, his wife peering into them and taking out square foil boxes – he had been into Presteigne to pick up a takeaway.

Harriet was an ordinary looking woman, her hair grey but cut in a flattering bob. If they had passed in the street neither women would have recognised one another and yet they had blighted each other's lives. Weenie realised that everything she knew about this woman and this marriage had come from Roger, and anything Harriet knew about her would have been from the same unreliable source.

She felt a strange mixture of power and excitement, seeing them and not being seen, their conversation with each other silent like an old cine film. She watched as his wife loaded up a tray and Roger came into the conservatory and began to light candles on the table. He returned to the kitchen for glasses and a bottle of wine and before he sat he bent over his wife, his hand on her shoulder, and kissed her on the cheek.

Weenie felt as if a frozen fist had gripped her insides and the ice was spreading through her organs. They had been a team, her and Roger. Nearly two years of innuendo and teasing had made Weenie believe they had a relationship of sorts which had culminated in a night of passion less than forty-eight hours ago, yet here he was lighting candles and pouring wine for the woman he had been married to for over thirty years and it broke her heart.

Several times Roger looked right out of the window at Weenie but there was no reaction at all – she must have been invisible standing back from where the light spilled out into the garden. She watched them talk in a silent mime, Roger chewing and helping himself to seconds, but suddenly he looked straight out into the darkness and pointed.

Weenie fled swiftly through the dark garden, down the long drive and out into the lane. She heard the slam of the heavy front door and, terrified he would catch up with her, squatted down behind the wall of a garden a few yards up the road. She heard his heavy footsteps on the drive but when he reached the lane he must have stopped to look around because when they started again they were receding. She peeked over the wall and saw Roger walking the other way from her up the road, looking around, a white napkin still grasped in his hand, and she took the opportunity to slip from the adjoining garden and down the lane where she had parked her car.

As she drove back she was overwhelmed with shame and remorse. What madness had gripped her, had sent her over there to stalk and spy on him? Had he seen her? She so hoped he hadn't. But along with the shame she felt for her behaviour, part of her was glad to have seen him in his true environment. It looked humdrum, it put Roger in a context she had never imagined – an ordinary man unpacking a takeaway under the directions of his wife in a kitchen full of knick-knacks and mementoes of a dull, ordinary life.

– 17 –

'Can I offer you a coffee or tea?' Simon Keane said as he held the door open for her.

'No, thank you,' Sam said. 'I've just had one.'

'I do hope coming over to the estate office hasn't put you to a lot of inconvenience at such short notice but I need to touch base with you about a rather serious incident that occurred on Friday night during the party.'

Sam sat down opposite the CEO, who unfastened the middle button of his jacket and took his seat across the desk from her.

'Incident?'

'It appears that during the celebrations, the Golden Hand was stolen from the dining room.'

'Really?'

'The Earl is insisting that this news doesn't get out – he doesn't want the papers crawling all over us, particularly after the furore over poor old BS Moreton in the spring. The replica is back up there to prevent any speculation in the short term. We're confident that the original will turn up – the police have been notified and dealers up and down the country put on alert so if it hits the market, it'll come straight back here.'

'As simple as that?' Sam said, surprised at the CEO's bullish manner.

'Usually. This doesn't look like the work of master criminals and the majority of felons who have tried lifting stuff from here get caught because they are extraordinarily stupid. However, the Earl is angry about it because apparently the alarms weren't set.'

'At his request.'

'I know – but that was because they kept going off at night due to the dust from the building works.'

'The building works finished months ago. I have tried to reassure the Earl that the alarms can be set again and are unlikely to malfunction but he's been insistent that they stay off if he's in residence.'

'I agree – it is awkward, I do understand – but he's concerned that if the Hand doesn't show up and we try to make a claim the Hall may be in breach of the insurance cover. He's also worried that this new find of yours will create more dust and put the alarm system out of action for even longer, leaving all the treasures in the Hall and on the private side in danger.'

'All of which can be solved, but not if he insists on having the alarms off when he's here.'

'I have tried to explain – I will have another shot at it – but I wanted to give you the heads-up before he comes over this evening to have a look at the machine.'

After leaving the estate office Sam crossed over the lake and walked into the cool glade of trees which flanked the eastern end of the drive back to the main Hall. The morning was fine and the walk took less than ten minutes. As she approached the front entrance she saw that Max was on the door checking the tickets of a group of Japanese.

'No photo,' he said, miming the action of taking a picture to the group who bowed and waved their cameras at him then shook their heads. He gave them the thumbs-up and they chorused their approval. By the time he had sorted them out and moved them on their way she was on the top step.

'Hello, Max,' she said.

'Oh – it's you.'

'It's a lovely day.'

'Yes.'

'Busy?'

'Steady.'

'Enjoy Friday night?'

'Not much.'

'Oh.'

Sam left him checking tickets and as she walked away she sighed. She had assumed that wherever their relationship led them her friendship with Max was inviolable. They had a connection which was effortless – almost instinctive – and its sudden loss mystified her. She had felt it was part of her, part of him, to talk with an easy banter, confident of their bond, but recent events had swept it away so effortlessly that what had once felt solid now felt ethereal, a dream she had woken from with the memory of it holding her in its aura but the chance of regaining it as impossible as falling asleep again and continuing the dream. She mourned its passing. It was if she had plopped down a wormhole into a parallel universe where the same figures move around but had no connection with the present or one another and she didn't have a clue how to get back again.

In her last relationship she had worked out the rules of the game – an unanticipated trigger followed by muscular arguments which would rage for days until she eventually wilted and submitted and he soothed and apologised until some sort of obscure agreement was reached, the terms of which never seemed to count when next it happened. At first it was stimulating but then it became predictable and eventually – as far as Sam was concerned – pointless. Self-inflicted pain in a relationship was fruitless unless it led to a deeper understanding, another detail on the road map which would stop you both taking the wrong turn next time. Her communication with Max had been different from the start – in particular she admired his lack of guile and now she had to accept that it was his probity that stopped him from continuing a stream of charming badinage when she turned her attention away from him and onto Hector.

Sam checked her watch – the Earl had been due forty minutes ago and she was obliged to wait. She wasn't looking forward to an audience with him – like everyone else at the Hall she found him difficult. It wasn't just because he was a cantankerous misogynist – working in museums and galleries over the years she had grown used to men such as him – it was his lack of mental acuity that she found the most difficult to deal with. She was accustomed to discussing problems with people of a fairly equal intellectual capacity as herself but the Earl, despite having had the opportunity for the best education available in the land, was not a canny man and covered his shortcomings by behaving in a boorish manner. His inflexibility was a result of his inability to grasp a concept rather than any deeper desire to maintain a status quo at Duntisbourne.

He eventually arrived with Simon Keane and it was the CEO who apologised for keeping her waiting. She held back the sheet of blue plastic and the Earl stepped warily across the floor between the piles of rubble. 'You're going to have to get this cleared up, you know. The dust has played havoc with the security system and I can't have the alarms out of action any longer. I hold you responsible for Friday night's theft.'

'I know you do,' Sam said. Keane caught her eye and smiled. 'Shall we?' she said and ushered them into the room. Both men

paused on the threshold and gazed up at the monumental structure that towered above their heads.

'My word,' Keane said.

'What in hell's name is it?'

'We think that at the beginning of the eighteen hundreds your
ancestor commissioned this to satisfy his predilections as his age
and weight became an increasing hindrance.'

'Hmm.' The Earl pointed towards the couch. 'And that?'

'Probably so that he could satisfy himself with more than one
cocotte at a time.'

Sam felt herself relaxing – the discovery was sufficiently
remarkable to momentarily deflect the Earl's ill humour but as he
rounded one of the stout pillars he recoiled and barked, 'What the
bloody hell is that there?'

'Well – that's a bit more of a mystery. It's a monkey of some type
but we're not exactly sure.'

'I think we are,' said a voice from behind and Sam turned
round to see Hector dipping under the plastic sheet and walking
towards the Earl. When they parted on Saturday he had given the
impression he was returning to London but clearly that had never
been his intention.

'Who the bloody hell are you?'

Hector put his hand out but when the Earl did not reciprocate,
he let it fall once more and patted his thigh in a carefree manner.
'Hector Schofield, My Lord. I was at the Slade at the same time
as your daughter, Lady Elizabeth – class of seventy-seven.' The
Earl stared at him with a disagreeable expression on his face but
unperturbed Hector soldiered on. 'And I know everything there is
to know about this fellow here.'

He reached out to touch the monkey but Sam said, 'Please don't touch anything,' and she was aware that her surprise and irritation at his sudden appearance must have been obvious from her tone.

'I believe, My Lord,' Schofield continued, 'that this fabulous little fellow once belonged to John Wilmot, the second Earl of Rochester, and that it was brought here many years after his death by a relative of his. As a matter of fact, I'm writing a book on the subject at the moment and would be more than happy to involve Duntisbourne Hall in any of the publicity surrounding its publication.'

The Earl stared down his long nose at him and flared his nostrils. 'I can assure you that the publicity about this find will come from us and if you think your book is going to sweep in on its coat-tails, you are mistaken.'

'No, My Lord, I didn't mean that at all – of course not – but I have been working in close conjunction with your archivist here.'

The Earl turned to Sam and frowned. 'That's not totally accurate,' she said, shooting an angry look towards Hector who winked at her.

The Earl sucked his teeth and surveyed the room once more. 'How long before we can get the public paying to see this thing?' he said.

'With your permission, I can organise a team of conservators to give us an estimate,' Sam said.

'Of course, of course. Soon as possible. What about getting some sort of waxwork model strung up there and a couple down here on the couch?'

'I don't believe that would echo the intent behind the rest of the exhibition.'

'What the bloody hell do you mean?'

Sam took a deep breath to stop herself feeling riled and continued, 'The success of the Dywenydd Collection depends on a study of craftsmanship not lubricity. In order to present this machine in the same way, we need to concentrate on these fabulous carvings, this exquisite metalwork. If we string up some type of mannequin in a gimp mask we'll look like every other sex museum the length and breadth of Europe.'

The Earl's eyes darted over towards Keane, probably trying to ascertain if his CEO had managed to follow her line of reasoning. Keane nodded encouragingly at the Earl and said, 'I'm sure Mrs Westbrook is right in the centre of the swim lane with this one, My Lord. The focus on craftsmanship and historical provenance has received praise from exactly the type of institutions we strive to be associated with – it is probably the single most important factor when we consider the demography of our visitors.'

The Earl ran his eyes across the structure once more and said, 'All right then, do as you think fit – just get rid of that hideous primate,' before turning and dipping out under the plastic.

'I think that went quite well – in the circumstances,' Keane said to Sam in passing as he exited the room fast on the heels of the Earl.

The plastic crackled as it settled back into position and silence ebbed back into the room, fissile with tension as Sam considered how to deal with Hector, but as she stood staring down at the floor with her back to him she heard a clicking sound like a radiator heating or cooling and swung round, certain that he was trying to move the machine again, but he was also listening, his head cocked to one side.

'What's that?' he said. 'Death-watch beetle?'

The clicking slowed and quietened but then began to accelerate again accompanied by a soft creaking.

Distracted from her ill humour, Sam came across the room towards Hector and looked above her head. 'It may be the weathervane,' she said. 'You can hear it turning on windy nights.'

'It's as calm as a millpond out there this evening.'

The clicking began again almost imperceptibly and they moved forward, listening with extreme concentration until they came to a halt beside the couch.

'It's coming from here,' Hector said.

Sam bent down and turned her head to bring her ear closer to the seat, and as she did so the clicking increased in volume and frequency and she looked up at Hector and said, 'It's coming from the monkey.'

'What?'

'The monkey's clicking.'

'Oh, Christ – something horrible's eating away at it.'

Sam stood and gazed down at the little body. 'Is he looking a bit tauter than he was on Saturday?' she said.

Hector circled around to her side. 'Possibly – yes, he does look like he's put on a few extra pounds.'

'I think I need to get the conservators in here immediately. The change in humidity – in temperature maybe – is bound to affect everything because it's been sealed away for so many years, but I think the monkey's the most vulnerable – particularly if he wasn't properly preserved in the first place.'

'You think he could be rotting?'

'Want to sniff?'

Hector bent forward and cast his nostrils along the length of the animal. 'Mmm,' he said, straightening up, 'he is smelling a bit gamey.'

'Is he? That's worrying. I'll have to get someone over from London tomorrow.'

'You don't think someone local could help? I'm sure it's just the sort of thing they'd be good at down here in the Marches.'

'I don't think so.'

Hector continued to stare down at the monkey and there was a stubborn set to his shoulders. 'You're not that good at taking advice, are you?' he said without looking up.

The observation was sufficiently unexpected to catch Sam off guard. She had been irritated with him when he first arrived this evening although it would be too strong to say she felt this was none of his business because she was culpable – in her excitement at the find she had invited his involvement. It was disingenuous of her to criticise him now for being over-zealous. She had rather enjoyed these past few minutes of bantering with him and her pique had softened, her guard had dropped. His criticism reminded her once again of her earlier vexation but she ignored his remark and said, 'Incidentally, I thought you were heading back to London on Saturday.'

She thought she saw a tightening of the muscles in his jaw but by the time he looked up at her he had superimposed a shallow smile across his lips.

'How could I leave after Friday night?'

'Nothing happened on Friday night.'

'Well, less happened than I would have liked but I wouldn't have called it nothing.' He leant in closer to her, reaching out and running his fingers down her arm. Imperceptibly she found herself leaning towards him. He gathered up her hand and said, 'Come on, let me take you out to dinner.'

By the time Max got home he was freezing despite having the heater turned on full in the Land Rover. 'Whatever's the matter with you?' Charlotte said. 'It's like an oven in here.'

'I can't seem to get warm, chick.'

'You got 'flu or something?'

'I don't think so. I'll run myself a hot bath and fix us some supper in about an hour.'

Upstairs he stripped off his suit and pulled on a towelling robe before shivering his way along the corridor and into the steaming bathroom. He couldn't understand how he had managed to get so cold – it was as if his gelid heart was freezing him from the inside out. He discarded his robe and stepped carefully into the bath, the water almost too hot for his feet as he dipped his toes under the surface before lowering himself in. He had been submerged for little more than a few minutes before he turned the hot tap on again and let it dribble scalding water into the space by his feet. He swirled the water around to disperse it and when the bath became almost too hot to bear, he turned the tap off and lay back under the surface watching the steam make patterns on the enamel. Under the assault of these extremes of temperature he gave a couple more shudders which sent goosebumps radiating out and down his limbs but gradually, as his skin flushed with the heat, he felt his body warming and relaxing. The roof window above his head was angled up towards the sky and he watched the clouds colour as evening approached. Swallows like tiny black crosses weaved and darted hundreds of feet above him, and higher still he recognised the wide and rounded wings of a buzzard soaring up above the house on the warm thermals. He heard Charlotte making her way upstairs but instead of her footsteps receding towards her bedroom there was a gentle tapping on the bathroom door.

'Mmm?' he said.

'Dad. You asleep?' she asked through the closed door.

'Nearly.'

He waited, his lids heavy, but as the pause continued he opened his eyes fully, the water sploshing gently under his arms as he pushed himself higher in the bath. 'What is it, lovey? Do you need the bathroom?'

'No.' There was another pause but Max sensed Charlotte was still outside the door. 'Will you be long?'

Her tone was so gentle, so placid that Max looked towards the door as if trying to read her expression through the wooden panels as he pulled himself out of the bath, leaving the tidal wave of water running up and down the tub. He grabbed a towel off the rail and gave his ankles and calves a cursory dab before wrapping it around his waist and flinging open the door. Charlotte was leaning listlessly on the architrave looking down at her mobile phone and when she raised her eyes towards her father she was no longer a woman but a child – a frightened and vulnerable little girl.

'What on earth's the matter?' he said and she turned the screen to face him.

At first he couldn't work out what he was looking at. The image was blurred but as he took the phone in his hand, a face swam up towards him, the pupils of the eyes tight semi-circles of black at the base of a dome of white sclera, veins snaking across the tough fibrous tunic of the eyeball and as the forehead disappeared out of focus, vessels across the brow distended and twisted underneath the skin, the lowering eyebrows drawn together, the cheeks raised as if in a smile but the mouth pulled taut in a grimace of intense strain.

Max was about to shake his head and groan that Rufus was up to his tricks again but he had seen the look on Charlotte's face and sensed that something was very wrong. He unhooked his dressing gown from the back of the door and pulled it on over his still wet skin then put his arm around Charlotte's shoulders and led her back downstairs.

'And you honestly don't think one of your friends sent this as a joke?'

'It wasn't sent, Dad – it's on my home screen. Someone's used my phone to take this picture – it's on the camera roll – and then they've gone to settings and made it my home and lock screen so it's the first thing I see when I use the phone.' She pressed the hold button and the screen went black. Then she pressed the home button and the hideous face loomed out at them. Charlotte flung the phone away onto the sofa between them. 'It's horrible,' she said.

'It's curiously disturbing,' Max said. 'I don't understand when this could have happened – you're never without that thing.'

'I've been without it since the weekend. I lost my charger – Rufus dropped his off late last night and I left it charging today when I was at work.'

'Good job I didn't need to get hold of you then – I would have been beside myself with worry.'

'It must have been done when we came up to the Hall on Saturday. Rosemary told us if a mobile went off inside the Hall we'd be in serious trouble so I left it down in the booth – in my bag.'

'Your bag? Christ, you'd better check there's nothing else missing. If someone got hold of your phone, they may have taken your credit cards, wallet – anything.'

'I've looked. It's all there.'

'Didn't you lock the booth when you came up?'

'Of course we did.'

'How peculiar – and you're absolutely certain this isn't Rufus or Jess or even Robyn having a bit of fun?'

'There's nothing funny about this. It's some loathsome old bloke.'

'Was there anyone like that hanging around?'

'I can't remember that far back and besides, on Saturday I was up at the Hall, in case you've forgotten.'

'All right, lovey – don't get snappish.'

'Sorry!' She looked down at the phone. 'What are we going to do?'

'I don't think there's anything we can do. No crime's been committed here – I can't make out what this man's up to but the image isn't obscene or anything.'

'It's seriously weird. That look on his face is foul.'

'I'll grant you that – and putting it on someone's phone is intrusive and unhinged, but I can't offer you any more advice except don't leave your phone lying around.'

'I didn't.'

'I know, lovey.' Max rubbed her on the shoulder. 'Delete it. Why don't you just delete it and try to forget about it?'

'I don't want to do that. Supposing there's something hateful going on – I could be destroying evidence.'

'I think that may be a bit dramatic . . . ' Charlotte flashed him a look but he held up his hand and made an appeasing face, 'but how about you download the picture onto your computer – or mine, if it really freaks you out – and then delete it from your phone?'

'OK,' and she picked up the phone and went through to his study.

— 18 —

Hector insisted on driving the Mazda so that Sam could enjoy a drink with her meal. He had tracked down a restaurant in Shrewsbury which he was eager to try, reassuring Sam that he intended to leave his prejudices about out-of-town culture behind for the evening and expected to be pleasantly surprised with the quality of the food served in the panelled dining room under the whimsical gaze of the Black Prince. He seemed keen to recreate the closeness they had enjoyed down by the river that hot afternoon which now seemed months ago.

They were shown to a table in a bay window which opened out onto a courtyard, and as the gentle light of the evening dimmed the night-pollinated blooms began to pump perfume into the air to lure nocturnal creatures on the wing.

'What do you think they make of us?' Hector asked as he waited for Sam to get comfortable on the banquette before easing the table back towards her.

'Who?'

'The other diners, of course.' He took his seat opposite and shook out his linen napkin. He had offered his credit card as warranty to the bar man forgetting that he was no longer in London and to cover his embarrassment had insisted on choosing the wine for their meal at the bar so that it could be brought to their table without delay. He nodded to the wine waiter who stepped forward to pour a splash of wine into his glass. Swirling it around the goblet he took a deep sniff, then turned to the waiter who hovered nearby with his eyes averted and said, 'That's fine.'

Sam looked out into the pretty courtyard – the wine ritual always struck her as comical particularly as she could see the bottle had a screw top and couldn't possibly be corked – while the waiter filled their glasses and promised to return to take their order when they were ready. Once he was out of earshot Hector asked again, 'So? What do you think our fellow diners make of us this evening?'

'I have no idea. Very little, I should imagine.'

'Come on, Sam – don't tell me you didn't notice the approving glances we got when we walked in tonight.'

'Did we?'

He took another sip of wine and when he replaced the glass on the table, he twisted the stem back and forth before looking up at her from under his brows, and Sam felt that jolt of physical attraction fizzle between them once more.

'We make a handsome couple,' he said. 'Don't you ever look at two people having a wonderful time together over a meal in a restaurant and imagine how they are going to make love when the evening ends?'

Sam felt a slight warmth rising up her neck and took a draft of mineral water. 'I can't say I do.'

Hector tipped his head to look across his shoulder and with nothing more than the raising of an eyebrow he indicated a couple on his left. Dropping his voice even lower he said, 'Those two over there will not end the evening making fabulous love.'

'They won't?'

'No. He's brought her here to impress her but he's out of his depth. Look at the way he gazes at her, trying to read her mood. She, on the other hand, is constantly scanning the room in case something better happens along.'

'You don't know that.'

'And over there,' he nodded towards Sam's shoulder and she

twisted slightly in her seat to steal a glance, 'is a couple who have been married for well over thirty years. They haven't spoken a word to one another since we came in – in fact, she despises him. Look how thin and mean she is, how corpulent and distended he is. She can't look at him but she watches his plate as he shovels food off it, hoping no doubt that every ounce of that cholesterol is clamping onto his heart and hastening the day when he clutches at his left arm and crashes to the floor like a felled tree.'

'Perhaps a night of passion would consolidate her aspiration.'

'I would guess there are certain limits to her ambition. No, she'd be better off encouraging him into the arms of a younger lover. A friend of mine had a heart scare last year and came home with a booklet of advice which warned against sex in a car with a stranger – I suppose sex in a car with your wife is OK, or sex in bed with a stranger, but the combination? Lethal.'

'Perhaps you should tell her.'

'It's a high-risk strategy. He could leave all his money to his paramour. The most interesting couple – apart, of course, from us – are the two women along the banquette from you.'

Sam swept her gaze around the room as if taking in the decor and finally alighted on their dining companions several places away. One was in her forties, clear-skinned and well-dressed, and the other several years older but bohemian with ranks of beads around her neck and grey hair piled up on her head and secured with enamelled combs.

'They will have fabulous sex tonight.'

'Come on, Hector – don't disappoint me. Can't two women dine together without middle-aged men fantasising?'

'Of course they can, but those two are different. They are the perfect love story. The older one, the one with the beads, was married for many years. She had sons – only sons – and ran a masculine household until she was widowed, quite suddenly.'

'Her husband in a car with a stranger?'

'I don't think so. I think it was something else, a tragedy. She isn't looking for anyone else but she finds companionship with the younger woman who has never been drawn to men, and their friendship blossoms and finally they realise they have fallen in love.'

'Why are you telling me this story?'

'It's a lovely story. They hesitate on the precipice of intimacy – it's the widow who's nervous – but when they fall the plunge is deep and eternal. They understand men but they understand themselves even better and they offer one another everything they've always wanted a man to give them.'

'As I said – classic male fantasy.'

'Mock if you want but those two have a connection and it isn't new – they've been lovers for several years and yet the relationship remains as fresh and exciting as it was in those early tentative weeks of courtship and discovery, and we both know how that feels.'

'We do?'

'You're laughing at me.' His expression darkened and he leant back in his seat and looked around. 'Where's that damned waiter got to? I'm starving.'

The moon was rising above the Red Lake when Hector drove in through the Dolley Green Gate. He parked the car and offered the ignition keys to Sam, holding them between thumb and index finger until she placed her palm underneath and they dropped with a jingle.

'Your keys, madam,' he said.

'It was very kind of you to drive.'

'My pleasure – but do you know what? I could really do with a nightcap now. I'm so stone cold sober you smell positively inebriated.'

'How charming,' she said but realised she could not very well refuse and besides, she had enjoyed his company throughout the meal. It may have had something to do with drinking the lion's share of the bottle of wine but as they walked into the deep shadow of the brick arch she slipped her hand into the crook of his elbow and leant her cheek against the rough fabric of his jacket.

While she opened another bottle of wine in the kitchen she heard Hector push up the sash window in the sitting room, and when she joined him he was leaning on the sill looking out across the estate.

'What a beautiful evening,' he said, taking the wine from her hand and turning to toast her with a dip of his glass. The smell of dried hay drifted in through the window and a moth banged around underneath the lampshade on the desk.

'So, Mrs Westbrook, what now?'

'What had you in mind?'

'Well – as the only sober person in this room for the present I should probably ring and order a taxi to collect me and take me back to my hotel in what? About an hour?'

'And as the only inebriated person in the room . . . '

'You could tell me not to bother.'

'Because?'

Hector grasped her by the waist and pulled her towards him, his breath hot in her ear and scented with wine. 'For God's sake, Sam, you know what I want.'

'The monkey?'

He drew back, a delusive smile on his face, and laughed softly. 'I often wonder if, like the gossips used to say about Wallis Simpson, you learned some fiendish Oriental foreplay to torture and inflame your suitors. Surely we're both too old for this cat and mouse game? Let's just go to bed.'

'I'm not sure that's such a good idea.' Sam placed her palm against his chest to strengthen her resolve. 'I think I've had too much to drink.'

'Seems the perfect moment – I haven't.'

In a bid to marshal her impulses Sam withdrew to the sofa and Hector followed with a look of resignation on his face. He sat down and reached out for her hand, 'All right then,' he said, 'let's talk about the monkey.'

Sam laughed and shook her head. She didn't want to talk about the monkey – if Hector had been more astute he might have realised that the wine, the smell of the summer night floating in through the open window and the strong physical presence of a man who desired her meant she was moments away from surrender.

'It's hot tonight,' he said and Sam kicked her shoes onto the floor and turned on the sofa to face him.

'It certainly is.'

'Do you think he's OK?'

'Who?'

'The monkey?'

Sam scanned Hector's face, trying to work out if this was part of his seduction, a bid to distract her or amuse her, to laugh her into bed, but his expression was austere. Without waiting for an answer he said, 'We should have asked the caterers if we could pop him in one of the freezers overnight. You know what, Sam, if you've got your pass keys, that's exactly what we ought to do, right now.'

His change of conversational direction took her by surprise. Moments earlier his eyes had been dark with yearning, the strength of his passion had hardened his posture, his breath on her cheek had been urgent with lust and the fathomless pit of her own desire thrummed in synchrony, but he had pinched it off so abruptly she felt guyed and rather angry. She swung her legs back down onto the floor, searching out her shoes with her toes and smoothing down her blouse. 'We couldn't possibly do that,' she said, feeling quite sober all of a sudden.

'If we piled up the contents of the freezer on the floor and insulated them with a rug or something they wouldn't thaw before the morning and there'd be room for the monkey.'

'What are you talking about, Hector?'

'Or I could take him back to the hotel in the taxi with me and get them to chill him down for the night – they'll probably have a walk-in fridge.'

'No. A thousand times no. This is madness. Moving him would cause more damage than leaving him where he is.'

Irritated, Hector stood up and began to pace back and forth, his jaw tensing. He came to a halt and emphasising his words with an index finger said, 'Look, Sam, I don't think you fully grasp how important this find is to me.'

'It's important to me too.'

Hector huffed quietly and shook his head, his expression one of fatalistic surprise. 'And it always has to be about you, doesn't it?'

'What?'

'Whenever we get down to brass tacks it always has to come

back to you – what you want.'

'That's not fair.'

'Isn't it? Night of the party – I want to sleep with you, you don't. Who gets their own way? You. I want to see how the trebuchet works – in my opinion it's stable enough to get it moving – but oh no, I'm not allowed to move it one little inch because you don't want me to. "Don't touch this, don't touch that," the whole time we're in there. Same thing tonight – lovely meal, getting on famously, only one possible way to end this evening in my opinion but oh no, Sam Westbrook says no and what Sam wants, Sam gets.'

'What has that got to do with the monkey?'

'Everything! When I first got in touch with you it was because I thought you could help me debunk centuries of theory about John Wilmot by finding an artefact you didn't even know about, and yesterday we found it.'

'I found it.'

'The builders found it – actually,' Hector said widening his eyes and jutting his jaw out.

'This is getting ridiculous.'

'I'm a hair's breadth away from an even bigger story now. What if it turns out that far from being a Victorian prig, the tenth earl was fascinated by the simulacrum that may be lying up there rotting as we speak? Perhaps he went on to create other creatures in a similar vein. I would have another great book in the pipeline and all the publicity I could want. We know the tenth earl was as eccentric as his father – why did he even embark on stuffing a full-sized Hereford bull? And what was behind his overtures to Queen Victoria after she was widowed? Perhaps when he suggested preserving Prince Albert as a mount he meant it in every sense of the word. I could change public opinion about Queen Victoria herself.' He finished his diatribe and stood in front of Sam full-square, panting slightly. The moth inside the lampshade tapped the vellum a couple more times before dropping onto the table and lying on its back, its legs feebly stroking the air.

'It's not your monkey,' Sam said.

'You heard the Earl. "Get rid of that hideous primate" – he said it himself. Why shouldn't I have it, take it up to London tomorrow?'

'He didn't mean that.'

'He did.'

Sam got to her feet and, going over to the table, gently scooped the moth onto the palm of her hand and cupped it. It fluttered against her skin with an encouraging energy and, pushing past Hector, she made her way to the window and tossed it out into the night.

'It'll just come straight back in,' he said.

She watched its pale shape dip and flap and diminish as it flew towards the light of the moon and with a sigh she turned round to face him and said, 'I think you'd better go.'

He stared at her, his lips tightening, and turned to snatch his jacket off the back of the chair but once he had it in his hands he stalled and she saw his shoulders drop before he turned. 'Oh God, Sam,' he said, 'I don't know what's just happened here.' He came towards her, contrition in every step. 'I am so, so sorry. I beg you to forgive me.'

He looked so dejected, so penitent that Sam nodded her pardon but when she said as gently as she could, 'I still think it would be better if you went – we can talk again in the morning,' she saw the red mist of anger come down over his countenance again, and flinging his jacket to the ground, he grabbed her roughly by the shoulders and pressed his mouth onto hers, the stubble of his chin rasping across her skin, his lips enveloping, his teeth glancing against her own. She pushed her hands up between their bodies and shoved him away but he dashed the back of his hand across his glistening lips and pounced towards her again, swinging her off balance and across the room towards the sofa where he pinned her down with his weight, grasping her by the wrist and holding her restraining arm aloft. She struggled and shouted at him in her throat, the sound muffled by his mouth as he clamped his lips over hers, but it just seemed to inflame him to further heights of domination until she finally managed to free her other hand and grasping a fistful of thick hair, she wrenched his head up and sideways.

Caught off guard he lost his balance, putting a hand and knee down onto the floor to steady himself, and with a strength born of pounding adrenalin, Sam swung the bulk of his weight off her and managed to scramble up the back of the sofa and down onto the floor. Wild-eyed, with her heart pumping, she ran around to put the dining room table between them and stood glaring at him as he hauled himself up from the ground.

He walked slowly towards where his jacket lay and dragged it up off the floor, watching Sam with contempt as he pulled it on and adjusted the collar of his shirt before running his hands through his hair. 'This isn't over,' he said. 'I will have that monkey.' To maintain their distance, Sam moved a couple of steps further around the table as he approached the door. When his hand was on the latch he turned to her once more and said, 'And I will have you.'

The moon was high in the sky and flooded the great courtyard with a light as thick as spilled white lead. The shadows cast by the pillars lay across the ground like black carpets and along these bands of ebony an intruder moved, witnessed only by the gargoyles which gazed down on him from the eaves. Despite the warmth of the night he had a waxed coat draped across his shoulders like a cape, the pocket on one side bulging and heavy. When he reached the door of the music room he dragged at the hem of the coat to bring the pocket into reach before pulling out a metal hoop festooned with keys. He heaved at the collar to pull the coat back into position on his shoulders, the remaining contents of the pocket dragging it down, and as he flicked through the keys they chimed dully against one another, a noise so slight it was only audible because of the hush of the night.

Hearing a door slam in the archway to the left of the courtyard, he pressed himself deeper into the shadows and from his vantage point he saw a tall man stride out across the gravel, his mobile held to his ear. The man's voice seemed shockingly loud as it echoed across the empty courtyard, his demand for a taxi to pick him up from the entrance of the park urgent and angry. He was still giving directions when he disappeared through the arch on the opposite side, his voice fading moments after he vanished.

The watcher puzzled to himself then, dropping the bunch of keys back in the pocket of the coat, he made his way with great stealth towards the arch from whence the man had emerged. Once inside he leaned against the wall to look up the stone staircase and took no more than three or four steps to raise himself to a point where he could see the door to the upstairs flat. A strip of light shone out from underneath and he descended again, the leather on the soles of his shoes crunching on the particles of gravel which had been carried in on people's feet over time. He then made his way out from the courtyard, his footsteps muffled by the grass as he walked around to peer up at the only lighted window on the east side, but moments after he gazed up at it, the light was extinguished.

He had a routine but tonight's events had disrupted it. When he was out and about on the estate in the evening, he knew that the woman who lived in the flat usually went to bed after midnight. She was careful to draw the curtains of the rooms during the evening but when the light in the bedroom went on he knew he would only have to wait for approximately ten minutes while she completed her ablutions in the bathroom. Then, whatever the weather, she would open the window in the room and draw back the curtains before getting into bed. He assumed she liked to sleep with plenty of fresh air in the bedroom but he also knew she liked to sleep completely naked.

When he first noticed the window from the other side of the lake in the spring she was circumspect, crouching a little before whipping the curtain aside and scuttling for the safety of the bed covers, but as the months progressed and the weather improved, he assumed she had become inured to the possibility of any witnesses out on the estate and quite frequently he was able to enjoy the curve of a breast, sometimes even a nipple if the night was dark enough to let him get close to the wall where he could gaze up and feel a tweak in the floor of his pelvis as the light shone on the pigmented skin, round and smooth like a chocolate penny.

He stared up at the east flank of the wall and checked his watch. He had no idea what had been going on in there this evening but it seemed to have altered her routine. However, he had a more exciting plan for tonight and was eager to press on with it.

– 19 –

As so often happened with Charlotte, she didn't stay down for long. She transferred the spooky picture onto Max's computer but kept a copy on her phone because she had texted it to Robyn and they were all meeting up in the Duntisbourne Arms for a drink to discuss it.

'Do you need a lift?' her father said.

'No – I'll walk down.'

'It'll be dark when you come back.'

'They always come back with me,' and she bent to kiss him on the forehead. 'You worry too much,' she said.

'A couple of hours ago you were worried.'

'I'm fine now.'

Max made himself a cup of coffee and wandered into his study. Charlotte had left the file on the computer open and when he moved the mouse the screen saver disappeared and he stared at the contorted and twisted face. He found it difficult to define what unsettled him so much about the image – it might have been the lack of any tangible or distinguishing features which left the mind free to fill in disturbing details – but as he looked at it he felt the follicles around his temples prickle.

Max was a past master at catastrophising and the first line of horror down which his mind ran was the thought of this hideous demon stalking the hedgerows under the moonlight watching his innocent daughter tripping her way back through the empty village at the end of the evening after the pub had closed. He pulled himself up short, consoled by the thought that Charlotte's new friends always ended an evening back at his house because he had a fridge full of beer which he was happy for them to enjoy. He sighed and smiled to himself with relief.

He half turned away from the screen when another scenario burst in on his imagination and propelled him through an even more terrifying series of events – he saw the gruesome figure slinking out from the back of the booth having planted its horrible image on Charlotte's phone before slipping through a gap in the stones so slim that his joints seemed to dislocate in order to flatten. He imagined him lying in wait until darkness fell and then creeping out once more, drawn like a moth to a flame towards the only lighted window in the whole of the vast Jacobean edifice, the window Max had so longingly looked up towards when walking around the park in the spring, the window of Sam Westbrook. He saw the stooped figure – which by now had taken on a form not dissimilar to the diabolical bell-ringer with his hunched back and giant wart covering his right eye – advance with a spider-like gait up the stone stairs towards Sam's flat where she lay helpless with no one to protect her.

'Jesus Christ!' he said so loudly that Monty ambled in from the sitting room and stood staring at him before approaching and sniffing his footwear to see if this burst of activity might be leading to an early evening stroll.

Sam sat on the sofa in the dark and listened. She was sure she heard someone at the foot of her stairs long after Hector should have left, the faintest scratch of stone against stone amplified by the acoustics of the staircase up to her front door. She had pressed her ear to the panel and heard footsteps across the flagstones which suddenly stopped, and she realised that with the window open and the curtains drawn back he could look up and see her in the room. Turning the lights off at the switch by the door, she manoeuvred herself between the shadowy shapes of familiar objects towards the window. She dropped onto her hands and knees and crawled the final few feet to the edge of the frame where, shielded by the gathered fabric of the curtain, she carefully raised her head above the sill and looked down at the grass below.

She flung herself away and sat with her back against the wall. Someone was there, out on the grass – she had seen a figure, the outline clearly visible in the light of the moon. She knew it was Hector although in that split-second glance he had appeared fore-shortened by the height of her viewpoint. What was he doing still here?

With her heart thumping in her throat she turned, raising her-self very slightly above the sill once more until she could see the grass. The light of the moon washed it with silver and it lay below her, cool and deserted. She rose higher to bring more of the grass into view but still she could not see where he had gone and then she heard the gravel at the side of the grass crunching again and realised he must have slipped out of sight against the wall of the building and was making his way back round – with what intent?

She sat on the floor with her back against the wall, straining her ears in the silence of the night, breathing in shallow breaths through her mouth as she listened. She stayed in this position for a long time, unable to move in case he saw. How secure was her flat? She suspected the answer was not very. The front door was fitted with an archaic lock, the housing to receive the latch carved in the soft wood of the architrave and easily pressed aside, she imagined, with a credit card. Security had never crossed her mind before – living in the courtyard was like living in a gated com-munity and she had let her guard drop, lulled by the false sense of sanctuary it offered. It wasn't like living alone – there were always staff over in the private side, and Pugh in the gatehouse.

She wondered if she should call for help, disturb Pugh or Dean the butler, but felt foolish for putting herself in this compromising situation. She hadn't given a second thought to inviting Hector up to her flat at the end of the evening: she was confident she knew him, understood the way he would behave. No, that was wrong – she didn't even question if he would behave inappropriately and she was even angrier with herself for flirting with the thought of the night ending with some sort of encounter. She certainly hadn't intended inviting him to stay the night, but that physical attraction between them had encouraged her to imagine how pleasant it would be if the liaison ran a bit further than it had on the night of the party.

She was angry with herself for ignoring the numerous indications of his baser personality – a flash of fury, a tug of control, a pout of petulance – and doing what she always did. She had felt an instant attraction to Hector which he had fuelled with his own desire and his pretentious actions, so she had turned a blind eye to all the indications that he was manipulating her, that he intended to have his way come what may, and tonight she had given him every reason to believe his goal would be achieved.

She had been sceptical of the 'no means no' brigade, having in the past believed that no encounter with the opposite sex should ever get that far, avoidance being the route an intelligent woman should follow to ensure her physical safety, but tonight, to her shame, her own conceit had allowed her to put herself in a compromising position with a brute of a man and she rued having ever held such preposterous ideals. He had frightened her with his sudden strength and loss of control and he was frightening her still. His behaviour had been unpredictable and she had no idea what his continued presence might mean.

Her whole body jolted when the mobile in her handbag vibrated then began to ring. She could see its light shining dimly on and off through the opening of the bag, the tone muffled but still exceedingly loud in the rarefied atmosphere of the darkened room.

Having frightened himself half to death with the thought of Sam in mortal danger, it crossed Max's mind that she might not be on her own this evening and resentful feelings about Schofield washed over him in jealous waves, blotting away much of his fear. Luckily the anger engendered by this jealousy wasn't directed at Sam – despite his earlier antagonism towards her, he was beginning to talk himself round to a more sympathetic attitude by blaming the Scoke for everything that had happened.

Max was in fact a very emotional man but his boarding school training had discouraged any outward manifestation of this to such an extent that his courtship of Sam was bound to fail when up against a man like Hector Schofield. Max despised elaborate displays of affection, regarding them as the worst kind of showing off, and as for expressing feelings verbally he found such protestations insincere and crass. He recognised that he was often a voice in the wilderness with these opinions – especially with his ex-wife who needed daily vocal effusions – but his principles remained unshaken. The only way to show your true feelings was through your behaviour and this – like a five-day Test cricket match – needed time, with ebbs and flows, exciting moments and more mundane ones, and it was only through this medium that you could truly show another person your loyalty and your commitment.

Hector Schofield had arrived with his smart country casuals, his preposterous masculinity and flowing hair, his flashy teeth and pungent aftershave. Max was in little doubt that he had wooed Sam with ludicrous bunches of flowers, elaborate and romantic meals and gestures, maybe even some mawkish verse following a pattern he probably repeated with every conquest he made. It was easy to see why she fell.

Max now began to worry that his own recent coldness towards Sam might have exaggerated the warmth of Hector's advances and he regretted behaving the way he did on the strength of hearsay and gossip. Noel didn't always get things right and he had been known to embellish stories from time to time. He could have been mistaken about Hector staying the night and surely the person to clear that up would be Sam herself.

'I'll ring her,' he said to Monty, who raised his head to look at him. 'What? You think the Scoke will be there?' The dog flopped his head back onto his paws and closed his eyes. 'It's a risk I'm going to have to take. I couldn't bear her to think I was sulking. Is it too late, do you think?' He rocked the dog's shoulder gently with his hand and Monty stirred again, moving further up the sofa and spreading out with a kick of his back legs. 'Not annoying you, am I?'

Max picked up the phone and walked about the room a few times, looking in turn from the sleeping dog to the French windows which were open onto the warm summer evening. He took a deep breath and dialled her number.

When she answered her voice was so breathless that a terrible image sprang up in his mind of her tumbling around in bed with the Scoke and reaching out for the phone in the middle of some passionate clinch, but then she said, 'Oh Max, I'm so glad it's you!'

'What?' he said, his mood soaring. 'Whatever's the matter?'

'There's someone outside.'

'Where are you?'

'In the flat.'

'Who's outside?'

'I think it's Hector. There's been a bit of . . .' she paused and he heard her catch her breath, 'an altercation.'

'What sort of altercation?'

'It's difficult to explain.'

'You sound upset.'

'I'm not – I'm being silly.'

'Silly's no good. I'm coming over.'

Having scribbled a note for Charlotte to explain his sudden departure, Max set off in his Land Rover thinking the worst – that Hector Schofield had taken his beloved Sam by force or at the very least subjected to her to some kind of physical threat – but as the countryside slipped past bathed in the cool light of the moon, he began to tell himself to stop over-dramatising the situation. Sam had sounded worried, not terrified. Hector had clearly done something appalling but she would have been far more distressed if the worst had happened. He could lay that worry to one side and instead concentrate on the encouraging thought that the Scoke had shown his true colours at last, his influence was on the retreat and he, Max Black, was rushing to Sam's side to protect her from any further upset.

The car park was deserted but for a few staff cars from the private side and Max strode across the gravel under the moonlight like a knight errant, scanning the courtyard for any sign of intruders. Over to his left he could see the cheerful lights of the private apartments spilling out across the flagstones in stark contrast to the cavernous windows along the north side of the Hall, the blackness disturbed here and there by the facets of handmade glass near the top of the building catching the moonlight which scintillated as he moved past. For a moment he had a sense that another light had passed one of the lower windows, a flicker of yellow among the black and silver, but when he looked directly over towards the building it was gone and he thought no more about it, so eager was he to reach Sam. He pulled his phone out of his pocket as he walked and dialled her number so that his approach would not alarm her, and as he ascended the stairs he heard her door opening cautiously above.

'Am I glad to see you,' she said, holding the door open just enough to let him pass through. He thought she was looking pale.

'Whatever's been going on here?'

'I just got a bit spooked,' she said, leading him through the sitting room which was in darkness and into the kitchen. 'Can I get you a beer?' she went on, shutting the kitchen door behind them. Max looked at her, puzzled.

'Of course,' he said.

She fetched one from the fridge and handed it to him unopened before realising and stirring around in one of the drawers to find the crown cork opener. 'Sorry,' she said. She picked up a full glass of red wine that stood on the worktop and Max saw that her hand was shaking as she raised it to her lips, staring off into the middle distance as she drank it down in one, gulping at it as if it was a half pint of lager, before putting the glass back on the surface and looking up at him. He took a sip from his beer. 'Better now?' he said and she nodded. 'Why don't we go and sit down next door?' he suggested.

'OK. But close the curtains before I put the lights on – please.'
He did as he was asked and she turned on a small lamp then sat
down on the sofa, her arms crossed, her shoulders slumped. 'I've
been such a fool.'

He took his seat next to her and reached out for her hand which
was tucked underneath her elbow. She didn't resist and when he
took it in his palm he felt it was icy cold. Putting his beer bottle
down on the carpet he rubbed her hand vigorously between both
of his and then gave it a pat to comfort her.

'That's hard to believe,' he said. 'Why don't you tell me what
happened?' He sat and listened as she related the events of the
evening. She was harsh on herself – too harsh, he felt, when clearly it was the Scoke who was at fault.

'There was such violence in his eyes,' she said. 'I can't tell you
what inflamed him the most, not having the monkey or not having me.'

'That monkey's no match for you.'

She smiled up at him, a hint of relief returning to her face. 'After
he'd gone I heard him creeping around outside. I've never got
used to how dark it is out here in the country and I had never
thought the flat was particularly isolated but I realised that if he
was still out there waiting, I was trapped – I couldn't leave or get
to my car.' She shook her head. 'I've been really silly. I'm sorry I've
dragged you over here on such a foolish pretext.'

'Not at all. Anyway, I rang you.'

'Why did you ring, by the way?'

'That's not important now. The thing is, I had a good look round
as I came in – there's no one out there now, except . . . ' and then he
remembered the glow in the lower windows of the Hall and Sam
frowned, trying to read his expression.

'What? What did you see?'

Max sat back against the cushions and puzzled to himself before replying. 'It was probably nothing.'

'What?'

'I'm not even sure I saw anything. It was just – well, I wonder if I saw the light of a torch through one of the downstairs windows in the Hall.'

Sam withdrew her hand and sat bolt upright. 'He's over there, isn't he? That bastard's got into the Hall and he's going to take the monkey.'

For the second time in three days Max found himself entering the Hall under cover of darkness but although it was a consoling thought that this time he wasn't breaking in, he was beset with concerns which Sam didn't seem to share. As she pulled on a cardigan and searched around the flat for her torch she was certain they were on their way to stop Schofield from whisking the monkey off to storage in some deep freeze somewhere in Shropshire, but when Max urged her to call the police, she insisted that as she knew Hector was intent on preserving the artefact as opposed to stealing it, no crime apart from trespass was actually being committed.

Max's concern was that if Schofield was as ruthless as she said, they could be putting themselves in physical danger by trying to apprehend him on their own. He wondered if it would be better to get some backup from the staff over in the private side but he didn't want her to think him feeble. Besides, his whole intention this evening was to be her protector so here he was, striding across the courtyard towards the door to the music room with Sam at his side.

'How did he get in?' Max asked as Sam struggled with the master key to unlock the door.

'I have no idea – but he did.' Max had one idea but this was not the moment to tell her what had happened on the night of the party.

She turned the torch on as they went in and said, 'I won't use the house lights – I don't want to alert the whole of the private side. We can sort this out by ourselves.'

The quietness of the Hall amplified the sound of their footsteps on the oak floorboards. The moon shone in through the windows in the great hall and moving quickly they made their way up the stairs towards the minstrels' gallery. As they rounded the corner Sam said, 'Look. The door up to the exhibition's open – I knew it,' and hurried forward to the foot of the spiral staircase. Up they climbed, round and round, and Max could hear that she was already quite out of breath – as was he. She paused momentarily by the slit window and steadying herself with her hand, turned to check how far behind he was.

'OK?' she said. Max looked up at her and nodded.

Suddenly both of them buckled and ducked simultaneously. A loud report exploded from above and echoed down the spiral staircase, bouncing around the walls. Sam looked upwards and around then back at Max, her eyes wide and staring.

'What the . . . ?'

Before he could answer, the crack was followed by a loud creaking and grinding which seemed to shudder through the stones around them and as Sam crouched even lower, Max leapt up a step towards her and wrapped his arms around her shoulders, pulling her head down and cradling it against him, certain that the very fabric of the Hall was about to fall and they were going to plunge, tumbling down with blocks of masonry crashing around them. The cacophony of grinding rose and he heard the sound of timbers smashing to the ground but the noise wasn't getting any nearer. He cautiously raised his head and realised that whatever was happening was way above them, somewhere in the exhibition.

The crumps and thuds lessened and finally stopped. As Sam lowered her arms from her head and raised her eyes towards Max they heard a noise like a rushing wind, and behind her Max saw a billowing cloud appear around the central column of the stone staircase a split second before it engulfed them. Covering his mouth with his sleeve he jerked her up onto her feet and pulled her head into the alcove of the window where a draught was coming in around the edge of the leadwork. They coughed and gasped, their breath forming steam on the glass as they pressed their faces to the leading to avoid the choking cloud.

Just as suddenly as it had started everything stopped and an eerie silence washed down over them, enveloping them as completely as the dust cloud. Still leaning their elbows on the alcove, Max turned to Sam. Her face was white, her hair the same colour, her mouth had taken on the look of the living dead, the flash of lip which the dust had missed as livid as if she had drunk fresh blood, her eyes oddly lustrous and glossy against the matt of the rest of her skin. He brushed his hand across his hair, dislodging a small shower of dust, and grimaced as he tried to swallow, wishing he could spit the grit out of his mouth.

'You OK?' he said.

'I think so.'

With silent agreement Sam pressed herself against the wall and let Max slip around her to ascend the final section of the staircase. The exhibition was still in darkness but a dim light glowed through the settling dust, and as they made their way towards it Max saw that a huge beam of wood had fallen out from the room which housed the trebuchet, tearing down the plastic sheeting in its path.

As they began picking their way over pieces of plaster that had been knocked off the temporary entrance, Sam rested her hand on the beam to keep her balance and said, 'Oh God. This is a beam from the machine – look, it's covered in carvings. Whatever's happened in here?' She played her torch into the room and as the dust swirled and thinned they were met with a scene of utter devastation. The mighty structure that had once filled the room from floor to ceiling was in pieces, beams and planks stacked one on top of the other, the metal bars which had held the sextant aloft sticking up out of the pile, chains still looped from one to the other like the rigging of a wrecked ship. The only illumination was a guttering candle standing in a pool of spilt wax.

From behind them another more powerful torch skittered around the room and turning, Max saw Dean the butler and one of the footmen dressed in their shirtsleeves climbing over the rubble towards them.

'What the hell's happened here?' Dean said, his tone a combination of anger and bewilderment. 'We heard the racket from the private side – I thought the building was collapsing.'

'I thought someone had fired a gun,' said the lad.

'Your guess is as good as ours,' Max said.

'The trebuchet's collapsed,' Sam added.

'Whatever will the Earl say?'

The four of them stood side by side staring at the wreckage, stepping back as another piece of wood creaked and swung down from the ceiling, tumbling down the pile before coming to rest on the floor with a puff of dust. Max thought he heard Dean groan and looked sharply at him but the butler was staring at the pile of rubble and he said in a whisper, 'What on earth was that?'

'I thought it was you.'

The lighter spars at the edge of the pile shifted again but this time not from above – something seemed to be pushing up from underneath and all four watchers stepped forward once again. 'There must be someone under there,' Dean barked. Dropping his torch on the ground he rushed forward and started hauling timbers away from the pile.

'Careful,' Sam said, 'it's very unstable.'

'Help me,' he said. Max and the lad joined him, pulling spars away and handing them back in a human chain. They worked feverishly and as they cleared the heavier timbers away another movement shifted the debris and they heard a long and terrible groan rise up from deep within the pile.

'Hurry,' one of them shouted.

'I've found someone,' said another.

'It's a leg.'

The three men scrabbled at the smaller pieces, Dean and the footman working in front of Max who was moving the waste away from the working area until the lad jumped back with a yelp of horror.

'Look away,' Max said over his shoulder to Sam, not wanting her to see a badly injured person, but when he looked back there was no gore, no blood, no devastating wounds or injuries – just a pair of white buttocks trussed in the leather straps that had previously hung from the sextant. Max tore his jacket off and flung it over the offending bottom and within moments they had freed the man from the rubble. He was white with dust, shaky and sullen but unharmed. They tried to move him away from the wreckage but he remained pinioned by the leather harness.

'Anyone got a knife?' Dean said.

'Who is it?' Sam said.

Max, who was struggling to undo one of the buckles on the harness, felt a bubble of laughter rising up in his throat because he realised for one glorious moment that Sam must have thought the buttocks belonged to Schofield, but the short balding man they were struggling to liberate bore no resemblance to him whatsoever.

'No idea,' he said over his shoulder.

Dean snatched the torch from the ground and the man held his hand up to shield his eyes from the light. 'I know you,' he said. Turning to the others, he added, 'This man used to work here. His name's Nigel Procter.'

- 20 -

Sam woke early and lay in bed hoping she might fall to sleep again, but after ten minutes she got up and went to the kitchen to make tea. It was six in the morning but the curtains glowed with the light of the rising sun. She threw them back and pushed up the sash window. How different the view was this morning compared to the night before, the grass moist with dew, the sun tracking up from the horizon and filling the estate with light. She gazed down on the spot where she thought she had seen Hector standing and knew it was Procter – Procter who was prowling around, stalking her. She regretted suspecting Hector and a pang of conscience somewhat mollified her feelings of anger towards him, but she knew she had a further confrontation with him looming once news of last night's debacle reached him. Before that happened she needed to work out what she was going to say to the Earl and the CEO.

She was uncertain of the extent of the damage. She had been unable to take a really good look last night, feeling awkward about rushing to help the men as they struggled to free Procter from the harness. Once on his feet he seemed to panic and began plunging and pulling against the harness like a horse shying away from a fallen cart, his exposed genitals, shrunken and dusty, bobbing from left to right between his legs making him look even more ludicrous. Max tried to save the man's dignity by getting him to sit down on the floor, covering the lower part of his body with a jacket but as they worked and pulled at the straps, the jacket kept slipping. Sam didn't want to watch someone suffer under such humiliating circumstances so she had taken the young footman out and gone over to the private side with him to call an ambulance.

When she returned, Max and Dean had got Procter free and brought him through to the exhibition where they had sat him down on one of the sofas. Max had put his jacket back on and was leaning up against a cabinet looking at the prisoner with an expression of ill-concealed contempt on his face. Procter sat poorly swathed in a large piece of builder's plastic which was bunched up in his lap where he held it to him. He didn't seem to be badly injured but there was a cut on his head from which some blood dribbled, cutting a channel through the soot on his forehead. From what Sam could see of his shoulders, his skin was crisscrossed with shallow scratches and an oblong bruise was starting to bloom along his collarbone. However, she thought he was a lucky man to have survived the catastrophe with such minor injuries.

He sat slumped and resentful but on hearing her approach his eyes flicked up and watched her cross the room, his tongue, incredibly pink against the pallor of his skin, darting out and running along his lips like a snake tasting the air. The lascivious look didn't go unnoticed by Max, who crossed the floor towards him in a single stride and shoved him on the shoulder as a warning, making the plastic crackle and sending up a puff of dust.

'Keep your filthy eyes to yourself,' he said before turning back to Sam and moving her out of the man's sight line.

'That was a bit harsh,' she said.

'Really? I don't think so – he's a despicable individual.' The intensity of his manner took her aback. 'I didn't recognise him until we got him out of the room and into the exhibition but that man there –' and Max stabbed his forefinger in Procter's direction before continuing through gritted teeth – 'that man there broke into the booth, searched through my daughter's handbag until he found her mobile and took a photograph of himself doing God knows what, then left it on her phone as a screen saver to frighten the bloody life out of her.'

'Really?'

'Yes – really. And although it sickens me to the very depths of my soul to say anything good about Hector Schofield, it wasn't him you heard creeping around earlier, it was that man.'

'I know. I guessed as much.'

'It's not the first time he's done it. I saw him weeks ago slinking away into the night one evening when I was here for a function. I don't know what his problem is but he's been haunting this place.' Sam felt an involuntary shudder tremble between her shoulder blades and Max came forward and placed a hand on her arm. 'Look,' he said, dropping his voice 'this is no place for a woman. Why don't you leave Dean and me to deal with things? The ambulance will be here soon – and the police no doubt. It could be a long night.'

'What was he doing up here?'

'Surely that's obvious.'

'Did he mean to bring the whole thing down?'

'I'm sure he'll be questioned – but not by you.'

'I can't leave without seeing the extent of the damage.'

'Yes, you can – you've had excitement enough for one night. Dean and I will secure the exhibition once this shocker has been taken away. You've had a terrible evening. You can deal with this disaster in the morning when you've got a bit more energy.'

She knew he was right – she felt utterly drained. 'But it's my responsibility,' she said. 'I was in charge of this. I let this happen.'

'There'll be plenty of time for recrimination and blame when we know all the facts. Go home. Get some sleep.'

'Are you sure?' she said.

'Completely. Things'll be easier in the morning.'

She picked up the site lamp which lay sprawled across the floor and checked the socket. It was switched on, which meant the bulb must have popped when the lamp went over. The other lamp was still upright and she manoeuvred it into a position where she could aim it around the pile of wreckage to the part of the room where the seat had stood. The bulb buzzed and glowed before flashing on and for the first time Sam was able to assess the full extent of the damage.

She was relieved to see that the beams of the structure seemed to have shaken free of their joints and fallen rather than fractured. In fact, the age and density of the wood used to form the main uprights of the structure meant that they had suffered far less damage than she had imagined, most of the debris being formed from the oak planking that had roofed the structure and which could easily be replaced with reclaimed boards.

Her next concern was the sextant and much of this had been uncovered by the men the night before. She lifted several more of the planks aside – she had had the sense to put on a pair of leather driving gloves to protect her hands from the splinters – and gently pulled the metal structure free of the pile. It was too heavy to set upright but it lay on the floor flat and true, unbent by the catastrophe that had befallen it. She noted that some of the chains had ruptured as the machine had folded in on itself but again she was confident these could be restored. Thanks to the men's care when releasing Procter from the harness, the leather on it did not seem to have suffered greatly.

By the time she made her way around the side of the wreckage, her spirits were lifting. It was an appalling mess but from what she had seen so far, it was recoverable. However, when she moved across to inspect the couch she was in for a shock. She could see the top of the two serpentine upper arms sticking out from under a couple of planks but as she moved these to one side she realised that the leather upholstery had taken a terrible pounding. The centre of the couch had all but disintegrated leaving a few wisps of singed horsehair and leather clinging to the brass tacks around the edge and when she moved forward to inspect a particularly large tuft she recoiled with horror – it was not a tuft of horsehair but one of the hands from the monkey still secured to the remains of the frame. The rest of the body was nowhere to be seen.

'What time did you get to bed last night?' Noel said. 'You look like death.'

'Why, thank you, Noel – you're never slow with an unkind word. About four o'clock in the morning, as a matter of fact.'

'Get any sleep?'

'What do you mean?'

'I heard you spent most of the night in the company of the fair Mrs Westbrook.'

'Yes, I helped out until quite late – but I slept in my own house.'

'Oh, really?'

'Yes, really.'

The two doormen stood to one side to make way for more clean-up equipment to come in through the front door. House maintenance had been working upstairs throughout the morning and any attempts at secrecy had been abandoned – all anyone could talk about was the discovery of the machine and its bizarre demise the previous night. Some attempt had been made to gloss over the identity of the person responsible for the disaster but speculation among the staff turned gossip to certainty, and as the day's visitors continued to arrive to the news that the Dywenydd Collection was closed for general maintenance, it became common knowledge among the staff that once again Nigel Procter had done something utterly appalling.

At around noon the number of people in the courtyard began to thin and Max was aware that visitors were drifting over towards the buttery. Lunchtime was upon them and until two o'clock the front door would start to quieten down but then he spotted a single figure striding in from the right. He recognised the long legs, the supercilious carriage of the head, the overlong hair and the black saddle-leather briefcase and felt his body pull up to its full height to meet head-on the man who had frightened Sam. Schofield – unaware, Max assumed, that his behaviour the night before was known to him – raised his hand in a jocular greeting as he approached and Max felt a wry smile begin to play on his lips because his rival, who had shamelessly used Rochester's ruddy monkey to woo Sam, was about to get the shock of his life.

'Morning, old chap,' Schofield said, coming to a halt on the top step with a stamp of his foot like a flamenco dancer.

'Afternoon, I think you'll find.'

Schofield checked his watch. 'Good God, you're absolutely right.' He gazed around the hall and ran his eyes up towards the minstrels' gallery. 'Sam upstairs then?'

'Of course.'

'She's probably got the conservators up there, has she?'

Max gave a huff and grimaced. 'Not as such.'

Something in his tone of voice pulled Schofield's attention away from the hall and he turned abruptly to Max. 'What do you mean by that?'

'I'm sorry to say a miscreant broke into the Hall last night after your ignominious departure–'

'My . . .?'

Max waved a dismissive hand towards him and continued, 'This miscreant entered the exhibition, lashed himself into the trebuchet, got himself underway all on his own and was having a fine old time up there with your monkey when the whole thing collapsed around his ears.'

Schofield gawped at him, then threw his head back and exploded with laughter. 'Very funny, Max,' he said. 'Very funny indeed.'

'It wasn't very funny for the miscreant – or the monkey for that matter.'

Schofield's affable expression of bonhomie began to falter and he looked over to Noel, who nodded in a matter-of-fact way and said, 'Dreadful mess up there.'

He glared at Max, struggling to compose his rage. His breath quickened and the pupils of his eyes shrank to hard black beads of fury – then he was off towards the foot of the staircase, bounding up the steps two at a time.

'Better follow him,' Noel said.

By the time Max reached the foot of the spiral staircase Schofield was already out of sight but he could hear his footsteps pounding up the stone steps above his head several turns ahead, his breathing stentorian and laboured. Max dashed into the exhibition in time to see the plastic sheeting dropping behind Schofield and before he made it to the inner room, he heard raised voices coming from inside. When he entered he saw that Schofield had Sam by the elbow and she was pulling away from him, looking surprised and shaken.

Max crossed the room, his feet crunching on the plaster dust, and dashed Schofield's hand away. The two men faced one another, Schofield broadening his chest ready for a fight, but Max had no intention of backing off. 'This has got nothing to do with you,' Schofield said.

'And precious little to do with you.'

'It's OK, Max,' Sam said, 'I can deal with this,' but the look she gave him reassured him that his intervention was welcome.

Schofield tipped his chin up towards Max then slid his eyes disdainfully away from him and back to Sam. 'How much damage has the monkey suffered?' he said, lowering his voice.

Sam took a step nearer to Max so that he partially shielded her and replied, 'It's not looking good.'

'You mean it's buried under this lot?'

'No.'

'I don't understand.'

'It looks as if by opening this space up we changed the atmosphere in here which triggered some sort of anaerobic activity inside the monkey.'

'You mean it was rotting. We knew that – I told you that was happening.' Schofield swung away from them and ran his hands through his hair, the muscle in his jaw twitching with tension. 'I warned you – I told you we needed to get it into some sort of stable environment. You wouldn't listen – you knew better.'

'It was perfectly stable until Procter punctured it and ignited the methane.'

'Methane? Who said anything about methane?'

'When we've gathered all the evidence we'll be closer to understanding.'

'Understanding what?'

'Understanding why it exploded.'

Max looked at Sam and felt that wretched uncontrollable urge to laugh rising up in his chest. He fought it for all he was worth, biting down on his lips, but it escaped in a sudden leathery chuckle and he was lost. 'I'm really sorry,' he said, holding a hand of apology up towards Schofield but it was too late. As Schofield's fist flew towards his face, he twisted and felt a thump on his shoulder, sufficiently hefty to throw him off balance and send him staggering across the floor. He heard Sam shriek as Schofield rushed after him, shoving him with a hand on either side of his waist and grabbing his jacket as he twisted the other way. Max put his arm up to defend himself but Schofield grabbed his elbow and landed an ineffectual slap across his cheek. Max shook him off and bounded back a couple of steps. Schofield took another swing at him but it missed and the momentum carried him forward so that he tripped and sprawled onto the dusty floor. He struggled onto all fours and tried to stand, panting and dishevelled, his face puce with rage.

'Stop it!' Sam shouted. 'This is ludicrous. Get up, Hector.'

Max came forward to help him back onto his feet but once up, Schofield irritably pulled away before smoothing his hair and patting the dust off his clothes. He shot Max a resentful look but seemed to have calmed down. Without a word he pushed past Sam and went over to where the arms of the couch could be seen rising above the wreckage and he stood staring down disconsolately. For the first time since entering the room Max noticed red flags sticking up among the wreckage.

'What are those?' he said quietly to Sam.

'I was marking out the body parts when I come across them so that we can collect them. Jenkins suggested it – he said he thought that's how they do it after plane crashes.'

'That bad, huh?'

Sam nodded.

'How did he manage to ignite it, do you think?'

'I'm still not sure but I've found several candles buried around the couch.'

'He was creating a romantic environment?'

'Evidently.'

During this short conversation their attention had moved away from Schofield and he had taken the opportunity to make his way further round the wreckage to the back of the room where he was surreptitiously lifting spars and peering underneath. 'Please don't do that,' Sam called across, 'I've got a system.'

'There's something down here,' he called back. 'I saw something white. It could be the skull.'

'Leave it,' Sam said, moving towards him, Max following closely, determined to prevent another confrontation developing.

Schofield turned towards her, his head tilted, his eyes looking up with a submissive and pleading gesture which didn't fool Max. 'Come and help me then,' he said. 'Look – it's there, you can see it.' All three stared at the base of the pile and sure enough, glinting away under the planks and twisted spars, Max saw a row of white regular shapes reflecting the glare of the site lights.

'Teeth, surely,' Schofield said, 'the most important part of the monkey, the head – the skull.'

'I'm not sure,' Sam said. 'They look too big to be teeth.'

'Help me, then.' Schofield began to pull away at the debris with renewed vigour and Sam and Max followed suit. As they worked Max manoeuvred himself into a position which put him in the vanguard, sidelining Schofield and Sam to the back, clearing the debris. As the pile shifted and rocked he was the first to realise what they had found and it wasn't the head of the monkey – it was the Golden Hand of Jerusalem.

He bided his time and when Schofield, hot and tired from the work, stood to strip off another layer of clothes he burrowed under the remaining pieces of wood and slid the giltware artefact free of its prison. With his back shielding it from view he held it between both hands, feeling the weight of the silver pulling it downwards. He blew the dust away and the pearls glowed brighter, then brushed the huge fingers gently with his own until the gold of the giltware burst out from under the grime. Max gazed at the craftsmanship, the silvered nails and the ring which encircled the pointed forefinger.

He frowned – he didn't remember the Golden Hand being adorned with any jewellery other than the pearls around the wrist. He stared at the puckered leather, rotating the Hand to left and right before clarification washed over him and he saw in a flash the explanation of everything that had happened in the last twenty-four hours. He stood and turned towards the other two, a half smile on his face, the giltware Hand lying heavy across his palms. Passing it to Schofield, forefinger first, he said, 'It's not the teeth, old chap – quite the opposite end of the monkey, I'm afraid.'

'You promise me you won't tell Monty,' Max said.

'Tell him what?'

'That I went for a walk round the lake without him.' Sam laughed. Max liked it when she laughed.

After Max had escorted Schofield out of the Hall and taken his place beside Noel once more on the front door he was noticed by

Bunty, who hurried across the hall towards him. 'Max!' she said. 'You can't stay on the door looking like that. You're covered in dust, absolutely filthy – what sort of impression is that going to give to the visitors?'

'Where would you like me then?' he said.

Bunty looked at her watch and then scanned the hall until she spotted Laurence on his way towards the guides' room for his tea break. 'Laurence,' she called, 'can you make it a very quick cup of tea then come and take over on the front door? I'm sending Max home.'

'I'm fine,' Max said, patting some of the dust off the sleeve of his jacket.

'Well, bully for you – I'm not fine with your appearance. Go home and get yourself cleaned up but make sure you change your time sheet. You don't get paid for a full day when you've only worked half of it.'

Noel rolled his eyes and Max responded a smile of resignation.

'At least it's a nice sunny afternoon,' Noel said after Bunty had gone. 'Make the most of it – have a beer in the garden.'

Instead Max caught Sam coming out of Rosemary's office where she had gone to report the discovery of the Hand. She was every bit as grimy as him but she also looked exhausted as if the past few days were beginning to take their toll. 'Do you feel like a bit of fresh air?' he said.

'That's a great idea.'

So here they were, walking side by side round the perimeter of the Red Lake. Max had dumped his jacket in his car, removed his tie and rolled up his shirtsleeves; Sam had peeled off her cardigan and tied it round her waist. Her sleeveless T-shirt exposed her shoulders and glancing across Max noticed how pale her skin was. 'Don't get burnt,' he said.

'Nor you.'

'I never burn.' He held up a swarthy forearm. 'Look at that. There must have been Mediterranean blood somewhere back in my ancestry.'

They walked together in silence for a while until by mutual assent they left the metalled road and wandered across the flat ground towards the edge of the lake, fringed with reeds, a great carpet of leathery lily pads rising and falling gently on the surface of the water.

'I owe you an apology,' she said.

'Whatever for?'

'You were right about Hector – he is a type.'

'A scoke.'

'If you like.'

Max gazed out across the water. Late damselflies twinkled over the water lilies and the mineral smell of moisture rose up from the surface. In the gaps of clear water between the groups of lily pads he could see their leathery stalks plunging down into the darkness, brightly coloured rudd weaving through the trunks of this underwater forest.

'Initially I found him very disarming,' she said.

'You don't need to explain.'

'I want to. I was attracted to him, I admit. I'm not blaming you or anything but you seemed to sort of cool towards me and he was there, being charming, being around.'

'I didn't cool towards you.'

'You did – after I came round to see you and Charlotte was a bit . . . difficult.'

'Was she?'

'Come on Max, you know she was.' Max tended not to dwell on that sort of thing. 'And then I saw things were going on between you and Robyn . . . '

'Robyn?' Max turned to look at her.

'Every time I tried to catch your eye at the party you were too wrapped up in conversation with her to notice, and then the two of you left at the same time.'

'Robyn?' he said, again too astonished to think of anything else to say.

'Yes – the girl I saw you hugging and kissing on the front door the other day.'

Max flung his hands into the air with exasperation. 'She's over twenty years younger than me.'

'That doesn't make any difference.'

'It does to me. She's not much older than my daughter, for heaven's sake. Do you think I'm one of those old fools who imagines that just because a young woman is amused by me and enjoys my company she fancies me?'

'It happens.'

'I'll tell you what happens. Men of my age have a certain style, a charisma that comes with the confidence of age, and young people find it attractive but the moment it's misinterpreted it leads to the most inappropriate behaviour. I love the company of women – I can laugh with a young girl, be amused by her, and yes, appreciate she's a pretty girl and she enjoys my company but I don't for a minute imagine she fancies me or wants to hop into bed with me. Blokes of my age make complete fools of themselves going down that route. They're deluded. It's ghastly in the extreme.'

'That's a very vivid denial,' Sam said.

'I have no interest in Robyn whatsoever other than a friendly one, and I guarantee she has no interest in me in the sense you mean. Which is more than can be said for the Scoke.'

'Oh, he was interested all right and he had me fooled – almost.' She paused then went on, 'It's your turn to believe me now – nothing really happened between us.'

Max looked out across the water again and said, 'I don't want to know what happened,' then he turned to her and added, 'I'm just glad it's over now and that irritating man with his great leonine head and pretentious flowing hair has gone.'

'He speaks well of you.'

As they resumed their walk Sam slipped her hand into the crook of Max's elbow and gave his arm a squeeze. 'Thank you for coming to my rescue – twice.'

'That's all right. I can't tell you the pleasure it gave me to see the Scoke sprawled and spluttering in the dust.'

Sam laughed and laid her cheek against his sleeve. 'Oh Max,' she said, 'you have something very decent etched right through you. Why can't I fall in love with you?'

'You need to try harder.'

– 21 –

Weenie assumed that Roger's coldness was a result of the tiff they had had about the French tour on Sunday but as the day wore on she began to worry that he had, in fact, seen her in the garden on Sunday night and was angry with her. She needed to explain to him that she had been driven to spy on him because of his behaviour towards her but the opportunity hadn't arisen.

It was late afternoon and she was sitting alone on security in the dining room, waiting to do a tour. When Roger came in and saw her, he did precisely what she had done to him a few weeks before – he put his chin in the air and stalked over to the opposite side of the room, confirming all her anxieties. Taking a lead from his strategy when she had frozen him out, she left her seat and risked the wrath of the head guide by crossing the room.

'Roger, please,' she said when he turned his back on her and walked into the china room, 'I really need to talk to you.'

'You'd better not leave your post unattended,' he said. As if on cue she heard the dining room door open and knew that Bunty was on the prowl.

'Weenie! What are you doing over there? For goodness' sake, if the Earl sees you jawing away with another guide we'll all lose our jobs. He thinks there are too many of us anyway. Get back over here.'

In her desperation Weenie called out over her shoulder, 'Just a minute,' then turned to Roger and said in a harsh whisper, 'I beg you Roger – wait for me in the car park after work. I've really got to speak to you,' but instead of replying he walked over to the pier glass and gazed at his own image with studied nonchalance before running a forefinger along the length of his eyebrow.

'Weenie!' Bunty said from behind and she knew she had to go. She sat down on the security seat on the other side of the room and watched Roger pacing back and forth in the china room, disappearing from sight and re-emerging with a sauntering gait, his hands behind his back, as if he was goading her. She stared across at him, her eyes pleading with him to look over but he never glanced her way. Her desperate peering was disrupted by Laurence who came into the dining room with a message that Bunty wanted her to do the next tour.

'Can't you do it?' she said, knowing that once she was out on tour she would never manage to corner Roger.

'No, sorry. Roger and I are down for the last tour so I wouldn't have time to do this one, have a cup of tea and be back down by four-thirty.'

'No,' she said slowly, 'of course you wouldn't,' but a plan was beginning to form in her mind. With a last desperate glance over towards Roger, she began to make her way out to take the tour but the idea ripened and burst and she hurried back to Laurence.

'Tell you what, Laurence, why don't we swop? It's a lovely summer's afternoon. I could do the last tour for you and you can go home at the normal time.'

Laurence looked taken aback – Weenie didn't often offer to help someone out. 'But you've been in since ten. It makes it a long old day for you.'

'I don't mind – anything to help a friend.'

'All right then. Why not? Perhaps one day I can do the same for you.'

'That would be lovely,' she said placing a hand languorously on his sleeve. 'Pop out and do this tour then – and tell Bunty we've swapped: it'd be better coming from you.'

Roger looked none too pleased when he sauntered out half an hour later and found Weenie chatting merrily to the handful of visitors who had arrived to take the four-thirty. 'Ah, and here's your guide,' she said.

'Not you dear?' one of the visitors said, 'I thought you were going round with us.'

'We take it in turns madam.' Two guides were needed for the final tour of the day, one to take the tour and the other to sit on security in the library until the visitors left the building. Knowing that Roger preferred to guide rather than sit and wait, Weenie felt it politic on this occasion to give him what he wanted. When he reached the library three-quarters of an hour later, she observed the unwritten rule that the person on security should wander a little way out of earshot, but before he began to wax lyrical about the mighty Wurlitzer she heard him say, 'And here we are in the last room of the tour and, I might add, the last tour of the season – for me.'

'Surely not,' said one of the visitors. 'But you're so good.'

She saw Roger puff himself up before saying, 'Thank you, madam, but as a Justice of the Peace I have rather more important fish to fry.'

Weenie waited for the group to leave and caught Roger on his way back to the office with the key.

'Roger,' she said, 'what on earth did you mean about that being your last tour?'

'Just that,' he said, brushing past her into the office. She waited in the dark corridor, there was no other exit he could use, and when he came out and began to make his way back up to the guides' room to collect his things she trotted after him saying, 'Roger, please stop. What are you talking about?' She continued her desperate pursuit and managed to stick to him like glue even though he was moving at some speed. Eventually, halfway across the courtyard, her persistence paid off and he rounded on her and said, 'Weenie! Will you stop hounding me.'

'I will if you just calm down and tell me what's going on.'

Roger looked up at the windows around the courtyard and said, 'We'll be seen – we can't talk here,' and grabbing her rather roughly by the elbow he led her on through to the car park.

'Give me lift back to Discoed,' she said. 'You didn't give me time to change into my walking shoes.'

Releasing her elbow, Roger pursed his lips and sighed but went around to the passenger side of his car and held the door open for her. Although he drove in silence, Weenie sensed that the act of agreeing to give her a lift indicated a small chink in his armour and when they reached her driveway she turned to him and said, 'Why don't you come in and have a little evening snifter?'

'I don't think that's a good idea.' Weenie's heart dropped – he hadn't turned the engine off and the tone of his voice was doom laden.

'Please tell me what's the matter. Is it because I was a bit snappish with you on Sunday? I know I was, it was stupid of me, I got in a bit of a flap when things started to go wrong and I took it out on you – but you can forgive me, can't you, Roger?'

'Perhaps – but I can't forgive you for coming to my house with the express intention of telling Harriet about you and me.'

'I didn't.' Weenie had never found it hard to lie but in this instance she genuinely felt she was telling the truth because she had no intention of blabbing to his wife.

'You did – I saw you, flitting around my garden like some crazy woman, gawping in through the windows at us.'

'Oh that,' she said, wafting her hand around. 'I was just trying to catch your eye and explain why I'd been a bit testy.'

'I don't care what you say you were doing – it was madness, pure and simple.'

'Madness is never pure and seldom simple,' Weenie joked.

'Rarely pure and never simple – and Wilde was referring to the truth, something else you seem to have trouble grasping.'

'Oh la-di-da! I stand corrected.'

They paused, this puerile diversion distracting them momentarily from the theme of the argument, but Roger pulled it back on course by saying, 'I have been very happily married to Harriet for over thirty years now – she is my rock, the love of my life, my best friend, and I will not let you or anyone else get between us. I'm a deeply religious man and have no intention of letting you destroy the sanctity of our marriage.'

It was Weenie's turn to goggle at this version of the truth and she snapped back immediately, 'Sanctity? Sanctimonious drivel more like. I don't think a hairless bottom is going to give you a free ticket to heaven.'

'Stop it, Weenie. I told you that in confidence.'

'And I wish you hadn't.' A tense silence descended and they both looked out of the windscreen in front of them as the diesel engine gently rocked the car. Eventually Weenie continued in a less strident tone, 'I didn't think you were that happily married – you led me to believe that your wife didn't understand you.'

Roger, somewhat chastened, said, 'She doesn't really but I thought you and I understood each other. I thought you knew it was just a bit of fun.' He looked across at her. 'It was fun, wasn't it?'

Weenie shrugged. 'I suppose so – but this isn't.'

'No, this isn't and I'm sorry. That's why I handed in my notice this morning to Rosemary. It's not fair on you if I go on working at the Hall when you still have feelings for me.'

Weenie let the magazine flop onto her lap, her mind unable to concentrate on mix-and-match menus or Shetland-style classics, and stared out of the window. Although it was late summer in the rest of the county, the garden of the care home was locked in a state of permanent gloom by huge Leylandii cypress trees which lowered along three of its four boundaries, smothering the beds with a felt of resinous needles, sucking the moisture from the soil and leaving the plants sickly from lack of light and nutrition. The skeletons of a couple of sparse rose bushes leaned in towards the mossy lawn desperately trying to escape the deep shadow, their leaves mottled with black spot, a few rose hips from the year before clinging resolutely to the tips of the branches. Weenie felt a great weight of despair pressing in on her as she surveyed the concrete ramps meandering around the lumpy lawn.

Please, dear God, she thought, let me stay fit and well until the bitter end and then let me get shot foiling a robbery or blown up by a terrorist's bomb or drowned trying to save a child – I don't even mind slipping away one night with crisp linen sheets drawn cosily up to my chin. Anything other than ending up here, clacking around the ridged concrete on a three-wheeled walking frame talking to myself.

She jumped at the sound of the door opening and got to her feet. A rather attractive young man in shirtsleeves and a tie, holding a manila file of notes to his chest, came across the room to greet her.

'Good afternoon,' he said extending a warm, strong hand towards her in greeting before gesturing to her to take a seat once more. 'I'm James Staunton. I've been taking care of your friend since she arrived and her niece was keen for me to meet you. I understand you worked together.'

Weenie turned on the seat to enable herself to observe Dr Staunton over a half-turned shoulder, her head tilted submissively to one side, her upper leg twining around the lower. She looked up at him and smiled the brave smile of a loyal friend. 'Yes,' she said, 'at Duntisbourne Hall.'

'Mmm. Duntisbourne – that place has a lot to answer for.'

'How is Nerys?' Weenie said.

'I'll be honest with you–'

'Oh, I do hope so.'

'She's very fragile at the moment. Sometimes the mind knows best and it can be extremely selective about the things it decides to remember and the experiences it would rather not think about again. Have you heard the term paraphilia before?'

'My bedroom's full of it.'

The doctor smiled. 'Not paraphernalia – paraphilia.'

'Yes, that's what I thought you said.' Weenie rolled her eyes upward as if deep in thought then said slowly, 'Do you know, I can't quite remember exactly what it means.'

'Well, let me explain. It's a term we use to describe sexual arousal from unusual objects, situations or individuals.'

'Oh, yes – I thought so.'

'Society regards a number of sexual desires as abnormal – in the past they were referred to as sexual deviations.'

'I know quite a bit about those.'

'Different cultures have different views – for example, men with a sexual attraction to feet are more likely to be regarded as having a fetish than men who are attracted to breasts, which in our society is seen as normal. However, most people agree that coprophilia – i.e. getting sexual pleasure from faeces – is unusual.' Weenie stared at the psychiatrist, an expression of academic interest frozen on her face. 'One analytic interpretation is that the excrement symbolically represents the male organ and in this particular case, in conjunction with the handbag as a fetish symbol of the–'

'Yes, yes – I think I get your drift.' Weenie was feeling exceptionally uncomfortable. The idea of her friend being turned on by anything was hard to stomach – but this.

'And of course Nerys,' the doctor continued, 'has carried the shame of what she witnessed a number of years ago.'

'What she witnessed? Oh, thank goodness – I thought it was the other way round.'

'Not at all. It has taken us a while to peel back the layers of the onion but several years ago she had a relationship of sorts which ended distressingly.'

'Oh yes, with Nigel Procter. She had a bit of a breakdown when that finished too, you know.'

'I know – my predecessor was in charge of her care but he never did find out exactly what had happened to her in the brown drawing room.'

'I can tell you – Nigel Procter did something appalling in the brown drawing room.'

'Yes – but we didn't know what until now.'

Weenie stared into the young doctor's beautiful brown eyes and gradually it began to dawn on her exactly what he meant. She clapped her hand over her mouth, the gold bangles clattering down her arm towards her elbow. 'Oh, good heavens – you can't possibly mean . . . ?'

'I'm afraid so. He defecated in her handbag.'

Weenie became aware of a steady drip outside the window, probably from a gutter blocked with moss and pine needles from the winter. She thought about Roger – how beastly he had been to her, how terrible he had made her feel – and for a brief moment she transferred those feeling to her friend and imagined what Nerys must have gone through and she felt true sympathy.

'Poor, poor Nerys,' she said. 'Would it be all right if I went see her now?'

− 22 −

'Come on in,' Simon Keane said, gesturing for Max to take a seat next to Sam. She looked up with a swift and secret smile meant only for him and he sat down, feeling a glow of amity. 'I don't think you've met DC Cragg.' Mercifully not, Max thought. 'But as you were an integral player in the discovery of the Hand, Mrs Westbrook–'

'Sam – please,' she said.

Keane nodded his assent – 'suggested you might like to join us to hear what DC Cragg's got to say.'

'Well,' the officer began, 'I didn't expect to have the Golden Hand back in our possession again in such a short time.'

'Yes, it does seem to have attracted a lot of undue interest lately among a number of less savoury characters,' Keane said. More than you can imagine, Max thought. Keane continued, 'DC Cragg will be advising on security over the coming weeks to make sure that the Hand can safely take its rightful place once more but in the meantime he has been speaking to the forensic team and has a fairly good idea about what happened on the night of the party and subsequently. I think you'll find it most illuminating but before he gives you the heads-up I'll bring you up to speed first, because neither you nor Sam worked here when Nigel Procter was alpha geek.'

'He was what?' Max said.

'Head of IT – and you may also have heard it aired out that a number of years ago something happened involving one of the guides, Nerys Tingley. In deference to her, I would prefer simply to say that when he left, an anti-social behaviour order was taken out preventing him from coming within ten miles of the Hall or having contact with members of staff.'

'His most obvious and provable offence,' DC Cragg said, 'was breaking the ASBO, and although this recent incident happened a few days ago we believe he has been in and out of the Hall for a number of months.'

'How come?' Max said.

'We can't beat the rap on that one,' Keane said. 'During his time here – completely unnoticed by anyone – he amassed a phenomenal assortment of pass keys and of course he knew the layout of Duntisbourne intimately. The intriguing aspect to all this is why, after an absence of nearly ten years, he started haunting the place again.'

'Nerys Tingley's return?' Sam said.

'The erotic exhibition?' Max suggested.

'That would be ironic,' Sam said.

'Explain,' Keane said.

'BS Moreton almost succeeded in persuading us that the collection should remain private because exposure to it would corrupt the general public,' Sam said. 'It would be embarrassing if he was proved right.'

'But that wasn't the real reason he was against it,' Keane said. 'Surely the real reason was that he'd helped himself to most of it.'

'Some of it – but I think his other concerns were genuine,' Sam said.

Keane raised his palms to feign surrender. 'The trigger could have been anything – we'll probably never know. Be that as it may, let's get back to the serious. Detective Constable Cragg?'

DC Cragg was sitting at the side of the desk, patiently watching the participants in the discussion as one would a game of tennis.

'Oh, right. Let me get my notes out again,' and he opened the folder that he had on his lap. 'We believe that on the night of the summer party Procter broke into the Hall and stole the Golden Hand. He admits he was in the Hall but maintains that the Hand was already missing from the dining room. Frankly, his version of the events of that night is bizarre to say the least.'

Max looked at his foot. When he first sat down he had crossed one leg over the other and he could see his foot moving in time with the throb of the pulse in his leg. He remembered a detective story where the culprit was unmasked because as the truth was revealed, the perpetrator's quickening pulse of anxiety was clearly visible to the detective by the bobbing of his foot. Max suspected that the version of events about to be put forward was going to answer a great many questions about that night and, concerned that he might inadvertently give away his agitation, he slowly uncrossed his legs and lowered his foot back to the floor.

'Procter maintains,' the officer said, 'that the Hall was full of people that night.'

'Full of people? That can't be true.'

'Agreed, but he is quite definite that two people were having sex in the library bedroom.'

'Really?' Sam said. 'Who?'

'He's refused to tell us for the moment – he says he knows who they are but he seems to believe that the information could give him some sort of leverage in the future.'

Max remembered rolling over the sill of the watercolour room, dropping onto the Savonnerie carpet in the darkness and hearing a rhythmic pulse like an ancient piece of machinery – he now knew why it had quickened and died.

'Procter says he watched them for a very short time before

making his way up to the exhibition where he found the Golden Hand thrust into an aperture in a Boulle-work box. He said he removed the finger of the Hand and,' here DC Cragg read directly from the typescript, '"finding the act of retraction sufficiently erotic" decided to use the box himself.'

Max remembered Laurence's expression of mild revulsion as he wiped his hand clean after touching something unpleasant inside the box. 'Of course,' he said. 'Why didn't we think of that?'

'Think of what?' said DC Cragg.

Max felt a cold sweat dampen his forehead. He had become so involved in the explanation of that night, he had momentarily forgotten he shouldn't have been there.

'Oh . . . that . . . well, that something like the brass-bound buggery box would tempt a man such as Procter.'

'I wasn't aware you knew him,' Cragg said.

'No, I didn't. I meant afterwards . . . after I found out about him, I should have realised . . . '

'Hmm.' Cragg frowned.

'Do carry on,' Max said. 'I shouldn't have interrupted you.'

Cragg returned to his notes. 'We have done DNA sampling and this has proved categorically that he did indeed use the box. However, no evidence that the Hand was ever in it.'

Cragg looked up at his audience. 'We assume that he took the Hand with him when he left. The police psychologist thinks he may have been carrying it around like a talisman, probably because it had become an erotic focus for one of his many fetishes because he clearly had it with him on the night of the explosion – which I will move on to now.'

'Everyone following this?' Keane said. Max and Sam nodded.

'From what we have managed to piece together, at some time

on Monday night Procter let himself into the Hall – probably at around ten o'clock when you, sir,' nodding at Max, 'saw a torch-light moving behind the windows. He could have let himself in earlier but Mrs Westbrook is certain she saw him underneath her window about twenty minutes to half an hour before so he couldn't have spent a great deal of time inside the Hall before the light was spotted.'

'It must have taken him a bit of time to get into the harness,' Max said.

'Well, according to your statement he did have quite a lot of time – the whole time you were with Mrs Westbrook.'

'OK.'

'Now we need to move on to the preserved monkey. As Mrs Westbrook had deduced, it had been constructed to perform a specific purpose and our Forensic Investigation Unit say there is no evidence whatsoever that the pelt was mounted on any kind of mannequin – they're usually made of wire and wood-wool apparently. They did however find quite a lot of tissue from the bladder of a pig – from several bladders in fact – and the theory is that these fluid-filled sacs were inside the pelt of the monkey and would have performed the same function as a modern high-end market sex doll which uses shape memory elastic gels. Unfortunately, when the room was opened up and the environment heated, bacteria sealed in the fluid of the bladders became active and created methane.'

'Which is why I thought the monkey was swelling.'

'Precisely – the pressure would eventually have built up sufficiently for the pelt to pop but the force of the explosion was down to Procter's intervention.'

'The candles.'

'Yes. He told us under questioning that he couldn't possibly have carried out his erotic plan under the brash light of the site lamps so he set up pillar candles – the way he described it, the room must have looked a bit like a landing strip at night. He got himself into the harness but after a few attempts at entering the monkey he lowered himself back down and proceeded clearing the monkey's – aperture, shall we say? – with the finger of the Golden Hand. This in turn released the methane under considerable pressure, it was ignited by the naked flames of the candles and the whole thing went up like the *Hindenburgh*. If Procter had not been suspended in the harness he would have taken the full force of the explosion but instead it threw him back and up – it probably saved his life when the structure collapsed around him. By the time the rigging of the harness fell, most of the heavy beams were down and he was covered with the lighter planks.'

'Awkward.'

'Yes,' DC Cragg said, closing his folder. 'Any questions?'

Weenie returned from the nursing home feeling despondent. She had been shocked by how much Nerys had changed in the short time since she last saw her. She seemed to have physically shrunk. A blanket made of multicoloured crocheted squares had been draped on top of her cardigan and she could see the outline of the dowager's hump at the base of her neck, the sharp line of her shoulder blades beneath the fabric. Weenie had drawn a chair over towards her and as she reached out to take her friend's hand, limp and icy cold like a dead fish lying in her palm, the rheumy eyes seemed to look through her not at her.

Weenie started to chatter merrily about everything that had been going on at the Hall but realised halfway through her tale that she was heading into dangerous waters because Nerys began to get agitated, her eyes darting around the room as she tried to withdraw her hand. Weenie decided the best policy was to talk about herself and regaled Nerys with a version of the story of splitting up with Roger without mentioning his name or saying that he was married.

'So you see,' she added, 'I do know what it feels like to be fond of someone and then find out that they weren't quite the person you thought they were.'

Nerys stared at her.

'Sunday went awfully well,' Weenie went on. 'You know, they made me head guide. Well, Rosemary came to me in the middle of the day to say what a very good job I was doing and I said to her, "My friend Nerys would have done it every bit as well as me," and she agreed. So you see, we all want you to come back otherwise they'll put one of those men in charge and we both know what a mess men would make of the Hall floor.'

When she got home Weenie fixed herself a stiff drink even though it was only two in the afternoon, and thought about her conversation with Nerys. She knew she hadn't been completely truthful about Sunday but she didn't want her friend to worry on her behalf. However, the more she thought things through, the more attractive the idea of spilling the beans about Max, Noel and Laurence seemed to be. Now Roger was out of the picture there was no one to censure her and she could mitigate her weak debut as head guide by currying favour with the management at the same time as removing three potential rivals for the job.

Galvanised into action she put the remainder of her gin and tonic onto a shelf in the fridge for later, popped a strong mint into her mouth and gathered up her bag and car keys – there was no time like the present. She would drive over to the Hall right away and insist she saw the CEO – that would test his 'open door' policy. Besides, she knew his PA Fissy quite well – they had been man-hunting buddies for several years before Fissy met a pleasant fellow online and married him.

'Fissy!' she said, plonking her things down on the seat in front of the desk in the estate office. 'How are you?' Weenie could see how she was – fat. The carbs hadn't wasted any time finding her former friend now that she was happy and settled once again. 'You look fabulous,' she said, leaning over to air-kiss towards her cheek.

'I haven't seen you for ages, Weenie, far too long. We must do lunch sometime.'

'Do let's.'

Fissy gazed across the desk, a fixed smile on her face. 'Anyway,' she finally said, 'what brings you up to the estate office?'

'I wondered if I could just steal a tiny little bit of Simon's time.'

'He's in a meeting at the moment.'

'Isn't he always? I thought he had an open-door policy – he always mentions it at the start of the season. I suppose I could just walk in through that open door and join them.' Weenie laughed loudly.

'I couldn't let you do that.'

'Joking, dear – I was joking.'

At that moment voices were heard above them and a group of people began to descend the stairs – a man Weenie didn't recognise followed by Max Black, Sam Westbrook and finally Simon Keane.

Sam and Max nodded a hello but Weenie felt herself beginning to blush, momentarily embarrassed that she was here to shop Max, so instead of responding, she dived down to pick her handbag off the floor, feverishly stirring around in it as if she was looking for something. Max and Sam left the estate office and Keane walked slowly towards the exit with the other man before shaking him by the hand and bidding him farewell. He returned with a thoughtful expression on his face.

'Simon,' Fissy said, 'Edwina is here to see you.'

'Hello,' he said without any sign of recognition.

'Can you fit her in now? Your four o'clock's running late.'

'Don't see why not – come on up. And Fiss, please could I have a coffee.'

'Now, Edwina–'

'Weenie, please. Everyone calls me Weenie.'

'Just refresh my memory – where exactly on the estate do you work?'

Weenie gawped across the desk but Keane wasn't looking at her, he was tidying some files and fiddling with a drawer while he waited for her to answer. When he found the small sweetener dispenser he had apparently been searching for he clicked a couple into his coffee, stirring it with his pencil before looking up with a distracted smile as if he was wondering why she hadn't answered.

Weenie, who had every intention of being as charming as possible, saw red and replied, 'I'll have you know that I've been a guide here for twice as long as you've been CEO. In fact, I'm the international guide and on Sunday I was the head guide. I probably know more about the history of the Hall and the way it should be run than the lot of you over here in the estate office put together. '

'Right,' Keane said, rather taken aback. 'And what can I do for you?'

Disconcerted by his lack of response to her provocation she shook her head as if tossing a lock of hair out of her eyes and, smoothing her skirt down her thighs, crossed one leg over the other, making the fabric of her tights sing against the silk lining of the skirt. Her heart gave a skip of excitement and she launched straight into her elucidation.

'On Friday night, during the party, three of your employees broke into the Hall and I know who they are.' She was gratified to see that although her opening salvo had somewhat confounded Keane, she now had his full attention.

'I see,' he said, reaching for the file he had recently tidied into a pile at the side of his desk. She spotted the crest of the Dyfed-Powys police. 'That's very interesting.'

Heading Roger's warning, she had dropped the idea of saying that she had seen the trio breaking in but she had come up with another version of events that was perfectly plausible and difficult to disprove.

'Well, it was interesting. I just happened to be feeling rather hot at the dance – I had been doing an awful lot of dancing, people just couldn't seem to leave me alone – so I went outside for a bit of fresh air and I saw these people inside the Hall when I looked through the windows. It was a little alarming as I have absolutely no idea whatsoever why they were in there.'

'Oh, I know why they were there.' Keane had opened the file and glanced down at the writing before looking up at her again, his expression open and interested.

'You do?'

'Yes. I'm obviously extremely glad that you've brought this to my attention – and I know the police would value another witness – but I can't really discuss the actions of one of them for legal reasons.'

'Legal reasons?'

'Yes – but you may well be able to help us to identify the other two and that could tie up the last few strands of a mystery.'

'I'd be delighted to.' Weenie leant forward and cupped her chin in her hand. She hoped this studious posture would show that their minds were thinking as one when in reality she couldn't work out why one of the men had been singled out. They hadn't stolen the Hand as she first thought because it was in the dining room for everyone to see. Perhaps one of them had blown up the exhibition? This was a great deal more interesting than she had expected.

'The mystery is,' Keane said, 'who else broke into the Hall that night with the express intention of having sex?'

Weenie experience an odd visual sensation as if Keane, with his eager eyes smiling across the desk at her, stayed in exactly the same position while the rest of his office seemed to stream past her and away into the distance. She dug her chin more firmly into the palm of her hand to slow the vertigo that swirled around them.

'Are you all right?' she heard Keane say. 'You look a little pale?'

'I'm fine,' she said, sitting back in the chair and holding onto the arms. Her mouth was feeling rather dry.

'OK. Let's go back a step – you tell me who you saw.'

The relief to get back on track washed over her with a shiver and she said, 'I saw Max Black, Laurence Cooke and Noel Canterbury inside the Hall that night.'

Now it was Keane's turn to look astounded and he also sat back in his chair with surprise and said, 'Having sex?'

'No – not having sex.' She screwed her nose up as if he had said something utterly stupid. 'I was looking through the window in the Hall – I was outside under the portico, looking through the window, I saw the three of them going up the stairs to the exhibition and I thought they were stealing the Hand.'

'What made you think that?' Oh God, Weenie thought, I couldn't have seen the dining room from the window in the Hall. 'Because before I looked in through the window in the Hall I had gone round to the west side of the Hall–'

'Why?'

'To see the sunset,' she plucked out of the ether. 'I looked into the window on the west front–'

'Weren't the shutters' closed?'

'Yes – no, of course not. Well . . . one of them was open . . . ' she waved her hand around in the air in a vaguely dismissive way and shook her head irritably. 'What does it matter? I looked into the dining room and the chains had nothing on them and I thought that the Hand had been stolen but later realised it hadn't been because it was there the next day and they said it had been taken down and cleaned.' She paused, aware that her voice was becoming shrill. She took a deep breath to slow herself down and said, 'I never went anywhere near the library bedroom.'

Keane watched her for a moment, his jaw cranked a little to one side as if he was investigated a back tooth with the tip of his tongue, then he said, 'I didn't mention the library bedroom.'

'You did – you said someone was having sex in there.'

'No, I didn't.'

'You said someone was having sex.'

'Yes.'

'In the library bedroom.'

'No.' His fingers drummed the desk, a single riff. 'Was it you?'

'What?'

'In the library bedroom?'

'Well, really!' Weenie scanned the room, glancing behind as if checking out an escape route before turning back to the CEO, who was watching her with a stern expression. 'Oh, what the hell!' she said, feeling a swell of pride, 'Yes, if you must know, it was me.'

Keane's austere expression began to lift and to Weenie's intense irritation he started to laugh, quite softly, then he shook his head and said, 'Unbelievable.'

Weenie sniffed and adjusted the scarf at her throat, the clatter of her bangles loud in the stillness of the office. Keane just kept swivelling his office chair left then right until the dead air became unbearable and Weenie felt impelled to speak.

'What are you going to do about those others? They were there, you know, I did see them – not through the window, that's all – but I saw them and they had broken in and they were going up to the exhibition.'

'How did you get in?'

'Through the front door.' Keane raised an eyebrow at her. 'With a key – Bunty had given me the key the week before when I closed up for her on a Sunday.'

Keane pursed his lips blew out a small puff of air. 'Quite a betrayal of trust all round then?'

'How dare you!' Weenie got to her feet and grabbed her bag off the floor.

'Please sit down,' Keane said. 'I haven't quite finished with you yet.' Instead Weenie stood by the chair and glared at him. 'The police will want to interview you. I assume they can contact you on your home number.'

'Well, obviously, but not tomorrow – I'm at work tomorrow.'

Keane watched her impassively.

'Now look here,' she said, raising a finger and wagging it towards him. 'I came here to speak to you today in good faith because those three men broke into the Hall. You should be thanking me. I've always been a loyal employee and–'

'As far as I can see you have been disloyal to the Earl, to the trustees, to the Hall and to your work colleagues. I certainly don't expect to see you here at work tomorrow or any other day for that matter. You are dismissed.'

'You can't do that. I have rights.'

'If you wish to discuss those with Human Resources feel free, but as far as I'm concerned you leave today on grounds of gross misconduct. I will recommend a week's pay in lieu of notice which will be forwarded to you. Good day.'

Weenie flounced over towards the door but before leaving she turned again and said, 'You haven't asked who else was there with me. Well, I'll tell you. It was Roger Hogg-Smythe, Justice of the Peace.' Keane didn't look up. 'What are you going to do about that?'

– 23 –

Max had trouble opening the front door – something was jamming it on the other side – but he managed to push it open enough to shout through, 'Charlotte! Move this ruddy bag. I can't get in.' He heard her footsteps thundering down the stairs.

'Sorry, Dad,' she said, hopping up on tiptoe and planting a kiss on his cheek as he came in, 'but Rufus will be here in a few minutes.'

'How much are you taking?'

'All of it – I may as well go straight back down to Bristol when the festival's finished. There's no point coming back here for a couple of days.'

'Madness,' Max muttered as he went into the kitchen and flicked on the kettle. Charlotte's plan to travel up to Edinburgh with Rufus and join his university friends for the final week of the festival seemed to have been jumbled together in the space of a few hours and although Max was initially beset with his usual neuroses – the safety of the journey, where they would stay, what they would get up to – it hadn't taken him long to see that after Tuesday afternoon's excellent outcome, Charlotte's departure would remove the final impediment to a headlong rush into a full-blown relationship with Sam. Monty appeared in the kitchen beside him shaking his plimby as an invitation to play and with an unusual spurt of energy brought on by extreme happiness Max chased the dog around the table in the sitting room a few times before he heard his daughter call, 'Dad. I'm off.'

He arrived at the front door panting a little and raised a hand to Rufus who was stuffing the last of Charlotte's bags into an overloaded mini. He put his arms around his daughter and squeezed before letting go and nodding towards Rufus. 'Good luck with that one,' he said to her and Charlotte pushed his shoulder and was gone.

It was a glorious day, the fields on either side of the road in various stages of harvest – some as ripe as burnt toast, others already ploughed, as neat and ordered as burgundy corduroy. Max could feel the heat of the morning sun on his back as he strode across the courtyard weaving his way between the early morning visitors. He looked over towards the stable block and up to the window of Sam's flat and felt life couldn't get any sweeter.

He was surprised to find Claude on the front door and wondered where Noel was – perhaps out on an early tour. He walked through the Hall to put his things upstairs and hailed the Major who was counting the cash float out onto the desk. 'Morning Frodders.'

'Max – over here,' the Major urgently gestured towards him. 'Have you heard the news?'

'That it's a beautiful day and all is well with the world?'

'No – they've sacked Weenie.'

'What?'

'Yes – sacked, she's had her marching orders, axed, given the bum's rush.'

'Why?'

'Apparently all the time you and Noel and Laurence were creeping around the Hall the night of the party, she was shagging Roger Hogg-Smythe in the bedroom next to the library.'

'Weenie? Never!'

'God's truth.'

As Max made his way upstairs an uneasy feeling began to worm its way into his head. He thought that all the pieces of the puzzle had been neatly slotted into place during the meeting with Keane, leaving him with a sense of relief that his daughter, his colleagues and indeed he himself had neatly side-stepped catastrophe thanks to Nigel Procter's dramatic intervention. Now he wasn't so sure. The drama of the past few days had superseded any speculation about who was having it off in the Hall that night. Max had subscribed to the general view that Procter was mad as a cut snake and nothing he said had any true validity, but now he began to wonder if by any ghastly chance they had been seen.

His fears increased when, as he approached the open door into the guides' room, he heard Bunty discussing the difficulty of manning the Hall with such a depleted workforce. This gripe wasn't new to her – it was a common mantra – but she stopped midsentence when he entered the room and cleared her throat.

Robyn was the only other person in the room and she looked up at Max with an expression of pity a split second before Bunty said, 'Message from Rosemary, Max – she wants to see you in the office immediately.' Without bothering to put his lunch box in the fridge he turned round and made his way back downstairs with a heavy heart.

His fears were pretty much confirmed when he entered Rosemary's office and found Laurence and Noel already sitting there, the former looking anxious, the latter affecting nonchalance. As Max took the only seat left vacant, Noel leant across to him and murmured, 'I think we've put up a bit of a black, old chap.'

Rosemary heard. 'I'm afraid you have,' she said, sighing heavily. 'Honestly, I can't tell you how fed up I am with the three of you. With Nerys's illness and Weenie's employment terminated, I was planning a shake-up of the floor. Bunty's not getting any younger and I had plans to get all three of you trained up as deputy head guides – but now? Hopeless.' She shook her head, her expression one of deep sadness as opposed to anger. 'Why ever did you do it?'

Max was about to speak when Noel cut in and said, 'We'd all had a bit too much to drink I suppose and it seemed a bit of a lark.'

'But what was the point? What were you doing there?'

Noel glanced over at Laurence, and Max got the impression the two of them had worked this out before he arrived. 'I don't think any of us can remember,' Noel said.

'Max?'

He was aware that the eyes of both his colleagues were turned towards him. He shrugged apologetically and said to Rosemary, 'No idea.'

'It's just ridiculous. You should know better. Now, if it had been one of the young ones, I could understand but you're all too old for this type of behaviour.' Max looked down at his fingernails, feeling very much as if he was under twenty again.

Rosemary gave another great sigh and continued, 'I championed your corner as vehemently as I could but this can't go unpunished, I'm afraid. The Earl has been informed and certainly until he departs for Florida all three of you are on unpaid garden leave.'

'Meaning?'

'It's the best I can do. Initial opinion was that, like Weenie, you should all be summarily dismissed but I talked them round – you've been suspended.'

'Does that imply,' Noel said, 'that we'll be back?'

Rosemary pursed her lips and said, 'I can't promise that – but I can promise that if any of you need a reference in the future I will be happy to provide it. I can't speak for anyone else here but I know you three and I truly believe this was a case of high jinks.'

Driving away from the Hall, Max slowed his car and took a long look back over the lake. He didn't want to leave – he liked working here. For the first time in his life, his days had taken on a kind of normality. He had made new friends – something he never expected to do at his age – and what friends they had turned out to be. As the three of them had walked back to the car park together, Noel seemed in good spirits, confident they would be back before long, looking forward to a few weeks off. Neither he nor Laurence would hear of Max falling on his sword or mentioning the part his daughter and her boyfriend had had in it all.

'Stop worrying,' Noel said clapping him on the back, 'I wouldn't have missed it for the world. Look, let's all meet up for lunch next week at The Blue Acorn and I guarantee you won't be feeling so chapfallen. Everything's going to be all right, you mark my words. They can't run that place without us.'

Above all the Hall meant Sam. He had never imagined meeting someone again in his later years who would mean so much to him and he had Duntisbourne Hall to thank for that. He felt he was on the threshold of embarking on a relationship that would change his life forever and yet he hadn't paused once over the past few weeks to wonder why he hadn't told her everything about the night of the party. For months he had enjoyed telling her all the funny little things he had heard and seen during the day and yet he had kept this to himself. She had given him the perfect opportunity down by the lake when he allayed her fears about Robyn and yet still he hadn't taken it.

His abiding desire had been to protect his relationship with his daughter. The two most important women in his life had not got off to a great start and although he was the first to roundly criticise Charlotte, heaven help anyone else who did the same. How could he tell Sam the true story of that night without damaging her opinion of his daughter? Particularly when she discovered he had been suspended while Charlotte's boyfriend had got away scot free. Sam may well put him under pressure to save his job, but how could he point the finger at Rufus without deeply upsetting Charlotte?

If he looked back over the chronology of events he could see why he had made each decision at the time. Sam seemed to be plunging headlong into a relationship with the Scoke which temporarily snapped their connection, shaking the trust he felt they had in one another. Without it he would have been foolish to have involved her – she was part of the management team after all. That factor was the other reason why he hadn't told her even when it became clear that the Scoke had failed in his conquest. He and his two colleagues were not strictly criminals but knowledge of what they did would put Sam in a very awkward position. It was this that caused Max to feel so bleak – how could Sam now embrace their relationship? He was *persona non grata* at the present – would she do her standing at the Hall any good at all by advancing this relationship? More importantly, how would she feel knowing that he had kept secrets from her when she had been so open with him?

He let himself into his cottage feeling dejected and low. Monty was at the door to greet him but even his salmon leaps of enthusiasm failed to cheer him. 'I may take you out later, you old stumper,' he said. The little dog sat at the bottom of the stairs as he went up to change, following him as he took a cup of coffee outside into the garden to think, and sat at his feet wagging his tail through the dust of the terrace. Eventually he slipped underneath the chair, sensing that all was not well with his master. The Japanese honeysuckle which scrambled through the hedge near the house was nearing the end of its flowering season but a few of the last blooms sent out wafts of sweet cloves and Max closed his eyes and tried to clear his head.

The phone in the house rang making him jump and spill his coffee. 'Bull shit!' he said, struggling to his feet and shaking the coffee off his hand. He picked up the phone. 'Yes?' he said irritably.

'Max, it's Sam. What on earth has been going on?'

'Sam,' he said. He wiped his hand down the edge of his jeans and squinted at the skin which was turning pink from the hot coffee. 'Sam,' he said again. There was only one way to deal with this – meet the problem head on. 'I'm afraid I have an admission to make,' he said. 'I'm sorry to say I haven't been totally candid with you.'

Acknowledgements

As with the *The Archivist*, the first book in the Duntisbourne Hall trilogy, my biggest debt of thanks is to my husband Chris for his invaluable and patient encouragement throughout the creation of Book Two. I would also like to thank my team of beta-readers – Boun Norton, Jane Gibson, Ginny Ifould and Antonia Keaney – who all did an excellent job of analysing how the narrative played out on the page. It is interesting how many of them were saddened by Weenie's demise, so much so that I am confident she will make a reappearance in the final volume of the trilogy. I would also like to thank science writer Philip Ball for his opinion on the plausibility of the denouement and Margaret Histed, my excellent editor.

The Hipkiss File

L.P. Fergusson
Publication Spring 2014

'I'd like to bring that man down,' says the disgraced BS Moreton, 'and I think I know just how to do it.'

Having completed his custodial sentence, the former archivist to the Earl of Duntisbourne is hell-bent on revenge, but when an ancient visitor to the Hall recognises his contemporary, Claude Hipkiss, as a retired agent living under an assumed name, BS's most important asset goes missing along with the dossier that holds the key to the Earl's demise.

As Sam continues to vacillate about her feelings for Max, outside events draw them both into a harrowing world of subterfuge and danger as the Duntisbourne Hall trilogy accelerates towards a thrilling conclusion.

www.lpfergusson.com